DEJA BREW

Deadlights Cove, #2

B. PERKINS

AIMEE VANCE

Revel Books

Revel Books
ISBN: 979-8-9863649-3-3

www.aimeevancebooks.com

For anyone who has put other's desires before their own, what you want matters, too.

Go for it.

I FLIPPED up the hood of my plaid flannel against the chill of the night, the crackling fire only warming half of me. It was the Saturday before Halloween, and every year, my friend and local demon bartender Sabazios, better known as Blaze, threw a rager at the beach in front of his house. The cool autumn breeze coming in off the ocean mingled with the scent of bonfires and barbeque. Several members of my fox shifter skulk stood around the firepit with me, joking and boasting about the latest prank they'd pulled on the wolf shifter pack.

"The key was," Casey said, all sly nonchalance, his pale skin a contrast to the solid black flannel he wore and his black hair, "I waited until the printer confirmed the t-shirt order with Julian. *That's* when I hacked into their system and uploaded Cole's design."

Akil — my eighteen-year-old highly influenceable younger brother, who shouldn't have even been here — was hanging on Casey's every word, practically bouncing in his crisp white Air Jordans. His features mirrored my own somewhat, but his skin was a slightly lighter bronze than mine, no doubt from all the hours he spent mixing music and editing videos indoors. While we had the same dark brown hair, his was cut short on the sides and carefully gelled up with pink-dyed tips. "What did you change it to?"

Casey smirked at Cole, his twin, who had longer, wavier hair than Casey, and, if it were possible, an even more conniving cut to his features. Wearing a black Cowboy Bebop tee over a maroon long-sleeve shirt, Cole pushed up the sleeves. Like most of our skulk, his forearms were covered in swirling tattoos, black against his pale skin. He pulled out his phone to show the design he'd made — a petite wolf in a butler's outfit, feeding grapes to a smug, lounging fox.

Just then, a few wolves passed our group, only making Casey's audience laugh harder at their unamused expressions. We had an ongoing rivalry between their pack and our skulk, which only got better every time we outsmarted them. It annoyed the pack to no end that our pranks were always successful, and their attempts at retaliation were thwarted.

I shook my head, but a smile tugged at my lips. I knew my father — our Alpha — wouldn't approve of their actions, but the joke was harmless. Like the foxes whose souls lived within us, we couldn't help causing mischief. Nevertheless, I felt too distracted to share completely in their laughter tonight, and it had nothing to do with the fact I needed to maintain a certain level of detachment from their antics. As the future leader of our skulk, I couldn't be seen condoning this sort of thing, especially not since my father's

Second, my uncle Jayesh, had stepped down, and I'd been forced to take his place.

No, the real reason I couldn't laugh alongside them tonight was something else entirely. Something that I then sensed with a jolt that shot through my entire body as a small group walked towards the beach from Blaze's house.

I willed myself not to look over at her, but the secondary soul inside me, the fox whose form I could take, won that battle. Even with the quick glance I allowed, I could tell Nimue Fitzpatrick was just as beautiful as the last time I'd seen her. Long brown hair flowed freely over her shoulders, curled lightly under the red Rockford Peaches hat she wore for her *A League of Their Own* costume. I didn't mean to notice how the pink skirt flared just right at her waist, stopping shorter than those uniforms did in the movie. And I definitely didn't notice the red knee-high socks with tiny bows against her alabaster skin.

When I returned my attention to our group, Akil's eyes were on me, the cup he held in front of his face barely hiding his cackling amusement.

"You're pathetic. Why don't you just go talk to her?"

I flicked his ear. "Did I just hear you say you want me to call Ma and tell her you're here tonight?" I looked pointedly at his red plastic cup that definitely did not hold soda.

His dark eyes blew wide as he snapped his mouth shut. The others chuckled at his fear of our mother, though at least my cousin Nadir and other brother Emerson understood why. As the youngest, Akil got away with far more than I ever had, but Ma was still a force to be reckoned with when angered. And she certainly would not approve of his being at this 21 and over event. With that, he muttered something about wanting to check on his set, and scurried off.

Even if I wanted to talk to Nimue, I couldn't.

What would I say?

It had been three years, nine months, and twenty-seven days since I'd last seen her, and not a day had gone by that I hadn't imagined this very moment.

I let out a breath, avoiding Nadir's knowing gaze as I stared into the flames. No matter what I wanted, I couldn't have it. I had to push her away. It would be cruel of me *not* to. Cruel to open either of us up to something that could only lead to more pain.

Because Nimue Fitzpatrick, a demon and my childhood best friend, was my mate. And she didn't deserve to either feel the guilt of rejecting that, or be doomed to live as a mate to a shifter.

With the full moon overhead, my senses were overloaded as I listened to Lysander and his band churning out cover songs. The Black Keys' *Howling for You* blared over the speakers by the stage, and I slipped away from the guys to get some air, moving down the beach. Usually, this party was one of my favorite nights of the year, but I couldn't handle it tonight.

The further I drew away from the stage, the smell of alcohol and sounds of rowdy laughter were replaced by the salty ocean air, and the crashing waves and pebbles crunching under my shoes.

Everywhere I looked tonight, there she was. Unavoidable. Even though I'd spent the last several years doing exactly that.

I couldn't leave — my father had put me in charge of my generation of shifters tonight. Everyone was excited to run in the forest outside of town in mixed company, away from our skulk's ground, and I could still hear the lecture that accompanied this responsibility.

Don't let them taunt the wolves; they get too riled up with the moon.

Yes, Pa.

And the alcohol. Don't let them drink too much. It makes them stupid. You shouldn't drink either.

I know, Pa.

Were we drinking? Yes. But technically, I hadn't lied because I *did* know that alcohol could make us stupid.

That's wolf territory. So if anything does happen, get everyone to leave. Don't escalate it. Nadir will help you.

I understand, Pa.

After the murder and magic-tampering here last month, you have to be more on guard than ever before. You have a duty to protect them as much as they have a duty to you. Never forget that.

At 29, I hardly needed to be reminded of this. Although I was still young for a shifter, I'd already been leading my generation for years. Even hours after his lecture, the heavy yoke of responsibility weighed on me, dragging me down. I wanted to run. To shift into my fox and flee. To get away from this. From her.

Besides, it wasn't as though there'd been any more signs of whoever was behind the rituals and sacrifices. For all we knew, they'd moved on.

The scent of rosewater hit right before Nimue dropped

onto the rocky shore beside me, bumping my knee. I stiffened on reflex, hastily shutting down my emotions before she could get a read on anything. As a demon, Nimue could sense impulses, and right now, mine were all over the place. I'd been tracking her every move all night to avoid this exact scenario. Being alone with her.

"Hey." She gave me a tentative smile, her black irises searching my face as she fixed her pink skirt, flaring it around her legs.

I swallowed, throat tight as my gaze flicked from her back to the Cove's open water. Despite that, I was still somehow hyper-tuned in to her every movement, every breath, and beat of her body. "Hey."

Her breath caught slightly at my response, or lack thereof, and I glanced back her direction. I hated to see her hurt or confused by me and my reactions, but wasn't it better than the alternative?

"Good party," Nimue remarked, trying again.

I nodded, sparing her a glance. "Blaze always throws a good one."

"I think I might have done something I shouldn't have." She pressed her lips together to contain a smile, but all it did was draw my eyes to them. I tore my gaze away and turned toward the ocean once more, watching the crests glint in the moonlight.

"What's that?"

Nimue leaned back on her hands, rotating to look behind her to see if anyone was nearby, and I sat up straighter, forcing distance between our bodies. Not sensing my own control slowly slipping, she leaned a little closer to me, her arm brushing mine, and my skin prickled.

"I think I talked Dev and Orion into giving it a shot," she whispered conspiratorially, giving me an overly-wide, uncertain grin that held absolutely no remorse for her actions. The sight of it had a smile pulling at the corners of my mouth despite myself, and something tugged against my heart. I missed her antics, her harmless and lighthearted fun, how easily she could put people at ease and —

"At least for tonight." She tilted back away from me. I had to stop myself from following, from closing the distance between us. Shit, I had to get a lock on that.

"You're kidding." I was gawking, I knew it, but no one ever surprised me the way Nimue could.

"What?" She smiled innocently, but I knew better than to fall for that. She always knew exactly what strings she was pulling. "They're both too uptight, and I didn't encourage anything they weren't already thinking. I just... nudged them a little in the same direction."

"And by giving it a shot, you mean…"

She lifted a shoulder with a playful smile. "That part is up to them. Maybe it's a handshake. Maybe he'll bang her. To be determined."

A laugh escaped me, and I shook my head, staring down at my hands draped over my knees. "I wouldn't go spreading that around to just anyone. Unless you want Dev to hex you."

A pause stretched between us, and I knew she was watching me. I willed all my impulses to the back of my mind, trying to replace them with other, less incriminating urges. I wanted to shift and run along the beach. I wanted to eat pizza. I wanted to taste her neck. *Fuck*. No. Okay. Well, now I wanted another drink.

"I'm not spreading it around to just anyone," she murmured. "Only you."

I needed to get out of here. I couldn't do this. I couldn't sit here, next to her, and keep pretending that I didn't want

—

"But I can see you're…" she paused. When I glanced at her, hurt flashed over her face, and I hated myself. I wanted nothing more than to open up to her, to tell her why I was behaving this way, but that would defeat the purpose entirely. "Anyway. I guess I'll see you around some other time, Kit."

She pushed herself to her feet, brushing sand off her skirt and sending her scent all the more strongly my way. Waiting a beat to see if I would respond, she gave a quiet huff of frustration. It was the only indication of her annoyance, but I knew her well enough to recognize it for what it was. Without another word, she headed back up the beach to the main hum of the party.

Once I heard her footsteps rejoining the others', I let out a breath, falling to my back as I stared at the night sky. I knew I was being an asshole to her, but what else could I do?

Several minutes passed while I contemplated dozens of scenarios where Nimue and I could be together, and I promptly found the obstacles to each one until I sensed members of my skulk approaching through the mental link we all shared through our shifter magic. I let out a slow exhale before a hand reached down to pull me to my feet. It was Nadir, his skin slightly lighter than mine due to his mother's German and English roots, followed by my middle brother Emerson, his face half hidden by the large hood of his sweatshirt as always, and the twins. Nadir's olive green eyes surveyed me knowingly, but he said nothing, and for that, I was grateful. The last thing I needed was for Emerson to realize what was going on with me, and let it slip to our parents. Well, more likely to Akil, who would tell our sister Lily, who would wait and play that card strategically to get herself out of trouble.

The twins had a dangerous gleam in their eyes. "Some of the wolves left their car windows open," Cole said, flashing his teeth at the rest of us.

Casey pulled open a backpack to showcase at least two dozen canisters of shaving cream. "Shall we?"

Nadir passed me a beer. "For courage," he teased, a challenging lift to one dark eyebrow. Unlike the others, I knew he was doing this to help distract me, and I shifted one claw to pierce the aluminum.

The twins cheered as I shotgunned it, Emerson critiquing my method the entire time. Crushing the empty can against my leg, I wiped my mouth before waving up the beach. This was probably not the best idea, but I wanted to do anything but think about the demon that haunted my every waking moment. Dominating the wolves yet again, even in this small way, sounded like a good enough distraction to me.

"Lead on, young pups."

Chapter Two

nimue

KIT SAYANA NEEDED to get a grip.

He'd been acting absurd ever since we'd kissed. The second time, that is.

The first time — twenty-one years ago — we'd been kids and were just experimenting. As eight-year-old best friends, we thought it was only natural. A quick peck, try it out and get a little practice in for later. For other times. It was awkward, but we laughed it off and stayed friends.

But the second time we'd kissed? That was right before I left town almost four years ago, and one I'd never forget. But Kit had been avoiding me ever since.

Maybe because I was a demon. Just like shifters had heightened senses of smell and hearing, I could sense intentions and urges. But so what if I'd sensed he had the urge to take the kiss further? In the heat of the moment, I'd had the same impulse before logic — and a bit more sobriety — had kicked back in. Kit was hot, nice, funny, and my best friend.

Every time I'd come back into town over the last four years to visit my cousin Blaze and my mother Mo, Kit had avoided me. I'd even stopped in his tea shop a few times, but he'd always been on break, probably hiding in the back. Even though I could sense his impulses just below the surface, I didn't understand his actions.

Maybe he didn't want to be friends anymore.

That thought hurt more than I cared to examine, even though it had been years since we'd been as close as we were as kids, just a demon and a fox shifter on the hunt for wild blackberries. We'd both grown up and changed in our twenties. He probably had a whole life I didn't know about now.

From my vantage point back amongst the crowd, I watched as a few young guys approached him by the waves — the members of his skulk closest to him, some of whom I knew from when they'd sneak out with us. My shoulders relaxed slightly when I saw Kit smiling with them. Even though he'd been kind of a jerk to me, I was glad they were trying to help him out of whatever funk he was in. He got lost in his own head so easily. Even if I wasn't the one bringing him out of it, it gave me some relief to know there were still people in his life who could.

Then I saw them cast a furtive glance back towards the party before slinking off into the darkness, and I knew they'd be up to no good soon.

I grabbed a glass of demon wine — not poison, my friend Devanna assured me since she'd made it herself — and slowly wandered through the throngs of people. I had half a mind to find Blaze and his new *human* girlfriend, Petra. My cousin was obviously besotted with her, and I was excited to get to know her. Hopefully, we could become good friends — I was ready to support her if she ever needed to gossip about Blaze. God knew I had more dirt on him than anyone. Except for Mo, of course, but her skills were unparalleled. If I ever had half the nose for mischief as the woman who raised me, I'd consider myself gifted indeed.

I got the feeling, though, despite what a reprobate Blaze could be, that he'd never do anything to make Petra need to vent about him. Even with the little I'd seen of them together, they seemed to fit.

Close to midnight, the wolves started leaving the party, many heading to their cars to strip, leave their clothes inside, and shift. As they approached their vehicles, shouts of, *"Fucking shit!"* and *"Goddamn foxes!"* reached me. I pressed my lips together to suppress my smile, even as I wondered what the guys had done. Hopefully, Kit and his skulk were already halfway home because they were about to have a pack of pissed-off wolves after them. But that wasn't my problem.

I passed Selene, complete with blonde wig and armor for her Daenerys costume, laughing and chatting with Mo, a slight flush to her tan face that was no doubt due to Blaze's Halloween punch. Finally spotting Blaze and Petra, I made my way over and sank down to the rocky beach to join them. Blaze's normally wild dark hair was gelled into a combover for his Casual Orion costume, complete with khakis and boat shoes — a sight I'd never forget. I pulled out my phone, holding it up to snap a picture of him, his arm thrown around his red-headed Alice in Wonderland, Petra, whose blue pinafore matched her eyes. He caught me taking the photo and gave his most serious, Official-Mayor-of-This-Town scowl for the camera — which looked absurd on him — and I laughed as I snapped a few more photos.

My phone was just back in my pocket before the demon

blood in me called so strongly that I couldn't help but stick my fingers in his hair, raking it back out of order.

Chaos.

Much better.

"How was it?" Blaze asked, wicked delight glinting in his dark eyes as he ducked from under my hand.

I leveled a stare at my meddling, nosy cousin. The male was as bad as Mo — not surprising, as she'd all but raised him too. "How was *what?*" I tossed back pointedly, and he let it drop, only smirking at me.

"Petey's decided to stay in town, Nimmie." He nibbled at his human's ear, and her bright red hair almost matched the deep blush that took up residence on her face, her freckles darkening.

"Maybe not if you keep calling me that." Petra narrowed her eyes at him, but I could sense the affection underneath it.

"Good. Maybe she can keep you out of prison for a little longer than usual." I tilted my head to the side before continuing, "Although, maybe not. Didn't I hear you were *with* him at the crime scene, Petra?"

I smiled broadly at her so she knew I was joking, then nudged Blaze's shoulder.

Blaze grinned as he tilted Petra's face up to kiss her. "And then she fought to prove my innocence."

I couldn't watch, even if my heart warmed to see my cousin so happy and settled. Blaze had always been a bit of a rolling stone, hopping from one thing to the next, never truly *criminal* in his impulses but causing enough trouble all the same. He finally pulled away to turn back to me. "So you should stay in town, too. It's all the rage."

"Uh-huh," I said, rolling my eyes. It was only the hundred-thousandth time he'd asked me, but I couldn't move back. At least, not while things were so weird with Kit. In a town this small, I'd see him everywhere, and I couldn't stand it if he wouldn't talk to me.

Chapter Three

KIT

AFTER THE SKULK emptied all the canisters of shaving cream into the wolves' cars, we threw our clothes in Casey's backpack, tossed that in Akil's car, and shifted to get the fuck away from the party before the wolves caught on to our prank. Shifters got over their modesty, if they had any, very early on in life if they wanted to keep an intact wardrobe.

We raced through the woods into town, foxes of every color scampering through the underbrush with the eerie howls of wolves at our backs. Another howl rang out, closer this time. Despite the ominous call of the pack, I wasn't worried. Even though our foxes were smaller than their wolves — but still larger than natural red foxes — we were faster than the wolves any day in a short race.

As future Alpha, I was the largest of us and had the brightest red coat; Nadir's was more orange with a black cross stretching over his shoulders and down his spine; Emerson had a black coat with a frosting of silver tips, a variation he inherited from our mother. The twins were nearly the same shade of tawny brown, the only difference being that the tips of Cole's ears were black.

I was *slightly* worried about leaving Akil behind. Not worried that anything would happen to him at the party in retribution — Blaze would take care of him, I was sure of that — but over my father's reaction if he found out I'd left Akil behind.

Technically, I'd left him with my sister Lily and cousin Sophie, Nadir's sister, who were still at the party. But Lily had been hanging around Julian, the wolf pack's Second, a lot lately — I didn't know if they were friends, dating, fuck buddies, or something else, and I didn't want to know. She might have left by now if she was running with the pack, and it was anyone's guess what Sophie got up to at these things.

It was well after midnight when my skulk and I made it to my apartment above Immortali-Tea, throwing on sweats from the bin by the door — a staple in every shifter home. My two-bedroom apartment was sparsely decorated — furnished with mismatched furniture I'd collected from members of the skulk over the years as they were throwing them out, and storage for the tea shop in the second bedroom. The living room was the beige color it had been when my grandmother bought the shop decades ago — I'd repainted it, but couldn't decide on a color, so I had settled on the same one as before.

The only real upgrade I'd made to the space over the years living here was the kitchen. All new appliances. Massive kitchen island with six barstools and open to the living room. It wasn't big enough for our group to hang out comfortably, but most of them still lived at home. The sight of my friends and family crammed onto my two couches and sprawled on the floor — a few others had shown up after we'd arrived — reminded me that someday, I'd need to abandon this place. My job as Alpha would demand I had enough room for the whole skulk to congregate.

"Pass me a slice of pepperoni," Nadir called to me from across the island. I opened one of the many boxes strewn across the counter, pulled out a slice, and handed it over. The heart-warming tones of *The Hero of Canton, the Man They Call Jayne,* reached me from the television as I made my way to the sofa. Nadir groaned as he sank beside my brother.

"Emerson, really? Firefly *again?*"

Emerson gave him his signature impassive stare and pointed at the TV. "This is a classic."

"Sure, but didn't you watch it last month?" Nadir gestured to the hand-held video game in his hands. "And you're not even watching."

My brother's eyes narrowed ever so slightly. To anyone else, he might have seemed annoyed, but I knew my family well enough to know that both males were amused. "I can do two things at once," he said. Nadir rolled his eyes as the twins slumped down on the light-grey sectional with their pizza.

"Napkins, boys," I shot at the twins where they lay. "We're not animals." At that, they laughed. "But seriously, if you get grease stains on my couch, I'll kick you out, and you can spend the night facing the consequences of your actions." I inclined my head towards the window, where the faint howl of wolves still reached us. The pack wouldn't hurt us, but I doubted anyone wanted to spend the night being chased down.

Casey glanced in my direction, and I could tell he wanted to flip me off, but I didn't break eye contact. My command suddenly became that of an Alpha, and he had no choice but to nod in agreement. I cared less about the stain itself than the lack of respect it implied, so it wasn't something I could let slide.

Asher, another member of the skulk who lived with the twins, was feeding a slice of veggie pizza to his new mate Mikaela. The scene was entirely too sensual for the rest of us to be present, moans and all, as she ran her hands over his plaid-clad chest. His eyes went fully golden as he watched her. Apparently, I wasn't the only one with this thought — a pillow zoomed across the room, slamming into Asher's head, knocking his backwards baseball cap off to reveal his dark russet hair, and jarring him from their intimate moment.

"Have you no decency? There's a child present!" Cole indicated Emerson with a wave of his hand. My brother, only a few years younger than the twins, flipped him off. "Get a fucking room."

"I never want to be mated." Emerson shook his head, pointedly not looking in Asher and Mikaela's direction as he played the video game in his lap. "That shit is gross."

Asher chuckled, a sly smile spreading across his face as he glanced from Mikaela at his side to Cole and Emerson, his eyes shifting back to blue. "You say that," his eyebrows rose, "but you'd be humming a different tune after you've felt your —"

Mikaela slapped Asher across the chest, stopping whatever he was going to say, and he brushed her blond hair out of his way to nip at her neck. I sighed heavily. The hormones in this room were stifling. And honestly, I didn't want to hear about it because then I'd know what I couldn't have with Nimue.

I still couldn't believe she was here, just across town. My fox was screaming at me for the distance I'd put between us, demanding I go and claim her in every way a mate could, but there were so many reasons I couldn't do what he wanted.

Occasionally shifters mated outside their species, but it was almost unheard of for a shifter to mate a non-shifter. There were too many aspects of our lives defined by our animal that a non-shifter would never be able to understand. The importance and hierarchy of the skulk or pack was one of them, but living with two separate but entwined parts of your soul was another. The fact that I would be the next Alpha to our skulk added another level of *don't go there*. I worked at the tea shop for now, but eventually, being the Alpha would *be* my job, and every aspect of my life would be consumed by responsibilities to the skulk.

Besides, what could come of a demon-shifter cross? A fire-wielding fox? We weren't Pokemon, for Christ's sake.

No. I was better off staying away.

"I saw you talking to Nimue at the party tonight." Nadir turned to me as the others continued their bickering and relentless teasing of Emerson. Nadir, my best friend, future Second, and cousin, had the annoying habit of picking up on exactly what I was thinking. That would be great when we were in charge of our skulk, but right now, it was fucking annoying.

I mumbled an assent but said nothing. Nadir only stared harder. "I said hi," I finally admitted, hoping he'd drop it.

Nadir nodded, tilting his chin up, *not* dropping it. "Must have been a really friendly hi. You both looked upset."

I swung my eyes to his, my Alpha energy rising as I stared him down. "Stay out of it, Nadir."

Instantly, he dropped his eyes at the reminder that I was his Alpha before his friend, and let it go.

Each time I had to pull rank rubbed me wrong. I'd watched my father order our skulk around my whole life, always with everyone's best interest at heart, but the constant need for discipline was draining. I knew that was my future, and I wished I could say I wanted it.

Watching out for everyone, keeping us all safe, that part I could handle. Gladly. I had always been the most cautious of our group anyway — not to say that I didn't take risks. I was a fox, damn it. Risk was my middle name. I just *assessed* the risks first. Calculated backup plans for everything. Safety meant we all got to live to our next prank.

CRACK.

Every head snapped to the windows facing the street, the sound jolting me from my thoughts. A sticky yellow glob slowly slid down the glass, and Nadir stood to look out the window. Cole and Casey were right behind him, peering over his shoulder into the darkness below.

"They're egging your shop!" Casey laughed. That got Emerson to set his game down as he moved to join them at the window.

I quickly hopped down the steps to Immortali-Tea, using only the streetlight outside to guide my way through the darkened shop. As a shifter, my eyesight was better than a human's, but I also enjoyed how the wolves' eyes widened as I stepped out of the shadow and stopped in front of the window, staring out at the wolves on the sidewalk.

"Thought you might need some eggs for breakfast," Julian called out with a smirk, and the wolves around him laughed. His light brown hair was tied up loosely on his head, his pack tattoos on full display with the sleeves of his denim shirt rolled up.

But it wasn't just wolves around him. I sighed internally as I saw my sister Lily, nearly a decade younger than him, at his side. In ripped jeans, motorcycle boots, and what seemed like Julian's shirt, she looked every bit the defiant female she was. I fought the urge to roll my eyes at my rebellious sister or order her into the shop with me, the second of which would indicate to these wolves that I thought they were a threat. At 25, she was an adult and could take care of herself.

Even when Julian slung an overly-familiar arm around my younger sister, brushing her wild brown hair over her shoulder, I showed no reaction. I only unlocked and opened my shop door, crossing my arms and leaning against the frame as I smirked at them.

"Wow. Vandalism from a law-man. Didn't see that coming. You guys think of this all by yourselves, or did you need to bring in the local middle schoolers for a professional consultation?"

A few wolves growled at my taunt, but Julian silently met my stare with one of his own, confusion playing on the edge of his features as he tried to puzzle out my reaction.

"Watch out, Jules. Wouldn't want you to hurt yourself thinking so hard."

He narrowed his eyes at me, a few of his wolves taking a step closer, but I only chuckled. "You know this building is a historical landmark, right?" I pointed to the side of the building where a placard stating as much was affixed to the brick. "I can't wait to show this video footage to the Ladies tomorrow. I wonder what they'll do about it?" I grinned at them, my lips pulling back to show my teeth, before turning my back on them and shutting the door.

Chapter Four

NIMUE

"CAN DEMONS ERASE MEMORIES?"

Devanna's blue hair was draped across the counter where she slumped over the kitchen island of my carriage house behind Blaze's cottage as I descended the stairs to the main floor. She looked a little worse for wear, and not only for the rumpled cat costume she still wore from the night before, having crashed on my couch after the party.

"Uh oh," I laughed, pulling my chestnut hair up into a loose bun as I rounded the island to start a pot of coffee. I pushed up the sleeves of my fuzzy pink sweater, which I'd paired with slightly faded grey jeans and black suede ankle boots. I could see Dev wincing slightly with each click of my boots, so I transferred my weight to my toes. "What happened?"

Only a groan answered me as she pressed her forehead into the cool grey quartz countertop. Of course, I knew *part* of what this was about, but I'd let her come to me with the details. Dev was like a cat, not only in costume — you could never let her know how much you wanted to connect, or she'd bolt.

"I think I made the worst mistake of my life last night," she mumbled into the counter. "Like, horrible. I can never come back from this."

When the coffee finished percolating, I poured two cups and slid hers across the island to her — black — and added a splash of cream to mine.

"Aw, Dev. I'm sure that's not true." I slid into one of the ballet pink velvet stools beside her, content to sip my coffee slowly and wait her out.

She was going to tell me eventually. She was dying to.

I glanced around the room, admiring the white back-splash, and how it contrasted against the pretty light wood cabinets and the grey counters. But the gold globes suspended over the island were my favorite — Blaze had done a great job renovating this space for me, and I missed it.

"No, Nims." She groaned again, pulling herself upright to take a long, desperate sip of coffee, adjusting her thick-framed glasses on her warm brown skin. "You don't under-stand. This was the *worst* thing I have *ever* done." She glared at me, willing me to understand her dismay, before her expression softened slightly. "But the worst part is..." she shook her head, taking another long gulp.

"Hmm?" I blinked innocently at her, knowing exactly where this was going.

"Okay. I'll say it." She took a deep breath. "I — we — *he* — I *might* have... complimented Orion's costume to him last night. God, I think I even *smiled* at him."

Only from my favorite blue-haired witch was being nice

to someone cause for so much angst. I gasped in shock like I'd had no idea. But, of course, I'd practically set the whole thing up. Nudging them towards each other. Nevertheless, I grinned like the Cheshire Cat.

"Niiiiims," she said, putting her head down again. "If you tell your stupid cousin, I'll hex that stupid smile off his face."

I mimed zipping my lips shut, locking it, and throwing away the key. "Secret's safe with me." I wasn't about to be the one to tell her that *smiling* at someone was hardly cause for gossip — though, to be honest, around here, and from Dev to Orion, maybe it was. I leaned in, nudging her elbow where it rested on the counter. "But I have to know… isn't there a *tiny* part of you that wants to know if he's as buttoned up in the passion department as he is in everything else? I bet not. I bet he kisses like —"

"I'm not talking about this." Her voice was muffled, face pressed into the counter still. "I regret telling you already. How's Colorado?" she asked, and I smiled at the drastic topic change; just like her to deflect away from something personal.

"Good, when I'm there. Boulder is fine, but everyone there is young, and usually high, or drunk, or both. So, inhibitions are low, and it's hard to block out all of the urges in a city of college kids. It's tiring." I didn't think I'd ever voiced that out loud before, but Dev had known me my entire life. She understood what I meant. "I did fall in love with this little shifter town up in the mountains, though. And I like traveling. I've traveled to so many places I've always wanted to photograph, and the portfolio I've built for myself while I've been there has made it worth it —"

Dev immediately put her hand out for my phone, and I swiped it open to my portfolio for her to scroll through while I continued. "To be honest, though…" I trailed off, unsure whether I wanted to give voice to my thoughts.

"You want to come home?" she asked as she sat up straight.

I shrugged, sipping my coffee. "I miss it here. Having a more permanent home base, having people around who understand you. I made friends with a few shifters, but I miss my Devvie." I leaned over, resting my head on her shoulder.

"For the love of God. No."

I laughed, trying to lighten the mood again. The fact that I was *slightly* discontent in my current life wasn't really Dev's problem. "But on the whole, it's been good for me, I think."

"I'm trying very hard to be supportive of you," Dev answered, and I smiled at her honesty, "but I'd really rather you just move home." Her head dropped down against mine. "I never have anyone to talk to here anymore."

"Blaze said you spend a lot of time at the bar with him."

Dev chuckled, her shoulder shaking lightly under me. "He doesn't count. But he does give me free whiskey."

"Self-service?"

Dev nodded. "Damn straight."

I couldn't help but chuckle at my challenging friend. She was as assertive and confident as they came, and on paper, we seemed opposites. But what you couldn't see on paper was Dev's fiercely protective side, and I was lucky enough to have earned that protection and loyalty from her. In exchange, my demon magic seemed to work in reverse for her, pulling on her desire, however buried, for calm. I loved providing that for her.

Her thumb stilled over a photo of a serene pond, the water perfectly mirroring the tall pines surrounding it and the stars and moon overhead. "Where was this one?" She cocked a too-knowing brow at me as she handed my phone back over, and I clicked it off.

I laced my arms around her, and she grumbled at both my lack of answer — though we both knew where it was — and the physical affection.

"You staying here?" I asked as I let go. Dev muttered something I couldn't quite make out, more of a groan than anything. "I'm headed to Mo's for breakfast, but I'll be back later."

Picturing Mo's house was enough to ignite my demon magic, and instantly, I slipped through the ether, flickering from my carriage house at Blaze's to Mo's across town. I smiled as I skipped up the steps to the magenta and teal house. The hydrangeas were pruned back for the season, leaving the yellow witch hazel to shine in full bloom in the crisp fall air. I'd loved growing up here — it was as magical on the inside as the bright paint made the outside. Nothing about Morgaine was ordinary, and I was lucky to have her as my mom.

"Morning!" I called as I pushed open the marigold door. The smell of coffee drew me down the hall into the kitchen, and the sight of the familiar room, its outdated parquet flooring, teal appliances, yellow bead-board walls, and exotically patterned textiles hit me like a hug from Mo herself. Mo was standing at the butcher-block counter, pulling out several mugs from pale blue cabinets, but stopped when I rounded the corner.

Her hands rose in the air, the sleeves of her rainbow leopard-print kimono that looked like something straight out of Lisa Frank sliding down her pale arms as she reached towards me for a hug.

"My baby," she said, yanking me into her hold. "Home at last." A wet kiss dropped on my cheek, and then magic tingled across my skin as she cleared the bright pink lipstick I was sure she had left behind.

"I've missed you," I said as I pulled back. Holding her at arm's length, I took in her gigantic pink plastic glasses, plaid pants, and clashing kimono. Her sleek white bob haircut was her most traditional feature, but somehow, combined with the rest of her ensemble, it was just as eccentric. "You look ridiculous."

"Exactly what I was going for, dear," she winked, and I grinned. Grabbing the mugs from the counter, I carried them over to the thick-planked wood table, setting them out at chairs. As I took over coffee duty, she slid back over to the stove, which was currently covered in a half-dozen different pans with pancakes of every size, shape, and color I never imagined a pancake could be.

"Who else is coming by this morning?"

"Blaze and Petra said they'd be in, and Selene stayed in town last night. I thought she'd be in Petra's carriage house, but I knocked earlier, and no one answered." Her eyes danced with mischief as she shrugged. "So I invited Ryker, too."

I shook my head with a chuckle, rolling my eyes. "So when are they changing your title from Aura Witch to Matchmaker Extraordinaire?"

"I don't need the title for it. They go hand in hand. I sense your auras, then find the match. Easy as that."

"You say that as if every witch can snap their fingers and find true love," I said as I poured coffee into my favorite mug — it was hot pink and said in bold letters, World's Okayest Sister. Blaze gave it to me for my birthday eight years ago, and we both knew it was more than a mug. He had a crappy history with his own family and intentionally chose me as his sister instead.

Demons didn't always make for the best families — I didn't even know anything about mine, beyond that, at one point, they'd been through Maine to drop me off at Mo's doorstep with nothing more than the blanket I was wrapped in and my name pinned to it. I considered myself lucky to have Blaze and Mo in my life.

"It is a fine art; I'll give you that." Mo smiled, switching off all the burners and turning towards the back door where Blaze and Petra stepped in. He was holding her hand, and the two were contentedly chatting. Blaze was in his usual black hoodie and ripped jeans, and Petra in an emerald green cable knit sweater that set off her red hair. Their conversation halted as Mo pulled them inside with a hand around each of their wrists.

"Mm. No babies yet, huh?" Mo tsked, and Petra's jaw dropped, her blue eyes popping.

"Mo." A tear leaked out as I convulsed in laughter, glancing between Petra's blanched face and Blaze's eye-rolling. "Stop."

"That's not—" Petra started, her mouth opening and closing, clearly at a loss for words, before she glanced at Blaze, yanking on his arm.

"Bit soon for that, Mo," Blaze sighed, pulling Petra into his chest as he dropped her hand and threw his arm around her shoulder. "But she did finally admit that she loved me yesterday, so that's progress. Maybe next week." He winked and Petra glanced up at him, panic written on her expression. I laughed harder.

"They're joking." I reached out, pulling Petra from Blaze's grip to free her from this awkward moment. "Mo can't resist. No one cares whether you have kids or not. We're just glad you're here, and a part of our little family now."

"That's right, sweetie." Mo smiled, patting Petra on the back as she passed us to grab the coffee pot. "Besides, Selene will be giving me babies around here first. It'll be years from now, but I'm a patient woman."

Petra's eyes settled on me with a confused expression. "With whom?" she mouthed, and I raised a shoulder, shaking my head.

"Knock knock!" The door opened and closed, Selene's voice carrying down the hall towards us. "Smells like pancakes. Am I too late?"

"In here!" Mo called back, and winked at me. "Come on in. I have plenty."

Selene rounded the corner wearing an oversized black t-shirt dress that dwarfed her petite frame, tied at the waist with a black hoodie. She was barefoot, but maybe she'd left them at the door. Her hair was up in a wet ponytail, curls forming along her hairline against her tan skin, fresh of any makeup.

Petra's eyes locked on Selene as well, taking in her strangely all-black outfit, but she said nothing. Mo finally spun in Selene's direction, and then cackled. *Cackled.*

"Did I miss something?" Selene said as she sidled up to my side by the table. "Mushrooms? Laughing gas, maybe? What's going on here?"

"No clue," I smirked as I sipped the coffee in my cup.

"Morning, guys," Selene said as she leaned across me to squeeze her best friend's hand and nodded at Blaze. "Have fun last night?"

"I did." Petra nodded, staring down her friend. "I looked for you at the party but couldn't find you. Did you leave early?"

Before Selene could answer, the door opened and closed again, and in strode Ryker dressed all in black.

What. A. Coincidence.

He grunted, not even bothering with a greeting, and swiped a mug off the table, filling it to the brim with coffee. Selene was pointedly looking anywhere but at the imposing dragon shifter, which was hard to do considering he was well over six-and-a-half feet of gigantic, tattooed, scary blond man and sucking the oxygen out of the room with his very presence.

"Was that Akil DJing last night, Blaze?" Selene asked, trying to push attention off herself, and Blaze nodded. "Kit's brother? God, I swear he was four yesterday."

"You've been gone a long time, hun." Mo sighed, a hint of longing in her voice. "But you'll return home before you have kids. Your mother Saw it before she passed. Could be any day now." Her expression danced with mirth as she glanced around the room.

Selene's eyes expanded in alarm as she glanced up at Ryker, who was *very* focused on his coffee. "And when did you get into Divination, Mo?" Selene asked, a hint of nervousness in her voice.

"You know I can't do that, darling." Mo smiled innocently as if she wasn't stirring a massive pot of drama in her kitchen. "Just my tiny little aura magic."

Blaze sputtered a laugh, coffee spraying across the table. "Sorry."

"Everyone sit. My children are here, and you've all made me one happy Mo. Let me feed you before you all scatter to the wind and leave me with only Blaze and Petra to pester once again."

Breakfast at Mo's was always my favorite — she made delicious pancakes of all kinds, some ordinary, and some so very Mo.

Plain. Banana. Blueberry lemon. Red velvet. Apple cheesecake. Funfetti. Maple bacon. PB&J and potato chips. Pumpkin spice latte.

The table was crowded, but it hadn't escaped my notice that there were still two empty chairs. Mo never did anything accidentally, so I was waiting to see how this would play out.

"There's too much food here." Mo acted shocked as if she hadn't prepared all this knowing she'd overdone it. "Call Devanna and see if she's up. Maybe she's hungry."

Dev and Mo weren't always on the best of terms when I wasn't home to moderate the conversation between the two of them. Both were powerful witches in their coven, and their two equally large personalities were a lot to handle in one room. I squinted at my mother, but she wasn't looking in my direction, happily chatting with Petra at her side. I shot off a quick text, then put my phone back down.

The doorbell rang shortly after, which was odd. No one rang the doorbell at Mo's. If you were here, it wasn't an accident — you just came right in. "COME IN!" Mo called, and the door opened and closed.

Orion ducked into the room, white wings tucked tight at his back and his silver hair perfectly combed, neat as ever with his crisp button-down shirt and dark jeans. "Thank you for the invitation, Morgaine. I wondered where all the normal breakfast patrons in my kitchen had run off to. Additionally, I wanted to speak to you and Blaze about the upcoming meeting regarding —"

"No business talk before pancakes, Orion," Mo scolded, spatula pointed at the large angel.

Orion's mouth snapped shut, his jaw working while he fought to obey her. I watched attentively, but, to no one's surprise, Mo didn't back down. With a heavy sigh, Orion pulled one of the two remaining chairs back gently, hardly scraping across the floor as he sat, wings draping over the back of the chair and almost to the floor.

"Could you pass the coffee?" he asked politely, pointing to the pot to my right, and I handed it to him. Mo's eyes met mine briefly, and I pulled my lips into my mouth, fighting the urge to laugh again. "While I was flying over, I noticed a new current in the water out by —"

The front door opened again, cutting off Orion's words, as heavy boots clomped down the hall. Orion lifted his mug to his mouth, stopping mid-air as we all glanced to the kitchen doorway.

"You know I can't skip out on panca —" Dev stopped, staring over the table, noticing the only chair left was right next to Orion. "Oh, fuck no." Dev spun on her heel and made for the door, blue hair swishing behind her, and Mo hopped to her feet. "You can meddle in everyone else's life, Mo. But leave me out of this."

Mo stopped in the hallway, her lips twisted to the side, but the door didn't open and close again, and her eyes sparkled with delight.

"I'm sitting in the living room by myself," Dev called back into the room. "I like pancakes more than I hate Orion."

Orion rolled his eyes, muttering an *unbelievable* before serving himself a plain pancake from the platter in the center of the table.

I shook with silent laughter as I cut into my lemon blueberry pancake. I forgot how much I missed my family, and the thought of leaving again sent a pang through my heart.

Chapter Five

IN AN EFFORT TO distract myself from the knowledge that my unclaimed mate was just across town, I stayed in my fox form as much as possible the next day. Tomorrow, I'd have to go back into town and open the shop, but Sundays were my day off, and I was intent on taking a break. Several of the skulk joined me, and we ran through our lands, skirting the trees and cliffs while we enjoyed our wilder side.

This was one of my favorite times of year to run the land, when the air was cool and crisp, leaves scattered on the forest floor, and the woods were settling down for the winter.

As dusk settled in, I shifted back, slipping into sweats on my parents' porch, and joined my family for dinner as I did every Sunday. We sat around the dining table, overflowing with food. Ma had made butter chicken and roti, and the familiar smell of garam masala and garlic wafted through the house. Everyone bantered and chatted easily, Akil trying to convince us he was old enough for his first tattoos, to no success. But I stayed quiet, my thoughts drifting back across town.

It seemed a lifetime ago that I'd sneak out of my house every night, shifting to scurry through fields, fences, and forests to wait in the hydrangeas outside Nimue's window. She'd hop out, and we'd spend hours running around the woods, playing and exploring together. Sometimes I was shifted, sometimes not, but always with her.

Our late-night rendezvous were a secret I'd never shared with my parents. Nimue wouldn't have cared if anyone knew, but she understood how important my parents were to me, and how terrified I was for them to find out.

I loved my family dearly, and had even taken over my grandmother's tea shop when she'd passed on so that it would stay in the family. The fact that I'd had to hide so much of my childhood from my parents had always eaten away at me. But they never would have approved of our creeping through the woods at night, or half the shenanigans we got up to.

In fairness, most parents probably wouldn't have been happy about their children running around unsupervised, but mine were especially strict. They'd seen firsthand how hard their parents had worked when they first came to the States, especially my father.

My grandparents had sensed his Alpha power growing even from a very young age and had left their original skulk behind in India to avoid a confrontation with their Alpha. They'd only stopped in the Cove to get the blessing from the then-Alpha of the Arrowwood skulk to start their own nearby, but instead, he'd welcomed them with open arms. Having no sons of his own, he'd taken my father under his wing to train him until he was ready to retire, and eventually, my father stepped peacefully into his place.

Even with the support of the Alpha, though, their first years here hadn't been easy, trying to get set up and settled while earning the trust and respect of a new community.

I knew my parents just wanted the best for me — for all of us — but their overbearing protectiveness often led to lies by omission so that my siblings and I could live a little and fit in with our friends.

Besides, as Alpha of our skulk, my father had an image to uphold in the community. He demanded nothing less from me, his eldest son — the one who would inherit his title when he chose to retire from his duties.

"Earth to Kit," Lily called, snapping her fingers in front of my face. My eyes swung to hers, flashing yellow for a moment as my Alpha side balked at her disrespect.

Lily's amber eyes, a hint darker than mine, dropped immediately, but her shoulders jerked at the unspoken command, annoyance ticking in her jaw. Julian's shirt was nowhere in sight today, but she couldn't honestly believe our parents wouldn't scent him on her eventually.

"We were just talking about plans for the next full moon, *jaan*," Ma spoke softly, and I glanced her way. The way she studied me made me feel like she could read into my soul. Though she and Lily were wildly different, often butting heads with their equally strong personalities, they loved with the same ferocity.

"What about it?" I asked. I should have been sorry I'd tuned them all out so completely that I had no idea what was being discussed, but I was too unsettled.

"I asked if you're ready to lead the run," my father's

deep voice rumbled, full of disapproval. His hair had turned grey long ago, having waited until far later in his life to settle down and start a family, but it still stood thick and straight on his head, and his thick beard was always neatly groomed. "But if you can't even follow our conversation, the answer is no." His frown was carved deep into his face, and I fought to contain my sigh.

"Not yet." I nodded, then pushed back from the table, heading for the door. I knew my father well enough to know a well-meaning lecture came next, and I didn't have the patience to sit through it.

"*Jaan*, don't run off," Ma called, and I paused.

"Thank you for dinner, Ma." I bent to kiss her cheek, then turned to my grandfather. "I'll bring some more of your tea next time, Dadaji." His eyes softened as he nodded; it was my grandmother's old blend, one they used to drink together. With that, I pushed through the door and out into the night.

Monday morning, I threw myself into my work. I not only opened the shop and served customers, but dusted every shelf and teapot, reorganized the mugs and to-go cups, and deep cleaned any and everything that could possibly be deep cleaned.

Like clockwork, Peg Fernsby and Eva Watford from the Historic Society swept in at nine, Peg lightly plumping her perfectly-coiffed purple hair as they approached the counter.

"Morning, ladies." I flashed the ancient witches a smile

that pinked Peg's cheeks as she tittered at Eva, and that Eva returned warmly.

"We weren't sure you'd be open so early today, Kit." Eva winked at me from under her pumpkin orange beret, complete with stem and vining leaves emerging from the top, her own short white hair perfectly styled. "Peg thought you might have spent the weekend with a young lady for the full moon after Sabazios's party."

Peg coughed a giggle behind her hand as I started heating water for their tea, assembled their usual assortment of pastries without even asking, and shook my head. Eva saw me as something of her long-lost grandson; as far as I could tell, she wanted to make me hand-knit scarves and freshly-squeezed blueberry lemonade for the rest of her days. Peg, on the other hand — well, some days, I wouldn't put it past her to try to slip me a love potion. But she was harmless. "Not this time. The guys and I were too busy cleaning up after the shop was egged."

They both gasped, hands fluttering over their hearts. "*No!*"

"*Egged?*"

"*Who?*"

"But this shop is a *historical landmark!*"

I nodded, my eyes wide and open to show I was just as appalled as they were. "I tried to tell them that, but would they listen?" I sighed, the sentiment echoed by both ladies, their expressions equal parts sympathetic and vengeful.

"I don't suppose you know who those ruffians were, would you, Kit?" Eva asked, raising a calculating brow.

"Well, it was dark." I grimaced, failing to remind them that I could see in the dark. Waited a beat to draw out the moment, knowing I had them on the hook. "But I did have the cameras on."

With a quick, triumphant glance between them, Peg turned to me, her eyes beaming with the chance to right this injustice I'd suffered. Right on cue, the two of them said in unison, "We'll need to see those tapes."

Both ladies assured me they would get to the bottom of this "abhorrent affair" after I handed them the USB drive with the footage, and I couldn't help but smirk as I wiped down the counters.

As they did every morning, the ladies sat at a table in the corner long after they finished their tea, gossiping in hushed tones. Thirty minutes passed before the bell above the door jingled, and a disheveled-looking Nox stumbled into the tea shop, slumping into a chair a few seats down from them. Our youngest local demon, Nox had blond hair that peeked out from under his black beanie, a handful of visible tattoos and piercings, and was startlingly out of place in my quaint tea shop in his all-black outfit, nevermind as company for the ladies. But he'd earned their ire for torching a historical property a few months ago, and since taking their meeting minutes was part of his penance, he'd become a weekly feature by their side.

I chuckled as Peg scolded him for being late — most demons struggled to rise before noon — and he snapped open a notebook as he grumbled under his breath, "One more month."

Leaving them to it, I boxed up an order of pies for Scallywags. Not much of a baker, Blaze was one of my best clients and had a standing order with me to offer at the bar.

The bell above the door chimed again, and I didn't need

to glance up to know my skulk had arrived, sensing their nearness through our mental link. Nadir, Emerson, and the twins entered the shop, greeting Nox with fist bumps and high fives as they made their way to the counter.

Nadir and Emerson worked behind the counter regularly with me, although both split their time between here and other jobs. When they weren't in the shop, Emerson was apprenticed to a local shifter tattoo artist, and Nadir worked odd jobs around town for the skulk, whoever needed help with a project. He was supposed to be the one to fulfill the requirement of having an engineer in the family, but dropped out of college his junior year when he realized he'd be committing to a lifetime in an office.

Casey and Cole both worked from home, the former as a programmer and the latter as a graphic designer. They were regulars in my shop, frequently choosing to use my Wi-Fi for a change of scenery, as was the case today. Settling into the table at the corner, Casey plugged in his laptop and secured his headphones.

"Wanna join us, Nox?" Casey taunted, then finger-gunned him. "Oh, right. Meeting minutes." He shot the young demon a smirk, and Nox's returning scowl had Casey snickering.

Cole was designing a new logo for the shop, and propped open his tablet on the counter to walk me through his initial thoughts for the new art. I motioned Emerson and Nadir to head into the backroom and start unloading the week's shipment before joining Cole at the counter.

After I approved his design — a tea stain blending into a fox tail looping around the shop's name — he took a seat across from Casey and got to work. Despite not being identical twins, when the two sat across from each other at the same table, intent upon their screens with nearly-matching flannel shirts, the resemblance was almost uncanny.

"Be back in a few," I called back to Nadir so he'd know to man the shop for now as I finished stacking the pies in a cardboard box to transport. He emerged from the back, giving me a nod and moving to wash his hands, and I grabbed the box and headed out.

Chapter Six

NIMUE

MY HEART RACED as I walked across town, steeling my nerves to talk to Kit again. Knowing he was here in town while we weren't on good terms was unbearable, and it needed to stop.

I repeated my reasoning to myself with every step towards Immortali-Tea. Could I have flickered there? Sure. But I needed the walk and fresh air to build up my resolve.

After pancakes, I spent the day with Mo catching up. All day, I'd checked my phone, hoping to hear from Kit. For some sort of explanation for his weird behavior at the party, or just a return to normalcy for us. But nothing.

We hadn't kept in touch the past couple of years as much as I'd hoped, but still. He had been my closest confidante since before I knew what friends were. That meant something. We were best friends. Right?

I guessed the past tense was the key there. I wasn't sure where we stood anymore, after the kiss. I'd freaked out, and fled town.

Maybe he was upset about *that*? That I hadn't sought

him out afterwards to make it right or acknowledge it? But it wasn't like he'd mentioned it either.

The truth was that the kiss had been phenomenal. The kind you only read about in a romance novel, with the freaking fireworks going off in the background. I knew he'd only kissed me because he probably felt like he had to after I drunkenly leaned into him, but then I'd panicked.

Now, years later, I understood my knee-jerk reaction better.

If I was being honest with myself, back then, I wanted it to mean a lot more than just a drunken mistake. Unwilling to risk my friendship with him, I'd bolted instead of telling him, since there was no way he would be interested in a relationship with a demon. We were notoriously bad at relationships and families. Shifters' entire lives centered around their skulks, their packs. Even if I had a much better upbringing than most demons, thanks to Mo, I knew Kit wouldn't want to risk it.

Rather than face him and the difficult conversation we needed to have, I had started taking more and more assignments out of town, *far* away from Deadlights Cove. I might not have realized at the time that I was running away, but in retrospect… It looked bad.

Maybe Kit was right to hate me. It was entirely possible he thought *I* had cut *him* out of my life and ended our friendship, which was not my intention.

Thoughts reeling, I stepped across Ocean Avenue towards the green in front of the gazebo, groaning internally. And maybe a little bit out loud.

Taking a deep breath to recenter myself, I approached the tea shop.

Kit and I were friends.

We. Were. Friends.

And I would earn his friendship back if it was the last thing I did. Even if he never wanted to be more than that, I'd rather have him in my life as my friend than not at all.

Nodding to my reflection, I pushed open the door. The bells jangled above as the familiar scents of black and green teas, peppermint, and cloves hit me like a wave, tension leaving my shoulders immediately.

Behind the counter, Kit's cousin Nadir popped up, a sly smile dawning upon his light bronze face as he spotted me.

"Hey, Nimue," he said, his sharp olive eyes studying me as he leaned his elbows on the counter, skulk tattoos covering his forearms. His thick dark brown hair stuck up slightly in the front, shaved shorter on the sides of his head, and he was sporting a short beard he'd grown since the last time I'd spoken to him. "Long time no see."

I smiled at him. "I must have missed you at the be —" My words were cut off when I was spun around from behind and embraced.

"Nimue!" I thought it was Cole, but it was hard to tell with my face pressed into his chest.

"Demon hog!" Before I knew it, I was ripped from probably-Cole's arms and pulled into a hug by probably-Casey, laughing as he tucked me under his chin.

"Oo, I should draw a demon-hog," Cole mused, grinning at me as Casey held me at arm's length.

"Hands off if you know what's good for you, cubs," Nadir scolded them with a raised brow, though the expression was more calculating than threatening.

"Oh, I don't mind," I assured him, throwing an arm

around each twin. "I missed you rascals. Get into any mischief without me?"

"Of course not." Cole's wide blue eyes conveyed total innocence.

"We'd never," Casey agreed solemnly, placing a hand across his heart, covering up the Stargate logo on his shirt.

"Isn't that right, Emerson?" Cole looked to Kit's brother for corroboration. I noted Emerson's gaze trailing along our entwined arms briefly before he scoffed, rolled his eyes, and turned to go into the back room. Emerson had always been a male of few words, and it seemed that hadn't changed even though he had to be 26 by now.

"Uh-huh." I looked from one twin to the other, Cole's longer black waves falling into his eyes as he smirked. "So the shaving cream I heard some wolves complaining about…"

"What shaving cream?" Casey deadpanned immediately.

"I don't even think I know what shaving cream is." Cole shrugged innocently. Shameless.

"Seriously, Nim, look at that smooth face. You think it's ever seen a razor?"

Cole coughed in indignation. "Hey, I could grow a beard if I wanted to."

I laughed again. "Sure. So, the shaving cream wasn't you then. But what about the shifter I saw angrily holding up a t-shirt with a wolf in a diaper crying as it reached out for a moon-shaped pacifier?"

"Well —" Casey capitulated.

"That one might have been me." Cole only grinned wider. I elbowed both of them in the ribs in turn and slipped from their arms, approaching Nadir at the counter, who watched our entire interaction with rapt interest.

Emerson emerged from the back room again, carrying out a box of teas. He began restocking the shelves behind the counter, pointedly ignoring all of us as we continued to catch up. I'd grown up with these guys, and I hadn't realized how much I'd missed them and their camaraderie until now.

"So, Nimue." Nadir's eyes flashed yellow as he straightened up, but when he blinked, they were back to light green. "You should come out hiking with us sometime. Like the old days."

"Almost like déjà *brew*," Cole sighed, a sly smile spreading at his own joke.

"That was both awful and genius." Casey slapped his twin upside the head. Nadir chuckled, but Emerson's hard gaze was locked on Nadir.

"I don't know if that's a good idea," Emerson said, voice low and eyes solely on his cousin.

I heard shuffling behind me, and half-turned my head to see the twins sidling off back to the corner table where their laptops were, my brow furrowing in confusion at their rapid exit.

Nadir had gone that preternatural stillness that only a shifter could achieve, though he hadn't turned to face Emerson, whose eyes were still boring into him.

"I'd love to," I said, hoping to diffuse whatever was happening between them. Sometimes shifters got into weird locked states like this, and a buffer could help shake them out of it. "I haven't seen the property in ages."

Nadir's jaw worked for a moment before he blinked and met my gaze again. "A lot's changed in the past couple of years," he said, slightly rigidly, but managed a tight-lipped smile. "The guys and I would be happy to show you. How long are you in town?"

"A couple of weeks." My gaze darted between him and Emerson, who was practically glowering at Nadir at this point, bewildered as to what was going on between them.

"Maybe this weekend, then? Do you have the same number? I can text you the details."

Emerson coughed, and I could have sworn I saw Nadir's hackles rise.

"Shouldn't we ask Kit before inviting her out with us?"

Was that a growl sounding from Nadir's throat?

"I don't remember asking your opinion." Nadir's tone was icy, low, and rumbling, his head tilting as he turned partially to face Emerson, eyes gone yellow again. "Keep out of this, Emerson."

I knew if I was a shifter, I would have felt the pulse of power that accompanied commands from higher to lower ranking shifters with his last words, and Emerson winced slightly, dropping his eyes.

Giving them a minute to regroup, I cleared my throat as Nadir's eyes returned to human again.

"Guess you're officially Kit's future Second, then?" I said lightly, though my eyes flitted to Emerson to ensure he was okay. The younger shifter seemed fine, though, as he resumed stocking the shelves and pretended to ignore us. I'd known it would probably happen — Nadir had always been close with Kit — but it was different to actually see him using ranked commands like that on the others. He would have come into his full power shortly after I'd left town.

"Why don't you ask him all about it on Saturday?"

Nadir turned that predatory, vulpine look onto me, teeth flashing, and I fought the urge to take a step back.

"He won't be back soon?" I looked to the shop's front door, hoping to see him on his way back in so we could smooth everything over and go back to normal.

Nadir pressed his lips together, and I could have sworn I heard Emerson muttering to himself.

"I think you should talk to him yourself on Saturday."

"YOU DID *WHAT?*"

I could have strangled Nadir.

"What? Aren't you two friends?" he asked innocently, but I knew the wily scoundrel better than that. He saw my reaction to Nimue at the party, he could feel there was a spot for my mate in our skulk bonds, and he was pushing his fucking luck.

"Told you," Emerson muttered from the back room.

"And I told *you* to shut your mouth about it," Nadir snapped back at him, his voice rippling with ranked command.

"Calm down." My order carried my power, and Nadir reluctantly took a breath, unable to disobey. I huffed a bitter laugh. "If anyone should be upset right now, it should be me."

I'd just returned from delivering Scallywags' pie order, which took considerably longer than expected. First, Blaze wanted to chat; then Morgaine; then I'd run into Caedmon, one-half of the dynamic duo who ran the coffee van; and finally Beverly, who owned the exotic pet shop. Ironic, in a town with shifters. On my return to Immortali-Tea, my future Second had informed me he'd invited my mate — though he didn't *officially* know that was what she was, even if he had his suspicions — to come hiking with us on skulk lands.

"Why would you be upset?" Cole asked as he approached the counter. He reached over the glass of the pastry case to snag a sugar cookie with a purple blackberry frosted on it, taking a bite.

"Yeah, Kit? Why would you?"

I merely leveled a glare at Nadir as I snatched the cookie out of Cole's hand, turning my back on them to storm off to my office in the back.

Despite my reservations about having Nimue on skulk lands — I feared the scent of our territory combined with her own would have my fox screaming at me to tie her down and never let her leave — part of me was looking forward to it. She hadn't been out there with us in years, and there were a few changes since she'd last seen it that I couldn't help but want to share with her. Though I'd never admit as much to Nadir.

Early Saturday morning, we all gathered on the wrap-around porch of my parents' white farmhouse. While we waited for Nimue to arrive, the guys loaded up the gear, dressed in flannels or sweatshirts against the day's chill. Most of the deciduous trees had dropped their leaves, but there were still some pockets of yellow and orange and red amongst the never-ending green conifers.

"Catch."

Emerson jerked his head up just in time to catch the water bottle Nadir chucked at him, throwing a middle finger at him as he stuffed it into his backpack. As the youngest and lowest ranked, Emerson would carry the bulk of our supplies for the day, though Cole also had a small pack.

"Where are we heading?" Cole asked from where he was shoving snacks into his bag. "Quarry?"

I'd thought about it, but most of our restoration work was focused further west, and I knew that was what Nimue would be the most interested in.

"Bear Pond."

Cole nodded, sliding on a black No Face baseball hat and rolling up his green flannel sleeves.

"Akil's not coming?" Casey asked from beside him.

I shook my head. "Not today." I didn't need to worry about him being an idiot in addition to myself. One idiot per trip, thanks.

I stepped away from the porch, wanting a minute alone before Nimue arrived. But as I could have predicted, Nadir was right by my side.

"Just say the word out there, and we're gone," he assured me.

I raised a brow at him in question.

"You know." He transferred his weight. "If you need time *alone*. With her. I'll take care of getting everyone else out of there."

Narrowing my eyes at him, I kept my voice low as I responded, "Why the fuck would I need that?"

Nadir's hands lifted in front of him, but he maintained eye contact. "Just in case."

I scoffed, turning away from him to head back to the others, but I could have sworn I heard him mutter, "Too stubborn for his own good."

Luckily for him, Nimue flickered out of nowhere, appearing a few steps from the porch, and my gut clenched to see her in such a familiar setting. My lands, my family's house, surrounded by my skulk.

I took a deep inhale. *Fuck.* I wanted to smell her and my trees in the same breath for the rest of my life.

"Hey, guys," she said cheerily, offering them a wave as she approached. She wore a pink Rocky Mountains National Park sweatshirt with grey quick-dry hiking pants and brown hiking boots.

The guys gathered around, welcoming and teasing her, but weren't stupid enough to try to hug her in front of me. Casey caught my eye, and I jerked my head towards her bag. With a nod, he slid it from her shoulders despite her protest that she could carry her own.

Not on my fucking land would she ever have to.

Confusion flitted across her face as she observed the exchange and then Casey slinging her pink backpack over a shoulder, but she laughed it off when he flashed her a grin.

"No worries, Nimue. Pink's my favorite color." He winked at her.

"It definitely does wonders for your complexion," she teased back.

I coughed to cover up the growl that threatened to start in my chest, and they both turned towards me.

"Take the lead," I ordered him, suddenly wanting to put

distance between him and my mate. With a shrug, Casey set off for the woods.

Hanging back to let the others go ahead, I rolled my eyes as Nadir passed me with a knowing look, and I fell into step with Nimue.

"It's okay that I'm coming with you guys today, right?" She shot me a quick glance before facing forward again.

Struggling to act normal, I answered, "You're always welcome here." She didn't know half of it. I slowed to let her climb over the rock wall we reached first, trying to force my gaze away from her ass in front of me and utterly failing.

"How's the shop and everything?" She waited for me on the other side of the wall — *like a good vixen*, my idiot fox purred at me — her eyes meeting mine as I caught up.

"Same old." I shrugged, but told her about Nox's new assignment, and she laughed.

"I wondered why he was there the other day."

"What have you been up to?" Through Blaze, I knew that she'd been taking photography jobs, but I'd purposefully kept myself out of the loop any more than that.

"I've been freelancing. Mostly I take jobs for smaller environmental groups to help promote their services and projects. Occasionally I work with larger firms who are suing companies for habitat destruction, things like that."

My fox did *not* like the sound of that. "That sounds dangerous." My voice took on a raspier quality all of a sudden.

She waved it off, winking at me. "I can flicker out of there like *that*, remember?" She emphasized her point with a snap of her fingers, smiling.

My steps halted, and she stopped with me. "Have you

ever had to?" The joking and shouts of the others grew distant as they continued, moving away from us.

Brushing back a strand of her brown hair that had fallen out of her messy bun, she gave a half-shrug that had me tilting my head. "Maybe once."

"Tell me." Fuck, my fox was trying to Alpha command her.

Her eyes flared slightly as she met mine — shit, had my eyes shifted? I pressed them closed, willing them back to normal as she started speaking, and I reopened them.

"The organization was suing a chemical waste company. The company claimed they were disposing of everything correctly, following EPA guidelines, even going above and beyond, but they weren't. They were dumping it up in a remote lake, polluting the lake and the water table." I nodded, encouraging her to keep talking. "I'd gone up to try to get photos of them actually dumping —"

"Alone."

Her nose scrunched slightly, but she kept going. "Alone, yeah. Anyway, it was night, and I'd been waiting for a few hours when they finally showed up to ditch some barrels of the stuff. They, um," she swallowed, her gaze moving to the needles of the red spruce she brushed with her fingers, "came prepared."

I moved in front of her, subconsciously squaring up and forcing her to meet my eyes. "You mean armed."

"Eventually, one of them sighted me." My whole body tensed, jaw so tight my teeth creaked. "Squeezed off a few shots. But I flickered out of there before anything else could go down."

"Fuck, Nim." I ran a hand through my hair to stop

myself from reaching out and shaking her for being so careless.

She shrugged again — fucking *shrugged* it off — and started to move around me to follow the others, but not before placing a hand on my shoulder that lit up every nerve in my body.

"It was fine, Kit. It'll always be fine because I can always flicker out. Not like a standard bullet would kill me anyways."

Pressing my lips together to stop my fox from trying to bark another useless Alpha order at her never to make another reckless decision like that, I forced myself to take one breath, then two. Then I followed her off through the woods.

Chapter Eight

NIMUE

LIKE NADIR back at the shop, it was one thing to *know* that Kit had come into his full power and another to see it like this. To see him ordering the others around with barely more than a glance half the time, and then watching them immediately jump to follow his direction. It was *hot*.

I also thought I'd heard the rumble of an Alpha command directed *my* way once or twice, but that was probably my imagination. What use would there be for that since they wouldn't affect me anyway? And it wasn't like Kit cared enough about me to bother with that. We'd barely spoken in four years.

Still, his eyes had *definitely* flashed gold when he made me tell him that story, losing control of the fox within for a moment. And I didn't know what to make of that.

He seemed to need a minute to cool down, so I picked up the pace to catch up with the others, falling into step between the twins like old times.

"Oh, good." Casey nudged me with his elbow. "Nimue can settle it then."

I was grinning already. "Settle what?"

"Would you rather eat your *least* favorite food every day for the rest of your life, or deal with slow, spotty internet forever?" Nadir, Emerson, Cole, and Casey all watched me solemnly.

"What did all of you say?"

"Oh, no." Cole shook his head. "Your answer first."

I hummed in thought, drawing it out to annoy them. "If I didn't *need* internet for my job, I'd say that, but —"

"Ha!" Casey pointed an accusatory and triumphant finger at the other three.

"You'd probably get used to the food over time anyway," I continued, Casey nodding along emphatically.

"That's what I tried to tell them! But these assholes don't need internet the way *we* do." He threw a conspiratorial arm around my shoulders as the others started arguing against us.

"The same fucking food *every day?*"

"It's just internet, for God's sake."

"No. No fucking way. You can keep your steamed Brussels sprouts."

I chuckled again, happy to be with the guys like this, not sure why I was surprised at how easily I fit back into their group.

They kept taking turns throwing out *Would you rather's,* the fallen leaves and needles crunching under our boots, until a low growl sounded behind us. The guys all froze in their tracks, the forest gone strangely silent. Casey quickly dropped his arm and stepped away from me, wincing.

I furrowed my brow, looking around at them before

glancing behind us. There, some ten feet back, stood Kit, having finally rejoined us. His eyes were glowing gold as they flashed between Casey, moving very slowly away, and me.

"Casey, what's —" but I cut myself off when I saw him flinch again, another low rumble reaching us.

"Casey." Kit's voice was barely more than a murmur, but even I somehow felt the Alpha power radiating from him. *How was that even possible?*

Slowly lowering my backpack to the ground, Casey put his hands up, his head ducked as he kept taking slow steps away and Kit stalked closer.

"Just meet us there, Case," Nadir told him from in front of us, his eyes fixed firmly on Kit's approach.

With the barest hint of a nod, Casey sidestepped until he was well into the forest, a good twenty feet off, before turning and taking off into the brush.

The others were still frozen, though waiting for what, I couldn't tell, as Kit finally met up with us and bent down to pick up my backpack.

"I can just —" I reached out for it, but a sharp jerk of Kit's head made me retract my hand.

He slid it onto his back, jaw tight as he ordered the others, "Let's go."

What the heck?

After a few minutes, the awkward tension dissipated, and the guys took up their chattering again, mostly Nadir and Cole going back and forth with increasingly ridiculous *Would you rather's*, with Emerson occasionally snorting and throwing his two cents in. Kit had taken position at the front, prowling silently through the woods and picking up the pace whenever I tried to catch up.

Eventually, I gave up with a mental shrug. Whatever had just happened, maybe he needed some space.

I caught Nadir shooting glances between Kit and me, but if he had something to say, he didn't share it.

Before long, we reached a large pond, and a gasp left me as I recognized where we were.

"*This* is Bear Pond?" I asked. A slight shiver of relief — was it relief? — went through me as Kit finally turned to face me again, setting my bag down on a rock by the shore.

The last time we'd been here, a fire had just torn through, leaving the entire hillside behind the pond bare of brush, with only blackened tree skeletons remaining. Now, the area was flourishing, with new growth coming in on the hillside, and a swath of healthy vegetation ringing the pond itself. One side was bordered in flashing red sumac, the slight breeze ruffling the leaves and the surface of the water.

Kit nodded, something like pride shining in his eyes, before a throat clearing drew his attention to Cole and Emerson.

Something unspoken passed between them before Kit sighed. "Move off down a ways, then. No flashing our guest."

The two of them and Nadir quickly moved around a large boulder, and the next moment, three foxes leaped into the lake, swimming and splashing around. I laughed as one of them pushed another under the water, and they both came up spluttering. The guys had always been as entertaining as foxes as they were as humans.

A whoop drew my attention from them, and I turned to see Casey rejoining us, stripping on his way to the lake.

"Oh, my." I laughed, covering my eyes, until another splash told me he was safely foxed and in the lake as well.

Kit watched his skulk members with avid attention, but a softening around his eyes betrayed how much he cared for them.

"Join them if you want," I said, settling cross-legged onto a flat boulder on the shore. "I don't mind."

Considering for a moment, Kit took a seat on the rock next to mine. "I'd rather be here."

Silence stretched between us, broken up only by the yips and splashing coming from the lake.

"What happened back there?" I asked, tilting my head back the way we'd come to indicate the whole backpack exchange.

His jaw ticked before he sighed. "Don't worry about it."

Frustration squirmed in my chest, but I brushed it aside. Probably just hierarchical business, and none of mine. "All right. Just a pack thing?"

Kit turned to look at me slowly, an unreadable expression on his face. "Skulk," he corrected, his eyes scanning mine. "You know that."

I laughed to diffuse the seriousness on his face. "Right, sorry. I guess I've been spending too much time with some wolves out in Colorado."

His eyes narrowed, and instantly I knew that was the

wrong thing to say. He was already on edge, for whatever reason, and I'd had to go and mention their nemesis species.

"What pack?"

I cleared my throat. "The one in Timber Creek."

He grunted in some recognition of the name, but didn't ask anything else even as his stare continued to pierce into me.

I turned to reach for my bag, and instantly found it at my fingertips, Kit holding it out for me.

"Thanks." Pulling out my water bottle, I took a long sip, racking my brain to figure out how to break this ice between us. "So, you guys restored all this?"

Leaning back on his palms, Kit nodded. "That fire tore through here a little over four years ago. July."

That sounded right. It was right before I left. Right before he and I had —

"It swept through here so well because a lot of these trees were already dead — hemlock scale. After the fire, we let it settle for a year to see what it would do on its own; see if the pests would come back," he continued. "Then we cleared out the worst of it, and started replanting. We set up a fire break on the other side of the hill, so it hopefully won't happen again, and we've kept a closer eye on this whole area for pests and parasites. The rest we let nature take care of. We've found a few infected trees over the years, but we treated or removed them before it could get as bad as it had been. Plus, things tend to grow quickly when you have green witches at your disposal."

I swung my eyes over the trees, avoiding glancing at Kit. "Well, I'm glad to see it healed." Taking in the whole landscape, the new growth trees, and the little meadow in front of the pond, a sense of peace stole over me. "This would be a beautiful place to build a home."

Kit went stock-still, not looking at me, but from what I could see of the corner of his eye, I could have sworn it flashed gold.

KIT

THIS WAS TORTURE.

We hung out around the pond while the guys swam, Nimue wandering around the area to snap photos. The others snuck out to grab snacks while she was occupied so they wouldn't flash her. She returned to my side after a while, having some trail mix herself, as the sun started to go down.

Her rosewater scent was driving me out of my mind, intensifying as the air cooled, stronger every time the breeze wafted it over to me. She was so close, within arm's distance — if I reached out, I could touch her. Every moment that passed that I didn't push Nimue down on the rocks next to me and seize her mouth with mine had my fox snarling at me.

He wanted to take.

To feel.

To own.

But I couldn't do that. Definitely not here, or now. Maybe never.

I scrubbed a hand over my face before pushing to my feet. As I stood, Nimue's eyes rose with me, but I forced myself to look out over the water instead. Placing my fingers in my mouth, I whistled loudly, and the foxes all glanced my way before starting towards the shore.

"Let's get a head start." I turned and snagged Nimue's bag off the rock.

"Oh," Nimue pushed off the rock, and made to follow me. "You don't want to wait for them?"

"They'll catch up," I threw over my shoulder, and Nimue joined me.

I needed to get out of here as fast as possible. This whole day had been a terrible idea. I heard her every footfall beside me as each step stirred up the scent of the earth and leaves under her boots, and I noted every breath as we tramped back through the woods. My thoughts were a lost cause; there was no way she didn't know what I wanted, unless she was actively trying to suppress that part of her magic.

My fox kept up a constant growl at me, demanding to know what was taking so long, and it sharpened into a pounding headache until I could barely see straight. Until there was just her scent and movements and breath and nearness.

By the time we made it back to the house, the others had caught up to us. Allowing myself only a second to pause, I handed Nimue her backpack and glanced at her, trying desperately to control myself. It would be so easy to push her back against the porch railing and — my eyes dropped to her neck, but I blinked, swallowing. "You can flicker back from here?"

"Sure." Nimue's eyes danced around my face, confusion written all over her expression, but I was seconds away from losing this battle to my fox.

I had to go.

"Right," I nodded, jogged up the porch steps, and turned into my parent's house, clicking the door shut.

Nimue didn't follow, and I leaned against the wall beside the door, closing my eyes as I tipped my head back.

"Ignore him." Nadir's voice drifted through the open windows. "It's his time of the month."

Nimue's laugh sounded forced, and my jaw worked to keep my Alpha side from ordering Nadir away from her. "It's fine. Thanks for today. I had fun."

"Anytime," Nadir answered. "We've all missed you. Even Kit."

"I can tell." Nimue's voice was full of sarcasm, but after their goodbyes, silence followed.

The door pushed open a moment later, and Nadir came through. "She's gone. You're a dick. You know that, right?"

His words raised my hackles, but I fought the urge to snap back at him. He wasn't wrong.

"I know," I muttered, and pushed back through the door, headed to town.

Days passed, and I listened carefully to chatter in the shop, curious to know if Nimue had left town yet. She hadn't sought me out again, but I couldn't blame her after how distant and rude I'd been to her.

The night before, the skulk had met me at Scallywags.

I'd wavered on whether or not to go, both afraid that Nimue might be there and hoping she would. After no sign of her, we all drank far too much, and several of them had crashed at my apartment rather than go home.

Slightly hungover, I forced a smile for customers, trying to be as pleasant as always, when, of all people, my mother walked in.

My mother, Aditi, stood at barely five-foot-two, but her small stature was deceptive — she was one of the most intimidating women I knew, right up there with Devanna. Despite the ferocity she could muster, she was also the warmest, most wildly loving mother a person could ask for. Her ruby sweater dress fell past her brown knee-high boots, and she tugged off her denim jacket as she stepped up to the counter.

"Is something wrong?" I frowned, coming around the front of the counter. She didn't usually frequent the shop, preferring to keep to the farmhouse out at the edge of town than come here into the center. If she was here, then it had to be something serious.

She brushed her long brown hair over her shoulder and pierced her shrewd eyes at me, setting a plastic container down on the counter. "You tell me. Emerson didn't come home until nearly three in the morning, and we still haven't seen Lily. Were you drinking? Are you hungover?"

I bit my lip, unable to lie to the woman, and pretended to be distracted by the Tupperware, cracking the lid open. "What's this?"

After another moment of assessing me, she waved a hand that clearly read, *my son is impossible.* "Your father always wants aloo paratha when he's been drinking."

I smirked as I shut the lid and tucked the container behind the counter, though not before I'd grabbed a piece and practically inhaled it. Her smug expression said she knew she'd caught me.

"Not that he ever drinks, though, right?"

"Of course not," she agreed sharply, but the corner of her eyes crinkled. Glancing around the shop, she asked, "Can you sit with me for a minute?"

As no one else was inside, I nodded and rounded the counter. She made her way to a table while I picked a few pastries out of the display, bringing them over as I joined her.

When she ignored the teacakes, opting to reach over them to clasp my hands, I knew something *was* wrong. My mother never turned down sweets.

Her swirling skulk tattoos were thinner and daintier than mine on the slightly lighter bronze of her forearms as she rubbed her thumb across my hand.

"*Jaan*," she began, pausing to find the words. "You're turning thirty next month."

Oh no.

"Soon, your father will want to retire. He will want to leave the skulk in good hands."

Please no.

"I know you've dated a little…" she trailed off. "But it's time to settle down."

Shit.

"There is a lovely young woman from upstate New York whose mother and I have been in contact." I flinched, and she squeezed my hands again as dread pooled in my stomach. "They're coming for a visit."

Right, I mentally scoffed. A *visit.*

I tugged on my hands, and she let me take them back.

"Ma." I raked my fingers through my hair, sitting back in my chair. "I can't mate some female I don't know."

"And why not? Many shifters, especially higher up, arrange their bonds. Often, it is the only way to bring in new genes." She watched me for a moment, eyes scanning my face, but I had to look away. The woman had an uncanny knack for seeing through me; maybe all mothers did.

I sighed. She and my father had met through an arranged mate bond, but they'd been lucky. Turned out they were also true mates. "I know, but I'm still young. I don't want —"

"Agree to meet her, okay? Then we can talk and go from there. Maybe you'll get lucky, like your father and I did. She could be your true mate."

Biting my lip because I knew she wouldn't let this go — the poor woman and her mother were probably already on their way up here — I conceded. It wasn't like I could explain to my mother, *No, Ma, actually, she won't be my true mate because I already found her, and she's a demon I've been best friends with since I was thigh-high to a grasshopper.* "Fine. I'll meet her, and then we can discuss how much I will absolutely not be doing anything else with her."

That smirk was back on her face, and my mother waved away my stipulation. "We'll see about that."

I rolled my eyes. "When is this *visit* then?"

Her amber eyes glittered. "Tomorrow." I groaned, rising to my feet and heading back behind the counter. She called after me, "Take a shower. And put on a nice shirt!"

Hours later, I sat at the counter in Scallywags again and tapped my glass.

"*Another?*" Blaze pretended to gawk at me. He knew I wasn't usually a heavy drinker, but I also knew he didn't care. I could only grunt in response as he took my glass and went to pour me another beer.

It wasn't the first time my mother had tried to set me up with someone, but this time felt different. Maybe it was because I knew she was right. My father had recently made several comments about me taking on more tasks, although he'd never outright told me he wanted to retire soon. As was the custom in most skulks, he and all the rest of the family would rather see me settled with a mate when I took over to lead. In normal circumstances, he would retain his position much longer since he was still young by shifter standards, but things had changed four years ago. It made this whole setup feel much more serious now than it had the last time, and it twisted my insides into knots.

Blaze had asked a few prompting questions throughout the night, but I wasn't ready to talk about it yet. I had texted Nadir to join me, but until he arrived, I waited in silence, alone with my thoughts as the bar bustled around me.

At some point, Petra came in, her red hair in a long braid that draped down her oversized olive green sweater, and took a stool beside me. She leaned over the counter to kiss Blaze before he handed her a drink.

"You seem a little worse for wear," she commented with

a tilt of her head. It might have been an insult from anyone else, but coming from her, it was just an observation.

A heavy sigh escaped me as the bell at the door jingled, Nadir finally arriving.

"I've just been informed my mother is trying to decide my future," I told her grimly as Nadir took the stool on my other side. A very nosy demon stopped cleaning at the other end of the bar and immediately appeared before me, leaning forward to hear what I had to say.

"Does that mean what I think it does?" Nadir asked, then glanced at Blaze. "Can I get the Gunnar's Daughter ale?"

But Blaze flapped a towel at him to shut it, and waved a hand for me to continue.

"My mother's having some female shifter over to visit," I grimaced. "For me."

The three of them seemed to be holding their breath. Blaze was the first to crack, and he and Nadir started laughing, but Petra pressed her lips together.

"And you don't want that?" she clarified, her blue eyes slightly narrowed.

A bitter laugh escaped me. "Definitely not."

Chapter Ten

NIMUE

THE MID-DAY SUN crept through the blinds as Devanna stood at the end of my bed. The suitcase she was supposed to be helping me pack lay open in front of her, but she was focused entirely on her phone, thumbs flying across the screen. After the eleventh *ding*, I finally threw my hands in the air.

"Who are you texting?" I raised an eyebrow. "Orion?"

Dev reared back, glancing up from the phone, nose wrinkling. "God, no. Petra is texting me."

I went back to folding sweaters. "You and Petra are friends?" Not that there was anything wrong with that, but Dev could be prickly about who she associated with.

She slid her phone into her back pocket. "Well, as Blaze's human, she's around all the time now. Unavoidable. And she's tolerable." I stifled my laugh. High praise from Dev. She glanced down at the clothes in a pile in front of her. Jeans. Boots. Jackets. Sweaters. I was headed straight to Yellowstone soon for my next contract, and was packing accordingly.

"These clothes are boring," she whined, dropped the cream sweater I wore most often back onto the pile, and drifted towards my immense closet. I *loved* clothes. While demons may not have ascended from Hell, we were undoubtedly ruled by our urges. I certainly fell prey to a little gluttony, especially when home decor, clothing, and jewelry were involved. I loved pretty, shiny things.

She flicked on the chandelier in the closet's center, running her hands along the rainbow assortment of fabrics hung inside. As her hands snagged on a red flannel shirt, her eyes drifted over to mine and she pulled it off the hanger. "Let's get dressed up and go out in Spring Harbor tonight, just us girls. It's Friday. We can call it the last hurrah before you leave me again."

I laughed, dropping the sweater back onto the bed before joining her in the closet. Snagging the shirt from her hand, I hung it back up, pretending it meant nothing to me. "Spring Harbor? Since when do you go out in Spring Harbor?"

Dev shrugged nonchalantly. "I happen to like human men. They're so unangelic."

I rolled my eyes, but glanced her way. "What are you going to wear?" I looked pointedly at her usual black leather pants and a black witchy graphic tee that said *Resting Witch Face*. "That?"

She circled my closet, pulling down a bright red bustier top I'd never actually worn but couldn't resist buying. "I'll wear *red* if you wear that flannel," she nodded to where I'd hung it back up.

I squinted at her, trying to discern what mischief she was

up to. I grew up with Mo and could spy meddling a mile away. "Why?"

"Just think how hot you'll look in this," she grabbed a black mini skirt, "with this top," a black lace bra top that covered practically nothing, "under it. I'll even let you wear my boots."

I glanced down at her black boots, twisting my lips to the side in thought. They were vintage Doc Marten leather platform boots, and I had always loved them. Swinging my squinted gaze back up at her once more, I snagged the skirt and bra-top from her hands to change.

We spent a half hour dancing around to music while I curled my hair — Dev transformed her hair magically, switching it from its usual blue to a ruby red, matching her corset — and we did our makeup. Dev insisted I needed black winged eyeliner and bright red lipstick to match the grunge-chic look I had going.

My stomach and legs were bare, showing too much skin for November in Maine, but I was a demon — cold wasn't an issue. Before leaving, I stood in front of the floor-length mirror, inspecting my reflection.

Dev's outfit choice for me was on point — I looked hot. In fact, I looked downright devilish, something I rarely felt, despite my species. I slipped into the red flannel shirt I'd had for years, pretending I didn't know exactly where I got it from, rolled up the too-long sleeves, and tied the hem into a knot just above the waistband of my miniskirt.

"I'd do you," Dev said as she slung her arms around my waist from behind, leaning her chin on my shoulder.

I glanced at her reflection in the mirror. "I know these are fighting words, but red looks so good on you."

Dev laughed, letting go, and spun to grab her clutch. "Black only. Except for you. Anything for you."

As we closed my front door behind us, Petra and Selene stepped out of the main house where Blaze and Orion lived, headed our way. Both were dressed to kill — Selene in a tight-fitting plum dress that hugged her every curve under a green leather jacket, and Petra in a burnt-orange jumpsuit and jean jacket.

Petra smiled as she waved, her expression a bit guarded and hard to read, but maybe it was just because I didn't know her as well. I could sense that she genuinely wanted to get to know me.

"I didn't know you were still in town," I said as I pulled Selene into a hug. I assumed she'd left after breakfast at Mo's last weekend. "Or are you back again for some reason?"

Selene flashed her megawatt smile at me, and I knew she was up to something. She slipped from my hold and pranced across the driveway to her blue sedan parked there. "Get in, girls!"

Dev climbed into the front passenger seat, and no one was about to argue with her about it, so Petra and I slid into the back. I opened my mouth to ask Selene again when Petra cut in, "I can't believe Dev loaned you her boots." I narrowed my eyes at her, then glanced back at the two in the front seat.

"She shouldn't get used to them," was Dev's only remark, but I could sense a distraction a mile away.

"What is going on here?" I leaned forward between the two seats, swinging my gaze from Selene to Dev and back. "What are you all up to?"

Dev placed her hand over her heart, jaw dropping — a perfect mockery of the look Blaze loved to give. "Is it so *impossible* to believe that your *best* friends in the entire world wouldn't want to just hang out with you for one last day before you leave town and forget to tell us if you'll ever return?"

I squinted at her, then turned to Selene. She was the weaker link. "Selene."

"I have to focus on the road." She cleared her throat, not meeting my eyes. "Safety first, right? So many deer. And moose. You know Winston — doesn't always pay attention to his surroundings. Absent-minded, almost. Wouldn't want to hit him, or another one. Dime a dozen up here, moose are. It would total my car, and weirdly enough, my healing magic doesn't work on animals. Or cars. Wouldn't that be amazing? Gosh, it's warm in here. Can you adjust the air, Dev? I worked up a sweat curling my hair. You know how it is."

Again, I squinted at her but sat back in my seat.

Chapter Eleven

FRIDAY MORNING, dread pooled in my stomach as I stood in the farmhouse foyer. Skylar and her mother, Susan, arrived after lunch, and we politely and awkwardly sat around my parents' living room, having tea. Skylar wore a grey turtleneck with navy slacks, blonde hair pulled back in a braided bun, and looked just about ready to do our taxes. I wondered if the conservative dress was her choice, her mother's, or if she thought this was how *we* would expect her to dress. Not that it mattered. I wouldn't have been interested even if she'd shown up in a string bikini.

Susan was mated to an Alpha, too, and she went on about how Skylar knew what it meant to be the Alpha's mate, the importance of it, and how to be responsible for a whole skulk. It was intended to be reassuring that Skylar would be able to take on that role and bond to me, but each word only hammered into my skull how impossible it would be for Nimue to ever understand it all.

Akil and Lily snickered, but pretended to be polite anytime an adult looked their way. Emerson had managed to get out of the whole event by working at his tattoo apprenticeship for the day. Lucky guy. Though my grandfather kept silent, he shot me a shrewd glance now and again that reminded me he saw far more than he let on, and I wondered just how much he knew.

After dinner, my mother practically kicked us out of the house, insisting I show Skylar a good time.

There was an innuendo I knew my mother did *not* mean in there, and Skylar looked at me uncertainly, probably wondering what the hell our skulk got up to on these types of meetings. Not sex, that was for sure.

To reassure her and to bail myself out of an awkward evening, I texted Nadir, who then texted everyone else, and we all decided to head to the Purple Dragon in Spring Harbor. With a quick call ahead to Lysander — his band was playing there later tonight — I reserved us a table. The music would drown out any possible conversation, and we could ignore each other until it was time to go home. Then, I never had to see her again.

Skylar swung back to me with an innocent smile as we stepped off my parents' wrap-around porch. "Could we stop by your place before we go out?"

I paused. Did this girl think I was seriously about to sleep with her right after leaving a meeting with her mother? I opened my mouth to clarify that was not my intention, no matter how suggestively my mother had unintentionally worded our dismissal, when she held up her hand, covering her mouth as she laughed.

"Sorry. That sounded bad. I want to change before we go to a club. No way do I want to wear this out."

Thank God I hadn't shoved my foot in my mouth by

denying her. I quickly recovered, glancing down at her, and noticed how large her handbag was.

Watching my line of sight, she held it up with a smile. "I always carry a change of clothes."

"Sure, no problem." I nodded, opened the passenger door of my hybrid SUV — safe *and* practical — for her, and helped her in. Shutting the door behind her, I circled the car, breathing deeply through my nose before climbing in.

After a quick pit stop for Skylar to change, Cole, Casey, Nadir, and Nadir's sister, Sophie, climbed into the car with us. This was why I drove an SUV. Lily opted not to come with us, instead slinking off without a word.

Cole slapped the back of my headrest excitedly, beaming over at Skylar as he took control of the AUX cord and fired up *Make You Mine* by PUBLIC. "Who doesn't love a night out on a Monday?"

I fought to roll my eyes for the 800th time tonight, and steered towards the highway.

Music thumped loudly through the speakers at the Purple Dragon, and I sipped on my APA as I sat back on the leather sofa in our section. The club was packed, but with the weather starting to turn, it seemed humans would make any excuse to go out and party before settling in for winter. Plus, Lysander's band, The Lost Talisman, would be on in an hour, and they always drew a crowd.

"Your skulk is so fun!" Skylar called out over the music from where she sat next to me, looking considerably more relaxed now that she was in a low-cut navy skater dress that barely reached mid-thigh, red heels, and a headband with a red bow. Through some mysterious female magic, she'd transitioned her hair from the bun to loose waves, and I had to admit she was pretty, even if she still didn't interest me at all. "Do you guys do this often?"

I sipped at my beer again, fighting the urge to get up and leave, knowing I had nothing in common with her. Or maybe just *determined* to have nothing in common with her. "Some of them do, but I don't always join."

"Oh," she said, bobbing her head along to the music. "I guess you're probably busy with the tea shop, right?"

"The shop, or whatever skulk stuff I need to do." God, this was painful. I fought a heavy sigh.

Skylar chuckled when a smoke machine began wafting fog out onto the dance floor, and Cole made his dance moves more elaborate to push it around.

"He looks like an air bender!"

I barked a laugh at that. "Please don't tell him that. He's already insufferable enough." She laughed again, and I glanced at her out of the side of my eye, watching as she smiled at the antics my crew got up to on the dance floor and finally put her out of her misery. "You do not have to sit here with me, you know. We're not mates. This won't work. Go have fun tonight, and then we'll never see each other again."

Her gaze swung back to me, momentarily shocked, and I kicked myself for my harsh delivery. "Sorry, that was rude. I only meant that because I already —" The scent of rose-water hit me, and my eyes drifted shut, sucking in a deep breath through my nose. When I opened them again, I rotated on the couch to look at the door where Nimue walked in, trailed by Devanna, Selene, and Petra.

My mate seemed oblivious to my presence, glancing around the dark club and already moving to the music, but her three friends had their eyes locked on me.

"Excuse me." I patted Skylar's leg. "Go have fun. Dance. Enjoy yourself. Drinks are on me."

She smiled hesitantly at me, then shrugged and was getting to her feet when Cole suddenly appeared in front of her.

"Hey, I just realized what you remind me of." He waved a hand to indicate her outfit, and I swore I saw a blush creep over her cheeks even in the dim light of the club. "*Kiki's Delivery Service.*"

She blinked at him, a shy smile tilting her lips as she toyed with the hem of her dress. "That's why I bought it."

Had her voice gone a bit breathless?

Cole flashed a grin, not even sparing me a look before asking her, "Want to dance?"

The two of them moved off, though I was hardly aware of their movements as I watched Nimue grin, my fingers digging into the cushions of the couch. Laughing with her friends, the four of them walked right out onto the dance floor. Her hands rose above her as she weaved to the center, friends trailing behind her like moths drawn to a flame.

The song changed, pounding out a rhythmic beat that had Nimue swinging her hips, her pale waist on display thanks to her crop top and her tiny skirt hugging her ass. Usually, I would cringe at a club song like this, but tonight it made me want to tip the DJ.

Chapter Twelve

NIMUE

MY FRIENDS HAD to think I was clueless. Not only were they acting incredibly awkward, but Dev had handed me a tumbler full of demon wine for the drive up to the ol' S.H. After taking several tentative sips, I'd decided it didn't matter and adopted the demon motto — only live once, right? And downed my glass.

The hint of a buzz combined with the dark, heady atmosphere of the club only ramped up my sensitivities to the impulses and urges of people around me as the four of us sang and danced out on the floor. We saw a few people we knew — there weren't any clubs in the Cove, our only watering hole being Scallywags, which could only boast Scrabble and cards' nights in terms of "partying" — so a lot of supes came up here when they wanted to let loose. Especially when Lysander's band was playing, which always drew a good crowd.

I smiled and waved at Nadir when I saw him with a mixed group of guys and girls, but he didn't wave back immediately. Instead, he narrowed his eyes as his brows drew down. I shrugged it off, though I noticed he leaned over to talk to Casey, and the other male's blue eyes scanned me, a smirk forming on his face.

Intrigued and maybe slightly empowered by my badass boots, I detached myself from my circle and headed over to confront them. Casey's nostrils flared as I leaned close enough to shout over the music.

"Something to say, fox?"

Casey grinned, his eyes trailing down my outfit, but he put his hands up. "Nope, nothing to say. I wouldn't dare."

I frowned at him. "What's that supposed to mean?"

He glanced at Nadir, the two of them in on some joke, as someone bumped into me from behind. The movement pushed me off-balance in the unfamiliar boots — the traitors — and sent me hurtling into Casey's chest. His hands grabbed my elbows to steady me, but he immediately dropped them and stepped back as something caught his eye to the left.

Kit stood there watching us, his deep blue button-down complimenting his bronze skin, his thick brown hair the perfect amount of messy that made my fingers itch to run through it. He had an unreadable expression on his face as he looked between Casey and me — or at least, to me, it was unreadable. Casey took another step back before turning and walking away, mirroring what had happened on the hike the other day. As Kit prowled over, barely glancing at me, I thought he would blow right past me, but a vice-like grip on my wrist, pulling me out through the crowd, said otherwise.

"Hey, what the hell?" I called over the music, my pulse ratcheting up, but Kit didn't even turn around. He tugged me out of the club's main room, down the hallway with the bathrooms, and into a storage room whose sign read *Employees Only* before I regained enough of my senses to pull my wrist away. Maybe I hadn't wanted to.

"Kit? Why are you and your whole skulk being so weird?"

Clicking the door shut behind us, Kit turned, nostrils flaring, one hand still on the knob, his every muscle locked and tense. "What the fuck are you wearing right now?"

I scoffed. "Really, caveman?" I looked down at my black lace top and mini skirt. "It's the new millennium, remember? Females can show whatever skin they want."

"Not that," he hissed, and his eyes tracked to the flannel. "*That.*"

Oh. Right. No, I could play this cool.

"What about it?" I traced my fingers over the knot of the shirt at my waist.

Kit's eyes shut, and his jaw worked as he pulled deep breaths through his nose. "It's mine."

"Really?" I glanced down innocently at the fabric. "Huh. It's been in my closet for so long. I guess I forgot where it came from. You can have it back, though." My fingers slid to the buttons just covering my lace bra-top, undoing them slowly, my demon blood humming in delight at how his nostrils flared again.

Suddenly, warm hands circled my wrists once more, stilling my movements.

"You can't fool me like that, Nim." Kit's voice dropped to a raspy whisper in my ear, and he stood so close that my nose was practically in his chest, the warmth of his body seeping into mine. His pine and rain scent hit me, and I fought to keep my eyes from rolling back into my skull. I glanced up at him and tried to pull back, but he didn't let go, keeping me all but pressed up against him.

A dizzying array of impulses swept through him, so many it was hard to sort out any of them individually. Usually, I tried not to read my friends like that too often; it felt like an invasion of privacy, but it was harder to control when I was drinking.

"Do you *not* want it back?" My voice was shakier than I'd intended, unused to being the object of his intensity in this way.

A laugh of disbelief left him as he let go of one of my wrists. My breath hitched as his fingers trailed first the bottom of my lace top, then skimmed down my ribs to the top of my mini skirt, leaving a tingling trail in their wake. Heat flooded through me, my pulse quickening, as Kit's amber eyes clocked every change he induced in me.

"No," he said finally. "I don't want it back. I want you to wear my scent every goddamn day."

My mouth parted at his words, and he tilted his head down into the crook of my neck, his nose skimming the sensitive skin there before his teeth grazed along it.

"You smell so fucking good," Kit growled the words against my skin, and I shivered. I'd never seen him like this, the Alpha in him coming out as he turned us around and pushed my back against the door. The pounding bass from the club reverberated through the wood at my back, matching my heartbeat.

I wanted to reach out and touch him, lace my fingers through his hair and draw his mouth to mine, but I was afraid of making sudden moves. Afraid any little thing could snap him out of this and make him stop.

And I did *not* want him to stop.

He gently nipped my neck, and then his mouth drew up, skating across my jaw. My breathing grew heavier, anticipation building within me as I willed his mouth to find mine. His body sank just an inch closer to mine, and as my chest grazed his, a light whimper escaped me.

Suddenly, his entire weight was pressing me into the door, and his lips finally crushed against mine. His palm rested on my jaw, tilting my head up for him as he deepened the kiss, and I raised my hands to grasp his shirt and pull him closer.

This. This was what my life had been missing.

It had been four years since our last kiss, but I didn't want to admit how often I'd thought back on it. I'd dated others since then, but I always compared everyone to Kit, consciously or not. Demons weren't known for long-term relationships, and no one ever caught my interest for more than a day or two — a week tops.

His tongue pushed into my mouth, demanding I open for him, sweeping against my own with a confident dominance. I moaned without meaning to, adjusting my hips as he pushed a knee between my legs, pinning me in place even more. The demon energy in me was humming as we both gave way to these impulses, and I was alight from within.

"Fuck, Nim," Kit groaned as I shifted along his thigh, unintentionally rubbing myself on him. His teeth scraped across my jaw as he returned to my neck, and a low rumble of approval escaped him when I arched to give him better access. "I can smell how wet you are for me already."

I smiled into the near darkness. My eyes shut as ecstasy swept over me, carrying away any sense of wrongness at this moment. Everything about it was right.

"We shouldn't do this." His words had my eyes snapping back open, jarred out of the moment until I saw the heat in his gaze.

I lifted a brow, letting my lips turn up in a smirk. "Why not?"

"Because I already dream of you every fucking night, imagining you underneath me, taking everything I have to offer." His hands drifted to my waist, yanking me closer to him, and I could feel *exactly* what he wanted to offer me.

The unexpected dirty words spilling from his mouth both shocked me and turned me on. My hands drifted to the hem of his shirt, slipping under it to feel his skin.

"You do?"

He hissed as my fingers scraped across his abs, skirting just above his waistband. "Keep touching me like that, and I'll fuck you right here."

"Promise?" I said on a breathy exhale. Kit's eyes flashed amber to gold, fire dancing in them that matched my own, and he moved to seal his mouth back over my own.

A metallic click sounded, and suddenly the door at my back disappeared.

"Oh, sorry," a voice said as we both tumbled out into the hallway, falling to the floor in front of the bartender standing awkwardly in the hall, mop in hand. She muttered something before heading back down the hallway, leaving us alone again.

A laugh escaped me as I stared up at the ceiling. Embarrassment wasn't an emotion demons felt often, but this was about as close as I came to it.

Kit yanked me to my feet, eyes meeting mine momentarily as he fixed the buttons on my — *his* — shirt, securing it higher than I'd been wearing it originally.

I watched his face, waiting for him to meet my gaze, to continue whatever it was we'd been doing, but he only nodded. Leaning down, he growled over the noise of the club, "Don't even think about taking this shirt off tonight."

My eyes expanded at the possessive command, my demon instincts fighting against it, but before I could answer, he strode past me and back out to the dance floor.

I stood in the dark hallway, still trying to understand what had just happened. We'd kissed. And not a quick peck, like when we were kids, or even the slightly more-than-a-peck that had happened four years ago. This one was an earth-quaking, knee-buckling *kiss*.

Kit just told me he wanted me. He said he wanted to fuck me. God, who knew he had such a dirty mouth? And who knew I'd love that? Because I absolutely did. I loved it.

Giddy elation bubbled in my chest. This could be so amazing, him and me. I'd wanted him at *least* since the kiss four years ago, though I'd begun to notice him before that, too. I couldn't pinpoint the day when I'd suddenly looked at him and realized he was all grown up, *we* were all grown up, and I'd seen him in a whole new light, but the change had happened long before I left town. I'd never imagined he might actually want the same thing.

Then, the elation began to retreat, and I sank back against the wall, the bricks of the hall supporting my weight. If he wanted this as much as I did — and I knew that he did, I could feel it with my magic as much as I felt it against my hip — why had he just run off, instead of making good on his supposed 'threat'?

Was it because I wasn't a shifter? Or because I *was* a demon? Did he think I'd just manipulated him into kissing me, stoking the impulse so he would be powerless to resist?

Demons did have that power. We couldn't create the urge, to begin with, but we could make those desires irresistible. Did he really think I would do that to *him*? I didn't know how he could possibly imagine that, but what other explanation could there be for his bolting right after the act?

Chapter Thirteen

I WALKED AWAY from Nimue as fast as possible, fighting the urge to claim her in every way possible. The music was pounding, and the cloying mix of colognes, perfumes, alcohol, and sweat overwhelmed my senses.

By the time I made it back to the booth, my mind and body started to calm with the distance I put between Nimue and me, but my heart… it fucking shattered.

I'd left her in that hallway. Alone. Like an asshole. I wiped a hand down my face. God, the shit I'd said to her. How could I ever look her in the eye again? I rested my elbows on my knees, raking my fingers through my hair as the Alpha power raged in my blood. I couldn't force this mate bond on her, or even explain my actions.

Half of me wanted to storm back into that hallway, throw her over my shoulder and into the back of my car, rip the clothes from her body, and show her how much my fox screamed at me to *take* what was mine. The other half was scared shitless. I'd hardly survived losing her as a friend — I couldn't imagine losing her as a mate.

That thought brought my mind to a stuttering halt. Horror settled over me as I realized how much of a jackass I was — I'd come here with Skylar, and almost fucked Nimue in a closet while she waited for me. My eyes came up, glancing out over the dance floor, and a laugh rose through my chest.

Skylar was apparently not a concern for me. Cole gripped her tightly around the waist, her back pressed to his front, the two grinding with not an inch left between them as he tilted her head back to suck on her face. My shifter magic hummed under my skin, prickling as a new awareness came through me. Shifters all possessed an internal awareness of the other members of their skulk or pack, strands connecting us through a mental link like a neural network or tree branch. The branch that led to Cole's connection with our skulk now split in two, a new presence now beside him.

Sensing the same thing I had, Cole's head pulled back from where he'd been attached to Skylar's lips moments before, his blue eyes flashing to glowing honey as he breathed heavily, no longer moving with the music. Skylar's eyes were locked on his as she spun around to face him, reflecting the same golden color as the two panted in unison, and I couldn't help but watch.

I couldn't hear him over the music, but I could read Cole's lips well enough as he growled, *"Mate."* Skylar pressed her hands into his chest, and a smirk stole over Cole's face as she flashed her teeth. He dipped down, grabbing her ass tightly as she laced her legs around his waist. Unable to resist the pull of the mate bond, Skylar was already tearing at his clothes, his button-down dropping to the dance floor as he carried her down the same hallway I'd just emerged from.

Nadir dropped to my side on the booth, amusement lighting his eyes as he watched the same scene I did. "Another one bites the dust."

I only grunted in agreement, hating how much I resented that I wasn't the one fucking my mate in that closet right now. First, Nimue deserved so much more than a dirty closet, and second… I would never get that chance.

"Nimue looked nice tonight," Nadir said, eyes drifting momentarily to me. "Smelled familiar."

"Quit it, Nadir," I snapped, Alpha power strumming in my veins with the new blood added to the pack power. He ducked his eyes, but didn't stop.

"Ignoring whatever that is — I won't name it — is only going to make you volatile, Kit," Nadir said just above a whisper. "Either do something about it or deny it. I can feel your," he was smart enough not to say it, clearing his throat first, "other spot in our skulk lines. It's like a vacuum, draining power away from the rest of us."

Shit. Why had I never realized that? Why had no one said anything? Was that why my mother pushed so hard for the arranged bond thing?

Without meaning to, my eyes glanced up again, searching the dance floor for the red plaid shirt I'd been missing for a decade. Nimue stood on the other side of the dance floor with her back to me, as far away as she could get. Devanna, however, was glaring directly at me.

If looks could kill, I was a dead man.

Chapter Fourteen

NIMUE

THE GIRLS and I more or less had to physically restrain Dev from storming over and hexing Kit, or worse, right there in the club. Even though I hadn't told them anything yet, her fury on my behalf was a force to be reckoned with. Eventually, after I promised to explain why I was flustered in the car on the way home, we convinced her we should leave.

Though if I was being honest, there wasn't much I could explain. Regarding Kit, I had far more questions than before we'd arrived tonight.

As we headed toward the exit, I risked a glance over to where I knew, without understanding *how* I knew, Kit would be. His stare was fixed on me, intense and still like the predator he was. He wore a pained expression as Nadir leaned close, speaking animatedly at his side. I tore my own gaze away, ignoring the concern etched on Selene's face, and pushed my way through the mass of bodies. After the stifling heat of the club, the chill air was a welcome relief when we finally stepped out onto the sidewalk.

At the car, Devanna had Petra sit in the front so she

could sit in the back with me. Taking my hands in a very Mo-like gesture, she waited until we were on the highway before clearing her throat pointedly.

"I've said this before, and I'll say it again, Nims," she began, as gently as she was capable of speaking, patting my hand. "You need me to kill someone for you? Just say the word. I've got the shovel ready and a map to the perfect dumping ground."

Petra coughed from the front, and Selene sighed. "God's sake, Dev. Let's hear her out before we start planning murders, shall we?"

Letting out a huff of disapproval, Dev said, *"Fine,"* but gave me a conspiratorial look that told me she was serious about her offer.

"So what happened?" Selene asked, her eyes glancing at me in the rearview mirror as she drove.

I wasn't entirely sure what *had* happened. I rested my head on the seatback and started talking. "Well, first Casey — one of the guys from his skulk — and Nadir were giving me strange looks, and then Kit showed up and dragged me into the storage room. I asked him why they were all being so weird."

"To the… storage room, you say?" I tilted my head up to see Petra turned around in the passenger seat, her lips pressed together with contained amusement. Her eyes danced between Dev and me in the back, and I glanced at Dev in time to see her roll her eyes.

"Just because you and Blaze get freaky in the storage room doesn't mean everyone does." Then Dev gasped, and whipped her head to me. "Or *did* you? What happened back there?"

"He was all hot and cold," I began. The haze of demon wine and wild emotions and the thumping bass of the music made the memory seem so far away already. "One minute, I thought he was angry at me for keeping his shirt." Looking down, I thumbed the hem of the flannel. "So I offered to give it back, and he got even weirder."

"I'll bet," Dev muttered, but mimed zipping her mouth shut when I shot a confused glance at her. She waved at me to go on.

"Well," I paused, unsure what sort of ammunition I was about to hand the self-appointed assassin to my left. "He sort of, um, kissed me."

Dev inhaled dramatically, turning her entire body to face me as she waved for me to continue even more frantically than before.

Slightly worried for her elbow joint with the forcefulness of her wave, I stuttered on. "He shoved me against the door and kissed the ever-loving life out of me. Said all of this dirty stuff I can't even repeat —"

Dev gasped, *"What stuff?"* at the exact moment Petra and Selene said, *"Kit?"*

"Then, he said we *shouldn't* be doing that, even though he definitely started it, but *also* that he wanted me wearing his scent every day. I nearly fainted when he said —" I paused again, a little concerned by how close Dev was leaning, hanging on my every word. Even Petra and Selene were shooting intense looks at each other and me from the front. "That he wanted to fuck me right there in the closet."

"Well, hot damn!" Dev slapped her knee, leaning back in her seat again as she whistled through her teeth, fanning herself.

"*Hello!*" Selene dragged the *o* out, surprise ringing in her voice. "He really said that?"

"Yes! Then an employee opened the door, and we fell out into the hallway. He picked me up and buttoned up my — his — shirt. All he said before he left me there in the hallway by myself was that I better keep his shirt on all night."

"And then he just *left*?" Petra asked, brow furrowed.

Dev had a shrewder look on her face as she all but chuckled, "Well, well, well, well, well."

What that meant? I had no idea, but she sounded more like Mo by the day.

Ignoring my inscrutable friend, I answered Petra instead. "RIGHT?" I yelled, hands raised in frustration. "What's his deal?"

Selene dropped me off at Blaze's carriage house, telling me to call her if I needed anything no matter the time as she hugged me outside my door. Dev mimed shoveling dirt behind her back and made a phone-call motion as well, and I had to duck my head so Selene wouldn't be alerted to our friend's murderous tendencies. Petra offered a wave, and the three of them drove off.

Back up in my closet, I sat on a pink tufted pouf and peeled off Dev's boots, stretching my now-freed feet with a sigh of relief. Sliding out of Kit's flannel, I paused next to the hamper with the shirt still in my hand, feeling the fabric between my fingers.

I'd known it was his the minute Dev had pointed to it

earlier. I'd kept it all these years, even as Kit and I grew apart and went from seeing each other every day, to at least *talking* every day, to only the occasional text. Then, nothing. No matter how the distance grew between us, I'd held onto his shirt, unable to shed this symbol of our friendship.

Slowly, I raised it to my face, pressing my nose into it as I inhaled deeply. Despite the fact the shifters had obviously still been able to scent him on it, my demon nose — though better than a human's, it had nothing on shifters — couldn't catch his scent. And my heart sank a little at its loss.

Still, something in me told me he'd be disappointed, upset even, if I washed it and eliminated his scent, so I slipped it back on a hanger, tucking it far back into the closet.

I didn't know what I would do about him; about us. He'd pushed me away almost as quickly and forcefully as he'd pulled me in and kissed me, and I didn't know what that meant. But I couldn't leave town without seeing him again.

Besides, I had the perfect, reasonable excuse to stick around with the harvest festival tomorrow.

Basically had nothing to do with a certain bewildering fox whatsoever.

Chapter Fifteen

MY EARS WERE RINGING between the music from the bar and the delighted shrieks of all of the women in my mother's house when I dropped Skylar and Cole back off after our night out. Nadir, Casey, and Sophie had wisely asked to be dropped down the street to avoid the oncoming hysterics.

I stayed long enough to be socially polite while everyone celebrated the new addition to our skulk, avoiding my mother's slightly disappointed gaze.

"Next time, *jaan*." She kissed me on the cheek as I said my goodbyes. I nodded, smiling to humor her, and made my exit.

The car ride back into town was blissfully quiet, but it left me finally alone with my thoughts, which was not a good thing. Every part of my body — one in particular — screamed for me to drive right past my shop, circle the town, head back up Ocean Avenue, straight to an extravagant carriage house I'd visited so many times before. I circled the gazebo once, then again, while my mind wavered on the decision. Even Winston, the local moose, gave me the side eye when he ambled through the square. Finally, I stopped, car in neutral, parked in the middle of the road, staring into the night. Not like I was holding up traffic.

A knock on my window startled me, which told me how distracted I was. Normally I could hear someone approaching from close to a mile away. I rolled down the window, staring at Mrs. Farrington, out for a nightly walk with her black cat, Bagheera, who was currently outfitted in a glowing collar that kept switching colors. Probably for visibility, since the cat was otherwise all but invisible at night, but the flashing lights didn't appear to improve his mood. He hissed at me, and I smiled, rather toothily, back.

"Are you lost, Kit?"

Her expression said she was more than a little worried for my sanity. Honestly, so was I at the moment. "All good. Just lost in thought." I glanced down at the basket she carried in her hands, and the blinking leash Bagheera was bucking against. "You getting ready for tomorrow?"

Her eyes expanded, and I sensed her pulse pick up. "Oh! Yes. I'm excited for the festival. Who doesn't love a harvest festival? I'm in charge of flowers tomorrow, and the mums are gorgeous. And the weather should be perfect. A great night for a new moon, new beginnings, and setting intentions for the new season. Perhaps new… relationships." She tittered a laugh, high and awkward, then waved a hand towards me. "I'm rambling. A handsome young male like yourself doesn't need to spend his night listening to a batty old lady in the middle of the street. Goodnight!"

I rolled up my window, but didn't move from where I'd paused, watching Mrs. Farrington sprint down the street towards her home, dragging the lit-up neon Bagheera behind her.

"That was strange," I mumbled, but the woman regularly walked her black cat in the middle of the night — not exactly the sanest of folks. She fit right in here in the Cove.

Hell. I was parked in the middle of the road. I guessed I fit here, too.

I forced myself to shower quickly and dress the following day, donning a maroon long sleeve henley and jeans. Our harvest festival was different here than in the human world. While it featured food vendors and games, it had a twist that was all Deadlights Cove.

The bell over the tea shop door jingled as the voices of Eva Watford and Peg Fernsby drifted back to me in the kitchen.

"Almost ready!" I called, stacking the last of the black and white iced skull cookies they'd ordered from me. My grandmother was an excellent baker, making these for the festival every year, and I was happy to carry on her legacy.

I pushed through the swinging door behind the counter, and stopped in my tracks. It didn't matter that I'd lived in the Cove my whole life — nothing could ever prepare me for the sight of my two most frequent patrons in full costume for the town's annual historical reenactment.

"Good morrow, Goodman Sayana," Peg said as she adjusted the corset tied under her low-cut peasant blouse. Her chest oozed out of the stays, more cleavage than I ever needed to see on the elderly witch.

"Already dressed and ready for the reenactment, I see." I stared at the ceiling, anywhere but at the woman who was now leaning over the counter in an attempt at seduction.

"Goody Fernsby, they'll hang you as a hussy instead of a witch if you don't rein it in," Eva said, her tone just as prudish as the Puritan she'd portray later. Her bonnet was fastened firmly under her chin and practically met the high collar of her modest black dress. Reaching across the counter, she grabbed the box of cookies and lifted it. "Thank you, Goodman Sayana. We always so enjoy the delectables we can count on from you, even if they are downright sinful." She winked, and I choked.

The women left, still speaking in character as if they'd lived through the Puritan era. I wasn't entirely sure how old they were, but I did know they weren't *that* old. Morgaine and Ryker, on the other hand… Neither had ever confirmed precisely how old they were, and they seemed content to maintain that mystery.

Blaze waltzed in next, leaning heavily on the counter. "Human girlfriends, Fox. Five Stars. Ten out of ten. Highly recommend. But, I can't find the coffee truck, and I *can't* disappoint her, not after last night's —" He broke off, probably realizing Petra might not want details of their escapades broadcast around town, and cleared his throat, grinning. "You have to help me out."

I stalled, hardly hearing his words and forgetting how my limbs worked as I stared at Blaze, whose cousin I'd pinned against the door of a bar closet last night. From his presence here and overall reaction to me, I assumed he didn't know. I'd be getting the Big Brother talk down if he knew, right?

What had he asked me?

"Don't tell anyone about this." I finally got my feet to move, waving for him to follow me back into the kitchen as I tried to act normal. His head popped up, unable to resist the hint of mischief, and he was on my heels as we spun into the kitchen, right in front of a state-of-the-art — though second-hand — espresso machine.

Blaze gasped, then glanced at me. "You've had this baby the whole time? And we don't have to go on a pointless scavenger hunt to find the coffee truck?" Then his eyes turned squinty, and his tone incredulous. *"You've had this the whole time?"*

I shrugged. "I don't want to put Val and Caedmon out of business, though I've never fully understood their business model. But the real secret is, I'm not typically a tea drinker."

Blaze laughed, running his hands through his hair like he'd had some massive revelation about my personality. He clapped me on the back, waving at the dials as he told me to fire it up.

If only admitting all of the other secrets I kept so close to my heart could be so easy.

Chapter Sixteen

NIMUE

STEPPING up to my favorite harvest festival event, I almost forgot why I ever left town. I sized up the field in front of me, dotted with Puritan-attired scarecrows, each placed in 50-yard intervals stretching across the meadow to the tree-line a quarter-mile off. I stood in line beside Blaze, dressed as a farmer for the evening's reenactment in an oatmeal linen shirt and brown wool breeches. I'd also gone with a farmer for my costume, but with a more modern spin of ripped overalls and a light pink plaid shirt and boots.

Next to Blaze stood Nox, another young local demon. I wasn't surprised to see him in his typical all-black, steadfastly refusing to dress up for the event. A few other demons from the area had come to the Cove for the festivities and stood in line with us.

The goal of this event was simple: the first demon to incinerate each scarecrow in their row to the tree line, waiting until each one was fully ashed before moving on — and without accidentally burning the rest of the field down, of course — won. Some of the younger demons might not even make it to their third one if they didn't have enough control over their fire yet.

Beverly, the owner of the exotic pet shop in town, stood to our right as moderator. On theme for the day's events, she was dressed as a stereotypical witch — only fitting, since she was one — in a black robe that made her pale skin seem ghostly white, and a pointy black hat, complete with sparkly stars.

"On your marks," she called in her airy, ethereal voice, and the featherless parrot on her shoulder squawked an echo of the command as she raised the flag. There was nothing for us to prepare, so we just waited, eyes fixed on those scarecrows. "Get set. Go!"

Immediately, a half dozen scarecrows burst into flame, set ablaze by our demon fire. Ah, torching Puritans on a crisp fall eve. What more could a demon want?

Blaze took an early lead, but he was half-witch, and started losing power faster than the rest of us. By his fifth scarecrow, he began to slow, his fire losing the heat needed to flash through the straw quickly. Nox, beside me, so young the tattoos on his body hadn't even burned off yet, flamed out only 200 yards in. Sweat dripped from his brow as he swore and kicked the dirt, stomping off.

I was neck and neck with one of the regional demons before Mo poured a bucket of ice water over his head. . The demon yelped, losing control of his fire, while my mother shouted at me, *"Go, baby, go!"* His fire sputtered on the scarecrow while it simultaneously licked across the field, immediately disqualifying him.

My secret was that I rarely used my fire, so I had more than enough banked up and ready for an event like this. Sensing the other contestants' power waning, I pushed through the rest of my energy, igniting one after another. Finally, the last one went up in flames, and I beat the others by seconds.

Clapping her hands giddily, Mo skipped over and pinched my cheeks. She was dressed as herself as always; her annual reasoning, which I had never been able to tell if it was a joke or not, was that she hadn't let the Puritans change her then and wouldn't now. Beverly brought over my prize — a Creepers the Skeleton Beanie Baby. The town was strangely obsessed with the tiny stuffed animals after something went down in the 90s that no one would give the younger generation a straight answer on. Beaming with excitement, I took it from her, as well as the cloud of cotton candy colored as flames — the only one made for the entire festival.

"I let you win," Blaze said as he nudged me with his shoulder, Petra on his other side holding his hand. She had a loose interpretation of "farmer's wife" for her costume, with a full tan skirt and a deep emerald lace-front jacket that set off her red hair.

"Sure." I raised my eyebrows, nodding. "I believe you."

"I didn't realize how much more powerful a full demon would be compared to this one," Petra jabbed her thumb towards Blaze, who coughed indignantly, but his eyes twinkled at her. "But really, that was intense."

Blaze squeezed her hand before pushing me back towards the center of town. "We have to hurry. Mo pressured Orion into an event today and refused to tell me what it was." Mischief danced in his eyes, and I couldn't help but laugh. How an angel and a demon had ended up such good friends was beyond me.

The gazebo was decorated with pumpkins and gourds, bunting flags with moon phases strung between each post, and fake spiderwebs dangling from the ceiling. Bright red and yellow mums circled it, painting it in fall colors. Petra was staring at it, blinking rapidly, before leaning over to murmur to Blaze. Seeing her confusion reminded me that the entire town was glamoured to look run-down to humans.

"What does it look like to you?" I asked Petra, curiosity getting the better of me.

"Well, when I first came to town," she paused, glancing at Blaze again, "the gazebo looked like it had been burnt to a crisp, tilting worse than the Leaning Tower of Pisa, rotted out, and covered in poison ivy. But now, it's beautiful. New white paint, bunting banners, and pretty pumpkins. The difference is still a little jarring."

We passed all the typical harvest festival booths — apple cider (in both liquid and donut form), caramel apples, pumpkin shot-put, witch hat ring toss, pumpkin carving, corn hole, etc. Then there were booths with a certain Covian flair, like the demon fire scarecrows. The witches' challenge was to spell demon wine, then taste test it for poison. A healer was kept on hand with the antidote, just in case, and was usually needed at least once a festival.

The shifters typically organized a maze with hidden items for their kids to sniff out, shifted or not — good practice for little noses. There was also an adults-only version where the organizers did everything in their power to overpower the scents of the hidden items. That ranged from throwing in red herrings to spraying sections with gasoline — slightly dangerous, but what Cove activity wasn't? — to coating areas in skunk spray, and even dousing some parts in the most noxious perfumes they could find. I'd also heard of them hiding rotten food, dead mice and fish, pungent cheeses, and sweaty socks. It typically overpowered their senses so much that they were all gagging — or worse — by the end. Finding anything at all in there had become a badge of honor. Such that it was.

Most angels typically didn't indulge in our pedestrian antics, though occasionally, like this year, someone managed to talk Orion into playing along. As mayor, it was explained, joining in helped him appear more approachable. He frequently countered that argument was more a mark *against* than *for* participating, at least for him, but he could be overruled if the other leaders in town ganged up on him.

As we approached the town hall, twin maniacal grins broke out over Blaze's face and my own as we saw what the others had chosen for Orion.

The practically perfect angel was sitting on a platform above a dunk tank in navy swim trunks and a grey quick-dry shirt that matched his silver hair. On the ground in front of him, a wooden sign read, *"Make the Official-Mayor-Of-This-Town pinch his nose or sigh. OMOTT does not know the rules."*

Blaze flicked his eyebrows up, shining an imaginary badge on his chest. "Oh, I was *born* for this. I think someone's been reading my Bucket List." Petra and I laughed as he rubbed his hands together, approaching the booth.

"Oh no," Orion muttered, seeing Blaze draw closer, then put his hands out, trying to wave him off, his white wings ruffling behind him. "No. No demons allowed."

"Hmm." Blaze scratched the beard along his jaw, drawing out the sound and leaning down pointedly to inspect the sign. He *tsk*ed and shook his head. "Does *not* say that in the rules, O."

Orion's eyes shot over to Petra and me, then back to me, and he tried again. "Nimue! Favorite quasi-little-sister of mine — "

"Aw, I'm touched," I cooed, hand placed gently over my heart.

" — get him away from here!"

I pointed a finger at Blaze. "You think I can control that thing?"

Straightening back up, Blaze tilted his head. "I'm equal parts flattered and insulted by that."

"Besides, you know I'm a demon too, right?" I added.

"Not like *him*." Sensing he wouldn't get my help, Orion turned pleading eyes on Petra. "Petra, remember how I welcomed you into this town and graciously granted you access to Rare Collections?"

"Actually, funny you mention that." Petra furrowed her brow, but shot a devious glance at Blaze that he returned with one glittering with pride. "That's not *quite* how I remember it. What about you, Blaze?"

"You're absolutely right, Petey, as always." Blaze grinned, and threw an arm around her shoulders, swinging her into him to plant a kiss on her forehead. "When you first came here, O had the biggest stick up his — "

"Fine! Fine." Orion pinched his nose and sighed deeply,

bringing the most gleeful gleam to Blaze's eye. "Get it over with. Do your worst —"

But, unbeknownst to Orion, he'd already triggered the mechanism; the tech was somehow bewitched to respond to his expressions. With a triumphant clanging, followed by a satisfying groan from the OMOTT himself, he dropped into the cold water below.

Chapter Seventeen

"THAT'S IT," I snapped from the back of my booth at the festival, having had enough. "You two — get the fuck out of here and don't come back." I didn't throw any Alpha command in; I knew it wouldn't be necessary.

At my words, Skylar detached herself from Cole's face. She was straddling her mate's lap on the folding chair I'd brought out for myself, grinding on him right there in the booth, as his hands gripped her ass. New mates were impossible to be around.

From what I'd seen of other shifters, I knew they would be like this for the foreseeable future. Once a couple gave into the mate bond, they usually spent the next week jumping each other's bones until they passed out from exhaustion, then started it up all over again when they woke. Just the thought of that made me miserable, knowing I couldn't have it.

Cole blinked, looking around like he'd forgotten where he was, which he probably had, then found my face. "Aw, I want to see Akil do the maze, though."

I raised one eyebrow at that, the slight motion saying very clearly that he wouldn't have noticed when Akil started or ended the maze. How the two of them had even made it here was beyond me.

Cole looked like he might have been about to protest again, but then Skylar nipped at his neck, and he groaned. "All right, we're leaving." He lifted her off him, placing her on her feet as he stood — a bit stiffly — and the two of them hurried out of the town square.

After they were gone, I dropped into my chair. Every year, I set up my shop booth for a few hours, selling pastries and tea for the festival. With its warm and seasonal spices, my grandmother's chai recipe was a big seller.

"*Can* I go in the maze yet?" Akil called out from where he was supposed to be helping me with the booth, but was instead seated on a cooler on his phone. He'd helped with approximately two customers before ditching me for social media. Having just turned 18, it was the first year he was allowed into the adults-only maze.

"You want to burn your snout until you're hacking your guts? Be my guest." It wasn't as if he was pulling his weight here anyway.

Akil let out an excited whoop, his ludicrous pink-tipped hair bouncing. Immediately, he stood, jogging out of the booth in a flash, and somehow found a group of friends heading for the maze.

Deciding to call it for the day as the sun crept closer to the tree line, I closed the booth, hauling everything back to the shop and locking up. After that was done, I had one last duty for the night.

String lights twinkled all around the square as the daylight faded. Locating Nadir in the crowd, I waved him over, and we both made our way to a white tent set up just outside the main hub of the event. Ducking under the flaps, we found our audience had already been assembled for us.

Every fox shifter in the region under the age of 10 that could walk looked up at us where they sat cross-legged in the tent. Their little faces alternated between eager and solemn with the knowledge of the task that awaited them. Around the edge of the tent, their parents and older siblings also stood, amusement written on their faces.

"Greet your future Alpha, pups," Nadir called to them, grinning at me.

A chorus of *"Hello, Alpha Kit!"* rang out, many sitting up straighter now that we had arrived.

"Good evening, cubs." I looked at each of them in turn to convey the seriousness of their work. "Tonight, you have the most important task of the reenactment. Do you know what that is?"

"Yes, Alpha Kit!" the children answered excitedly, a few bouncing around with giddy energy.

"Good. You are in charge of running the Puritans out of town to make it safe for our community. Nadir and I know you can handle this big responsibility, but what do *you* think?"

A series of cheers — and some downright shrieks — rang out through the tent. Nadir feigned terror, leading to a round of laughter and giggles. One small female in the front raised her hand, her brow drawn low in concern. I waited until the rest quieted down to crouch down to her level and call on her.

"Tara?"

"The wolves are so much bigger and scarier, Alpha." She stopped there, assuming I would fill in the rest of her comment for her. But it came up most years, so I knew what she was leaving out.

"The wolves are bigger, yes, but that doesn't mean you can't be just as scary," I assured her, then lifted my gaze to include the others. "As foxes, we have something the wolves will never have." I raised a brow, waiting for someone to tell us what that was.

Sure enough, a boy in the back stood and screamed *"INTELLIGENCE!"* at the top of his lungs, arm raised in the air proudly. Chuckles ran through the adults around the room, and I waved him to sit back down.

"Thank you, Nicholas. Yes, intelligence. Being able to outsmart others will always win over size."

Little Tara narrowed her eyes at me, trying to decide if I was just an adult lying to her as adults often did to ease children's fears. I flicked a finger under her chin as I smiled down at her, waiting until she nodded, accepting my judgment, before standing.

"Now," I said, letting my eyes sweep out over the children again. "When you get out there, what do you need to do?"

"Chase them away!"

"Scream as loud as we can!"

"Nip at their heels!"

"Tackle them down and sink our teeth into their flesh!"

"Whoa, whoa." I put my hands up, locating the last

speaker, a tiny pup I knew was several years older than his size would indicate. "No biting the reenactors, Oliver." The others laughed and joined in with *"Yeah, Oliver!"* and *"No teeth!"* as they'd been instructed for years. Oliver folded his arms over his chest, pouting, and slouched into himself. Maybe I needed to talk to his parents before the reenactment took off.

"You go out there and show those Puritans whose town this is!" Nadir called out, answered by another round of raucous cheers from the cubs.

"Make the Arrowwood Skulk proud, pups," I added, then nodded to a group of the parents. They took over the rest of the preparation, passing out the costumes for the evening, as Nadir and I turned and headed out of the tent.

The reenactment would start soon, so it was time for my skulk and I to get into position to watch. Nadir and I got to the shop's back door at the same time as Casey, Emerson, Sophie, Asher, and Mikaela. I unlocked the door to let them in, and we all took the stairs to the roof. Despite the size of our group, it felt strange not to have Cole or Lily — who was probably off with the wolves again — with us as Nadir passed beers and hard seltzers around. We sat on the edge of the roof, feet dangling off the building as we looked over the square and the sun slipped below the trees.

A few moments later, we all watched as Akil stumbled out of the maze, face as green as his brown skin would allow. His typically perfectly styled hair was rumpled and flat as he grabbed the conveniently-placed trash can outside its exit, puking as I'd predicted. The entire group around me burst into howling laughter; the rest of us were wise enough by now not to bother partaking in that particular activity. But then Akil's eyes rose to us on the roof, and he held up a victorious arm, hand clasping the most coveted maze item. A Gobbles the Turkey Beanie Baby — one of the twenty most valuable Beanie Babies, he'd told us a hundred times in the last week — tag intact. Casey, Nadir, and Asher cheered and whistled at him as Akil took a dramatic bow before collapsing to his knees and hurling again.

"What a moron," Emerson muttered, but I caught a glimmer of pride down the skulk ties and playfully knocked his shoulder. We both watched as our youngest brother drifted off to flaunt his hard-earned prize to his friends.

It didn't matter that I'd seen the reenactment dozens of times before; the sight of Caedmon in full Puritan costume, standing on the edge of the gazebo, was always priceless. Seeing him in anything but the bright Hawaiian shirt and shorts he usually wore — rain or shine, summer or winter — while manning the coffee van was jarring. He'd also exchanged his fedora and glasses for a stereotypical black felt hat, complete with a buckle, and a monocle. His stark black Puritan coat only made his skin seem even paler than usual. Translucent, even.

As he did every year, he gave his long and rambling speech about the town's history and how supernaturals came here until most of us were bored to tears. The skulk kept it interesting by taking a drink anytime he said *heresy* or *blasphemers*. We were currently at seven, by my count. But now he was getting to the good part, so everyone in town was perking up a bit.

"The Town of Deadlights Cove is hereby sentenced —" his voice carried over the crowd of gathered Puritans and captured witches, shifters, and demons. Peg Fernsby fought against her imaginary bonds, pretending her hands were tied behind her back, and this performance would be her ticket to the Oscars. Her corset shifted violently with the movement, and I cringed at the sight. " — to burn for the crimes of heresy — "

"Drink."

" — consorting with the Devil, and witchcraft."

"This is my favorite part," Nadir chuckled from next to me. I couldn't help but laugh with him as I sipped my beer.

"MORTAL FOOLS," Val's voice boomed as he stomped towards the gazebo, impersonating our town founder, Henry Rosewood. He stared down his partner with fire in his eyes, no sign of the loving adoration he usually wore when gazing upon the other man. "Your accusations are false, and there is nothing here for you."

"Here it comes…" Nadir whispered.

"BE GONE!" We all yelled his famous line in unison as Val lifted his hands. All of the lights in town flickered as Val smashed his hands back down.

On cue, a hoard of young shifters — wolves, bears, and foxes alike, though in different costumes — fanned out screaming from their respective tents. The children beelined for the reenactors dressed as the Puritans and townsfolk. The adult shifters in the audience, those on my rooftop included, cheered them on.

The foxes — some of the older ones shifted, but most not — wore their white ghost costumes, and, as directed, chased the townsfolk out of town. One small shifted fox, his costume already lost and his coat bright white in the moon-light leaped onto Blaze's back as he ran. Before Blaze could shrug him off, the fox started climbing, making for the neck. Luckily, an adult swooped in and gripped the cub by the scruff and hauled him off, shrieking at his thwarted violence, before his teeth could sink into flesh as desired.

Once the townsfolk were properly removed from the town, the most epic food fight ever seen broke out, rotten fruits and vegetables flying faster than the human eye could track. No one could remember when the food fight tradition began, but the goal each year was to top the one before.

"Oof. Sourdough. Cruel choice. That will hurt," Casey muttered from my left.

"Tomatoes are the way to go. Best splat-factor," Asher answered, as if this was just a normal conversation.

Val turned, covered in goo, but still in character. "From this day forth, we shall glamour this town to be so *hideous*, so *abhorrent*, that no human," he paused, scanning the crowd, and broke character for the first time in his illustrious career, with a, "er, *besides* Petra, I suppose," before continuing, "shall ever be tempted to step foot on our soil again."

Chapter Eighteen

NIMUE

I HAD FORGOTTEN how outrageous the food fight was every year after the young shifter ghosts, ghouls, zombies, vampires, and other absurd made-up creatures chased the "humans" out of town. Food stains were splattered across the usually pristine sidewalks — the thought being this was what the humans must see if they ever accidentally ventured into The Cove.

With a grimace, I tiptoed through the mess over to where Blaze, Petra, and Selene, who'd stayed up for the festival, stood with a few others by the gazebo.

"Is this what the town always looks like to you?" I asked Petra when I joined them, and she glanced around the town at my question.

"Well. I mean, Scallywags — the neon sign doesn't work, and the S is falling off." She pointed at Blaze's bar down the street, and I followed her gaze. Blaze wrinkled his nose in distaste, whipping his head to Orion with a whispered *"Really?"* Orion said nothing.

"And Devanna's shop just looks very dark and ominous," Petra continued.

"Just like its owner, no glamour necessary," Orion quipped, and Dev flipped him off.

"I've only seen the General Store open once," Petra went on, and we all laughed. That wasn't part of the glamour either. Endymion, the owner, was a demon, and a highly unreliable member of our community.

"Town Hall looks the worst, though, other than how the gazebo used to look," Petra finished, pointing at the two. "But the gazebo looks beautiful right now."

"So does Town Hall." Blaze nodded in the direction of the immaculate colonial-style building, refinished and cared for by the Historical Society. It was a shame that the glamour made it look so awful because it was Orion's pride and joy.

As if sensing my train of thought — or maybe he couldn't stand hearing the insults to his precious Town Hall — Orion scratched his nose, and a wave of power poured off him in Petra's direction. She gasped, eyes wide as she glanced around town.

"Oh, my God."

"If you can see wings and shifters running through town and still decided to stay, I'll allow you to see the buildings now, too." Orion nodded, and Petra smiled at him in return.

No way did Petra understand the gravity of what Orion had just done. I glanced at Blaze, who was staring at his best friend with disbelief.

"Well, Orion. Consider yourself prank-free for a bit. Blaze's adoration is reactivated." I smirked, and Orion rolled his eyes.

"He did throw me in jail for ten days." Blaze shrugged, as if being held for murder wasn't that big of a deal. "We can call it even now."

"We need to look into why the glamour wasn't working properly for her," Orion said to Blaze and me quietly as Petra walked towards Town Hall, chatting with Selene, admiring the architecture Petra could now appreciate. "I don't like that."

"Good thing the meeting is tomorrow." Blaze nodded.

With a burst of magic, Orion and Blaze worked together to clear the food fight remnants. Blaze incinerated the scraps into piles of ash while Orion gently swept everything through the air to the nearest trash receptacles. Mo and the witches from the coven swept the area for trash, restoring the streets and square as if nothing had ever happened here, then headed in for the night.

Once that was finished, Blaze linked his arm through mine, then Petra's, pulling us towards Scallywags for a nightcap.

"Oh, by the way, Nimmie," Blaze said, his voice full of mischief, "don't leave town yet."

I hesitated, glancing at him as we made our way down the street. "And why is that?"

"You have to come to that meeting with me tomorrow."

"... And why is that?" I repeated myself, not following his train of thought.

"You're my Second."

"Your second what?"

"No, my *Second*. Capital S. As in, Head Demon," he pointed to himself, "and Second Demon," he pointed to me. "By demon law."

I laughed, brows rising high on my face as I glanced at him in surprise. "Since when? Do we even have laws? Or Seconds?"

"Since," he glanced down at his arm that most definitely did not have a watch on it, "half-past a freckle. Standard Elbow Time."

Petra chuckled, and I rolled my eyes at my cousin.

He shrugged, then poked me in the arm. "Really, though. It's your fault. After you left town, the rest of the demons got me drunk and made me the de-facto demon leader. So, per my decree — which is the law — you are to be my Second. Non-negotiable."

"Everyone else is bringing a Second to the meeting, aren't they, Blaze?"

"Everyone? Well, not *everyone*, since you know that the nymphs won't show. But the others, yes. I think so. Good thing mine happens to be in town this week."

I shook my head, but I was curious to find out what could be affecting the glamour in town to such a degree that a human was able to see through it. Before I could ask more, Blaze called out to someone across the square.

"Hey, Fox!"

I would have stopped, but Blaze still had his arm linked through mine. Whether I wanted to or not, I was carried along as Blaze turned all three of us to face the other side of the square where Kit and his friends emerged from his shop.

Kit's head rose at the call, and he waved the others to go on without him as he finished locking up and strolled over to us. Decidedly *not* looking in my direction.

I tried not to notice how his maroon henley stretched across his broad shoulders, how its rolled-up sleeves revealed the intricate tattoos over his forearms. I didn't want to notice how his jeans hugged his trim hips, the casual confidence in his gait. He hadn't even looked at me, and my palms were warming, something kindling in my chest.

"How was the arranged bonding visit?" Blaze's grin, never far from devious, was much too wide to be innocent as he shot a glance my way before returning his attention to Kit.

I swallowed, then was sent into a fit of coughing on nothing as I fought to pull air into my lungs. Tears were streaming down my face as I turned away from the group, eyes wide with the words. Blaze slammed his hand down between my shoulder blades with a *"wrong pipe?"* I nodded, trying to regain my composure as my mind spun over the mention of an *arranged bonding.*

Kit, Blaze, and Petra all stared at me for several beats, waiting to make sure I'd recovered before Kit continued. Sliding his hands in the back pockets of his dark jeans as he tilted his head, Kit answered, "Better than I could have expected, to be honest."

"Oh, so she's the one?"

A tight-lipped smile tugged at the corner of Kit's mouth. "Not at all. She mated Cole. *True* mates." He nodded in the direction his friends had gone to indicate his skulk. I chose not to think too hard about why I felt so relieved to hear this news.

Petra looked between Blaze and Kit, one eyebrow up. "Does *mated* mean what I think it means?"

Chuckling, Kit shook his head. "No. I mean, *also* what you're thinking, but occasionally a shifter finds their true mate. Has Blaze given you the shifter magic rundown?"

Petra raised a wavering hand to indicate *somewhat*. Kit's eyes flashed to me momentarily before he continued. "We have the closest ties with soul magic, since we have two souls intertwined, our human and our animal. A true mate is when that magic recognizes its equal, its… perfect match." His voice caught a little on the last words, and he cleared his throat.

Throwing a glance over his shoulder in the direction his friends had gone, he continued, "I have to run — make sure everyone gets home. See you around, Petra — Blaze —" He opened his mouth, like he was going to say my name as well, but then closed it, clearing his throat again. Shaking his head, he turned and loped away, leaving the square on his friends' trail.

"Okay." Blaze drew out the word as he detached his arm from mine so he could face me head-on. "That was awkward, even for you two. Which is saying something because *that*," he waved his hand between Kit's retreating back and me, "has been awkward for years. What was that? Start talking, Nimmie."

I blinked. "What was what?"

He narrowed his eyes at me as Petra toed the ground, and he swung on her at the noise. "*You.* You know something too, don't you? What happened that I'm missing?"

It was then that I got the feeling that Petra was not quite so practiced at the art of impromptu subterfuge as a demon. Her voice came out far too high as she responded, "Nothing. What? What could I know? I don't even — I'm so new to all the — I mean, I *just met* him, basically, *and* Nimue, so —"

"Wow," I chuckled, cutting her off to end her misery.

"Seriously." Blaze met my gaze, concern on his face,

then placed a sympathetic hand on Petra's shoulder. "Petra. Babe. That wouldn't have fooled a child."

"Disgraceful." I nodded.

"We'll have to work on that, Petey. You can't be with a demon if you can't lie more convincingly. How are you supposed to defend my good name in court when the opportunity arises?"

"Um." Petra glanced between us. "*Opportunity?* Is that the word?"

Blaze waved a hand. "Opportunity, eventuality. Call it what you want." He rounded back on me. "But don't think you're distracting me from this. Don't make me get your mother involved."

Just then, my savior appeared at my side. Dev looked extremely comfortable in the full black witch costume she'd worn for the evening. "Come on, Nims," she stuck an arm through mine, towing me along. "I won the demon-wine contest, and you get to reap the benefits."

Blaze opened his mouth to interrupt, but I waved a hand at him over my shoulder as I let Dev drag me away. "Sorry, Boz — girls' night!"

I leaned into Dev as she threw me a knowing smirk, the plum-colored bottle in her hand swinging at her hip. "You're the best. You know that?"

She chuckled as we entered the bar and headed for our usual booth by the back corner. "And don't you forget it."

Chapter Nineteen

AS WE NEARED the treeline on the outskirts of town, my skulk began shedding their clothes, shoving them into a backpack I tossed near the base of a tree. One by one, they shifted into fox forms, yipping as they raced through the woods ahead. I went last, waiting until everyone had shifted before I stripped, added my clothes to the bag, then threw it high up into the tree. I'd come by and retrieve it on my way home later.

There was nothing as freeing as running wild in my fox form, letting my animal take control as it moved to the forefront of our shared soul. My eyes scanned the forest, especially dark tonight with the new moon. Small prey scurried in the underbrush, but my Alpha nature required my attention to stay on the foxes in front of me instead. Wolves howled in the distance, and I needed to stay alert. While the chances of true violence between us were low, there was always the risk that what might start as a playful, teasing hunt could turn serious if their animal took too much control. Then there was the matter of the witches practicing human sacrifice last month; they'd never been caught, and just because we hadn't heard from them in a few weeks didn't mean they were gone.

Scenting that we had crossed back into our territory, we slowed to a trot for the rest of the walk home. Even if it were a full moon, when the wolves were wildest, they wouldn't mess with us here. Legal agreement aside, we also had all sorts of traps and snares set up against intruders, and only *we* knew where they were and how to avoid them. A wolf only had to fall victim to one before they decided they were better off heeding the boundary, even if they were the apex predators of the forest and their Alpha was the head of the region's shifters.

If being Alpha only meant *this* — overseeing my skulk through runs in the woods, even leading the cubs before their time to shine in the reenactment — I'd be fine with it. I loved being surrounded by trees, my family, and the brisk night air. But it was so much more responsibility than that — the thought of having to keep everyone protected and safe at all times was daunting, to say the least. They'd all be counting on me. My father had been training me for it since I could control my shift, but I still wasn't sure I'd ever be ready.

When we reached the creek behind my parents' house, Casey, Asher, and Mikaela slinked off, their tawny brown, rust orange, and sandy coats disappearing into the under-brush. I watched as they headed for the house the twins and Asher shared with a few others in our skulk.

Nadir, Emerson, and I continued together. Even though I lived in the apartment in town, my mother had a connip-tion if I didn't stop by several days a week, and my father would chew me out if I didn't make sure everyone made it to the front door safely and checked in with him.

True to form, the male was standing on the porch of the white farmhouse, arms crossed over his chest as he watched us approach. He wore only sweats, but despite his casual attire, the subtle undercurrent of authority he emitted couldn't be denied by any of us as we slowed to a stop at the porch steps.

"I just received a *very* interesting phone call."

The phone tree in the Cove was incomparable.

"Emerson, your mother is warming food for you. Shift and take Nadir with you."

Shifting back, my brother and cousin grabbed shorts from the bin of assorted clothes we kept on the porch.

"Pa, we're not hungry —"

His penetrating gaze stared through Emerson as his bronze skin wrinkled across his brow. "I didn't ask if you were hungry. Your mother is up late making you food, so you will go eat it."

Emerson shot me a glance before heading inside with Nadir at his heels.

"Shift back so I can speak to you properly." He chucked another pair of shorts at me while I did as he asked, then slid them on. Leaning into one of the porch posts, he stared down at me, his body language still not allowing me to come up the steps.

"Where's Akil?" His tone was light, which set my stomach sinking.

"Still in town, I think."

"You think."

He let the silence do the scolding for him.

"And Lily? Sophie?"

I averted my gaze as I knew he wanted, a sign of respect. Sophie had taken off right after the reenactment, saying something about meeting friends, but I should have gotten more details from her. "I don't know."

"What was it I told you about the festivities in town this morning?" he scratched his beard, brow furrowed as he pretended to forget what he'd lectured me about over the phone before I'd set up my booth at the festival.

I contained my groan of frustration. Though I had no real desire to be Alpha, submitting to my father's overwhelming dominance was irksome. My fox bucked against his command.

"They were just having fun."

Turned out that was the wrong thing to say. He pushed off the post, straightening as his gaze sharpened on me. Before he could decide what to do, my mother came bustling out of the house.

"Mahit, what are you thinking, keeping him out here in the cold in only his shorts?" she scolded him, waving at me to come up the steps, knowing full well that the cold bothered neither of us. "Come in and eat before you freeze to death."

"Give us a moment, *shona*," my father told her, though in a much gentler tone than he used with me. She frowned at him, but went back into the house after shooting me an imploring glance. Pleading with me to submit and get this over with so she could feed me.

"Kit." He rubbed a hand down his face. "Mikaela's mother called to say she saw Lily and Sophie running off into the woods. To the *west*." Shit, that was wolf territory.

"You can't leave them out there. Find them and bring them home. And don't be long; I'm sure your mother will wait up."

My gaze slid to his without thinking, and his own eyes narrowed as he waited to see if I was challenging him. I wasn't — I was only thinking that I had no idea if Lily and Sophie would be running *with* the wolves, not just in their territory. But I quickly realized I had no way to explain that to the male in front of me. Maybe I would luck out, and all three of them would still be around town.

"Yes, Pa." It would be much faster to run as a fox, so I shed the shorts again, tossing them back onto the porch, and went to shift.

Only, I couldn't.

I frowned. Maybe I wasn't focusing enough? I tried again.

Again and again, but it was as if the soul of the animal within had gone to sleep, and I was unable to call on it.

"What is it?" my father took a step down, concern on his face as panic rose in me.

"I can't shift." My eyes were wide as I stared at my father, heart racing. This had never happened before, not since I'd learned how to control my shift when I was five.

"Of course you can." His words were encouraging, but his tone was still confused, worried.

"I *can't*." I shook my head. "My fox isn't there."

He descended the rest of the steps. "Yes, you can. You were just shifted. How much did you have to drink?"

"It's not that." No way I was answering *that* question. Not after our reenactment drinking game. "I just — you try."

He gave me an *I'll show you how it's done* sort of hand wave and peeled his clothes off.

After a moment, where he was no doubt attempting and failing to shift himself, an urgent energy stirred in him. He pulled his clothes back on, indicating for me to do the same, and hopped back on the porch. Flying into the house with me at his heels, he rounded on Nadir and Emerson in the kitchen, both eating at the kitchen island. Ma looked up from where she was slicing mangos, pausing as we barged in.

As Pa found his phone on the counter, he pointed to the boys. "You two — shift, now."

Confusion was written on their faces, but they stood to heed his command as he scrolled through his contacts and tapped one. My sharp hearing easily picked up the ring on the other end.

Soft gasps escaped my brother and cousin as they, too, realized they couldn't shift, their brows drawn as they looked between me and my father, phone to his ear.

"What the fuck?" Nadir whispered at me, hoping my mother wouldn't hear from across the kitchen. But she pointed her knife in his direction and hissed a warning to speak with respect — shifter hearing was impeccable. I shrugged, then my head jerked towards my father when he spoke.

"Kit, text your sister. Ask her if she can shift — and ask if the pack is having the same problem. Nadir, find your father, then contact the rest of your friends. Emerson, call Akil."

I tried not to let my jaw drop at my father's casual insinuation that he knew all about Lily hanging out with Julian and the wolves, silently making eye contact with Nadir and Emerson as we went into action. Our phones were back at my apartment since we wouldn't have been able to shift with them, but I could text Lily from Ma's tablet, and Emerson went for the house phone. Nadir took off to find his father at their house next door.

"Orion." Even from the living room, where I'd found the tablet on the coffee table, my father's voice seemed to boom through the sudden stillness that had invaded us, the quiet left behind by the missing pieces of our souls. "We have a problem."

Chapter Twenty

NIMUE

"WE HAVE A SITUATION," Orion called out over the crowd gathered in Blaze's bar after the mayor had announced an emergency town meeting. Every face turned to him as conversations ceased, and the silence rang louder than the noise that had just faded.

He looked over everyone, seeking certain people out. "Any shifters here — please try to shift and let me know if you cannot."

A ripple of unease went through the crowd at the strange request. I watched as people scattered around the bar began to gasp a moment later, Kit's little brother Akil included.

Nodding grimly, Orion continued. "I've received a few calls tonight from others. For some reason, it seems that shifters cannot switch between forms at the moment."

"Does that mean anyone currently in their animal form is stuck that way?" one of the wolves still among us called out.

Orion shrugged. "We'll have to find one and see. But at

the moment, I would say it is safe to assume that yes, they are currently stuck in animal form."

"Is it affecting shifters everywhere, or only here?"

Wings ruffling with discomfort — the male preferred having all the answers — Orion pressed his lips together grimly. "I'll call around to the other supernatural town leaders tonight to find out."

Murmurs increased, especially among the remaining wolves. It was a long-standing tradition to shift after the Harvest Festival. Many of their pack would currently be in wolf form, now trapped like that until we could figure out what was going on. Voices talked over each other as everyone began frantically calling and texting, trying to get in touch with friends and family to find out who was human, and who was stuck as an animal.

I glanced at Akil, who pulled out his phone and texted furiously. The urge to go over and ask about Kit, to see if he'd been able to make it home and shift back to human in time, was almost impossible to resist. I caught Blaze giving me a sympathetic grimace, whispering something in Petra's ear before slipping through the crowd to Akil's side.

"What do we do?" one wolf called out, turmoil written on his face.

"The Heads and I are meeting tomorrow," Orion said, trying to calm them. "We'll come together and see what we can find, then move forward. If we discover anything useful, we'll inform any shifter in our region as soon as we do."

Sensing the dismissal, the crowd dispersed, the after-party over now that half the guests had to go find out if members of their families were trapped indefinitely in an animal's body. Blaze reappeared at my side without a sound, squeezing my shoulder.

"Kit's human," he informed me, and a breath blew out of me. "He made it home and shifted, seemingly just a few minutes before this — whatever this is — happened."

I nodded, mouthing a thank you at him, then decided to turn in for the night. While there wasn't anything we could do about it yet, my heart was heavy as worry settled over our community.

The next morning, I found a chair along the wall in the large conference room in Town Hall as Blaze made his way to the oval table in the center. Orion sat at the head, with Blaze as demon representative to his right. Ostara represented the witches, the white streaks in her hair practically glowing against her rich brown skin. Ryker stood in for... I guess, Ryker — there were no other dragons in this part of the country that I knew of. For the shifters, a very flustered Julian represented the wolves, wearing a Deputy Sheriff t-shirt; and Kit's father Mahit for the foxes was to his left. I recognized a few other shifter Alphas from local packs, but none I knew personally. Maybe they were new since I'd left, or perhaps from some of the smaller packs that didn't live in town.

To my left and right along the wall sat the Seconds. Lysander — a witch, and Ostara's son — sat to my right, his pale green eyes and light brown skin contrasting against his dark blue button-down and green chinos, a bit more dressed up than when he played with his band. Raking his fingers through the black coils of his hair, he leaned closer to the female wolf on his right, whose name I didn't know, deep in conversation with her. A very quiet, very solemn Kit looked all around the room before realizing the only empty seat was next to me, and sank into the chair to my left.

"How did your skulk fare?" I whispered to him, trying to sound as normal as possible. If he wanted to pretend that nothing had happened at the bar, then fine. We had bigger issues to deal with now, anyway. The voices around the table spoke over each other, reporting the strange instances around town.

"No one has seen Sophie or Lily yet, and Cole and Skylar didn't manage to shift back in time, though they made it home. But they're safe, just stuck. There are a few others unaccounted for, but everyone else seems to be all right." He answered quickly enough, but I could feel the tension oozing off him in waves.

Even on good days, Kit had always taken responsibility for his skulk, and I hated seeing him so anxious about their well-being. Only when he thought no one was watching, when the reins of responsibility were lifted, did he ever relax. Only with me... or at least, it used to be that way. Now, I wasn't so sure.

The Kit that had pulled me through the crowded dance floor and shoved me against the wall, growling fierce and dirty words... I wasn't sure I knew that Kit. Wiggling in my chair at the memory, I also couldn't deny that I *wanted* to know that Kit.

"Are you worried about Lily and Sophie?" I asked, trying to pull my mind back to the topic at hand. I didn't turn towards him, not trusting my demon instincts not to override my sensibilities and cause even more trouble for me, and tried to follow the reports the shifter packs were providing to Orion.

Kit hesitated, and I glanced his way for only a moment, trying to read his body language. "I think Lily's seeing Julian. He's here, obviously, and human. So, I don't know what to think."

We both paused, listening as Julian reported on the wolves' missing numbers. "We had a cohort of pups shifting last night for the first time." He rubbed his hand across the back of his neck. "Darius shifted with them to help control their animals."

The room collectively sucked in a breath, and it suddenly dawned on me why Darius wasn't here — he was pack Alpha and the Sheriff in town; the only reason Julian would be here in his stead was...

"Oh no. Darius is stuck." My words were hardly above a whisper, distress settling in.

The room seemed to hold the same opinion as me, and they all began to speak at once. Kit's hand drifted over to mine, gripping it in a comforting gesture until he looked down at it, seemingly as surprised as I was by this reaction. He had always been able to sense my emotions after knowing me my whole life, and it seemed he still could, even as he let go with a gentle pat on my arm.

"What happens when you stay in your animal form for too long?" I leaned into Kit, trying to keep my voice low as he pushed his hand into his pocket. He smelled so good — like pine and petrichor, that fresh, forest rain scent — and I was momentarily distracted. "Or, I guess, vice versa?"

Kit puckered his lips, moving his mouth to the side, and

I... watched. I shouldn't have. Of all the times to think about Kit's perfectly full lips, this was definitely not the time. Infernal demon impulses.

"Our souls are connected. Two halves of a whole," he mused after a moment, half-focused on the conversations around us. "It's a delicate balance, and either way — shifted or not — tips the scales. As our animals, we have less of a concept of time, past and future; of consequences. There's just the present; our senses, our needs —" He licked his lips, glancing at me. "Too long as our animal, we start to become our wild brethren. Too long as a human, we lose the powers that gift us the ability to shift, to heal, to," he paused, listening as Julian reported 17 wolves trapped in their wolf form, muttering a "*shit*" that only I heard. "All of it. We lose all of it."

I cringed. That sounded terrible, either way. "Well, this sucks."

Kit chuckled, letting his eyes dart over to me for only a moment, and something inside of me eased at the sound." That it does."

Chapter Twenty-One

I BARELY NOTICED as Ryker begrudgingly took charge of the meeting. Orion sat back, frowning, but conceded control to Ryker as the strongest shifter in the region. Nimue was leaning towards me, and it took all of my control to stay in my seat; not to nuzzle into her hair or neck and breathe in her scent like a goddamn freak.

But when a dragon starts grumbling out orders, you listen. I forced myself to turn my attention back to the black-clad, blond-haired giant at the end of the table.

"Right now, we have a shifter problem. That is the immediate need," Ryker's voice practically thundered over the room. Even the non-shifters sat straighter, hearing the command of the most powerful and oldest being in attendance. "Orion and I spoke with the other territories, and whatever is happening, it's only here in the Cove."

"This has to be related to the witches last month, right? The schoolhouse attack?" Blaze said, glancing from Ryker to Orion. "Maybe they didn't stop as we thought — you said the glamour was still more affected than it should be, right?"

Ostara leaned forward. "If it is witches, we've still had no sign of them, or any further spell work."

"But sapping power from the ley lines, it would make sense that affects us shifters most," Winona sighed heavily. "Our magic is most deeply reliant on them as a source."

Voices spoke in hushed tones, but Ryker cleared his throat, smoke leaking from his nose, and silence reigned once more. "Though the town is glamoured, the animals are not. Foxes we can get away with, and the two bears we have missing. But how long do you think it will take to make it onto the human news that a pack of wolves randomly popped up in Maine? We cannot let these guys get picked up by wildlife control."

I leaned forward in my seat, not having noticed the bear's Alpha, Winona, present at the meeting, concern written all over her sun-tanned face. A middle-aged woman, she usually had a warm friendliness about her. Despite that, I knew she could be as fierce as any Alpha in here when provoked.

Orion's jaw was clenched tight, but he let Ryker continue to bark orders.

"Blaze, you're in charge of the nymphs. Get in touch with Maia. Find out if this is affecting the water shifters, too. Keep in touch with them." Blaze held up a hand as if to argue, but Ryker's eyes flashed green, and Blaze's jaw snapped back shut. He nodded, looking uncomfortable as he fidgeted in his chair.

"That has to chafe his demon instincts. He wants to disobey," Nimue chuckled at my side.

"Julian, you're in charge of the wolves for now. I need you to stay in town, keeping those who haven't shifted under control. With your animals trapped, your wolves are about to feel rather edgy, I'd guess." Julian nodded, and Ryker switched his gaze.

"Same goes for you, Mahit and Winona." They nodded as well.

"Ostara, take the witches in town. Divide and separate to the nexus points. Someone is fucking with them still — that has to be what's happening here." Ryker quickly glanced at Orion to confirm his suspicion, and the mayor nodded in agreement. "We've been watching them since the attacks, but maybe we missed something. Maybe these fuckers are getting better at hiding their tracks. Figure it out.

"You and I, Orion, will strengthen the town's borders. No one goes in or out without our permission." Several voices began to speak at once, and Ryker's blazing green gaze slid across the room. Silence descended once again. "Ostara — who is your most powerful cosmic witch? We need to harness the celestial powers to get this set up now."

Ostara threw an austere look at her son, then back to Ryker before answering, "Devanna." I glanced towards Lysander in time to see his jaw tighten; he was a man used to being the best at everything, but his ego was large enough to take a hit or two.

"Call her. She's coming with us then, Orion. The magic will be stronger if we braid more elements into the border. Make this thing an electric fence for supernaturals."

"You can't do that," Julian spoke up, and Ryker slowly turned his head towards the male. Julian swallowed, but maintained eye contact as he insisted, "You can't kennel us like dogs here in town, Ryker."

"You know the deal, Julian. The longer they're shifted, the less control their human soul will have, and they'll start to go wild. I could wait for them all to get tranq'd and shipped to Canada, or zoos all over the world, or I could put them all down like feral animals instead. How's that sound?"

"All right, that's enough, Ryker." Orion stood, hands on the table in front of him. "I agree with these plans, feral animal comment aside. That was too far."

Ryker offered no apology, and his words still hung heavy in the air.

"The rest of you," Ryker addressed those of us scattered around the edge of the room now, "Pair up, start hunting down the shifted, and bring them back into town. One should be a shifter on the off-chance you can still communicate with their animals, and the other should have magic in case the animals aren't responsive and lash out. Alphas, you can split up your territories to ensure it's all covered."

With that brusque dismissal, Ryker stood and strode from the room, unwilling for more discussion. People pushed to their feet, looking at each other as we all tried to process our current reality. Julian strode over to the other wolf to begin discussing logistics, and my father came over to me while pulling out his phone.

Our territory was split into different sections, with names based on either geographic features in that section, numbers, or historical residents. Pa was already texting other members of the family about what areas they were going to check.

"I'm telling Jay to find a witch and head to Reynold's Quarry," he informed me while typing, referring to my uncle. "And Kali and Emerson will go meet the witches headed to Oak Grove," referring to my aunt Kalini, my father's youngest sibling. He rattled off a few more assignments before clicking his phone off and sliding it back into his pocket. "You and Nimue take the pond."

I blinked at his order.

"Nimue doesn't need to come. I can handle it." There was no way I was spending the day in the woods with her, not after I'd barely held it together while we were hiking, then what I'd done to her at the club. I could still barely look at her after the words that had come out of my mouth that night.

The adjustment in my father's stance was subtle, but I clocked it all the same. "You heard Ryker. One shifter, one non. You might not be able to communicate to them if you can't access your fox, and then you'll need Nimue to subdue them with magic and flicker them home."

I could feel Nimue glancing between us, confusion emanating from her.

"I'm happy to help," she said at last. Reading my hesitation as not wanting to inconvenience her, apparently. "We need to get everyone to safety as fast as possible."

I couldn't even look at her, my gaze locked on my father's as my Alpha instincts fought to dominate this command. "*I* can subdue them."

Nimue cleared her throat as the tension grew between us. I wished I could pull my stare away, but it was too late.

"Kit," Pa's voice was low. "We can't do this today; we can't waste time. Go out there and bring them home."

Did he know about us? That Nimue was my mate? Was

that why he was pushing for this — to make me confront her about it, one way or another?

A soft hand clasped around my arm at the elbow sent a jolt through me that finally tore my eyes away from his. I looked down at it, and some of my tension eased. I followed the hand up the arm until I met Nimue's black eyes. They glimmered, shadowing further, and the pull of her magic sent a shudder through me. She had locked on to my desire to back down, *not* to fight him on this, and was pulling it out, increasing its strength until it won out over the deeper impulse to push him.

Sensing our confrontation was over, my father turned and headed out of the room to go home and secure the rest of the skulk as Ryker had instructed the Alphas.

Once I lost sight of him, I let out a breath, rubbing a hand over the back of my neck as I slipped from Nimue's hold.

"Let's go," I muttered, striding for the door without looking back to see if she was coming. I knew she would be.

The male was right; I couldn't challenge him today. I didn't *want* to fight with him at all, but my second soul had other plans. It had made them very clear on my twenty-fifth birthday when foxes finally sensed what their full strength would be. I far out-powered my father, which was why I'd had to move out. I hated it for tearing me away from my family, even if I saw them almost daily.

In the crisp fall breeze outside, I took a deep breath as I spotted my father crossing the square, and waited for Nimue to catch up to me.

"Should I flicker us there?"

I tried to hide my flinch. "Sure." Meeting her eyes

briefly, I aimed for an appreciative smile, but it probably looked like a wince. "Thanks."

Her lips pursed, but she only clasped my arm again, and I closed my eyes as the world spun around us. I knew she'd get us exactly where we needed to go. After all, she knew our lands almost as well as I did.

Chapter Twenty-Two

AS THE SCENT of sun-warmed pine needles and earth hit me, a wave of memories crashed through my mind's eye. Images of Nimue and me in these very woods, night after night, at different ages. I rubbed a hand over my chest, an ache there that hadn't existed a moment ago.

"So, what was all that about?" Nimue trailed a hand over the bark of a white pine, not realizing she was leaving her scent all over it.

As I set off through the trees, I drew my eyes away from her hand, keeping my ears and nose attuned for any sign of foxes. But they were probably all bedded down until dusk at this time of day.

"What was *what* all about?"

Gliding along at my heels, all unruffled innocence — but I knew better than to believe that — Nimue laughed. "That whole scene with your dad."

I sighed, not wanting to get into that right now. Or ever. Not with her.

"It didn't use to be like that between you two. Did something happen?" Her concern for me was so genuine that I'd never wished I could shift and run away more than I did at that minute.

"You could say that."

Her hand rested lightly on my shoulder again. I closed my eyes, lost for a minute to the feel of the warmth of her palm through my flannel, alone with her here under the trees, the wind picking up around us. I smelled a storm in the air.

"You know I moved out. Before..." I couldn't bring myself to say *before you left*. We'd never discussed her leaving town. "Well. It was getting to be too much with us both under one roof."

Her brows drew together. "You were fighting?"

I gave a stiff nod. "When we were shifted. We try not to be shifted together anymore. It was practically giving Ma a heart attack every time we did."

"Because you're next in line?"

Stepping out of her hold, I continued walking. "Yes. But also because I'm a higher level Alpha than he is."

Nimue let out a soft cough of surprise. "Wow. Why aren't you Alpha now, then?"

Without thinking, I reached over, bumped her shoulder, and then hastily withdrew my hand. "You know I never really cared about that. He can retire when he's good and ready, preferably in at least another fifty years."

Laughing softly again while she shook her head, she countered, "Kit, you'll be a great Alpha whenever he retires. You care about everything too much not to be."

We walked further into the woods towards Bear Pond in

silence, but I could feel the tension in Nimue's every movement.

"Is that why you've been so weird?" she finally asked. "Weird*er* than usual, I mean. Or is it because of what happened at the club?"

Shit. Obviously, I knew she could tell I was being weird, but I didn't want to tell her the real reason.

A few raindrops pelted us from above, and Nimue hissed. Demons — fire creatures that they were — did not care for water, though it didn't *actually* harm them. Nimue wasn't the Wicked Witch of the West — far from it.

"Come on." I jerked my head towards the pond. "I know a spot where we can sit out the storm. It'll pass." Though being trapped in an enclosed space with Nimue was the last thing I wanted to do right now, I didn't want to see her uncomfortable.

We reached the foot of a large tree shortly, and Nimue gasped as she looked up. "The treehouse."

"Yeah. Well, the old one burnt down in the fire."

Her gaze drifted from the treehouse above down to me, a soft smile playing across her lips. "You rebuilt it?"

"Seemed only right." I shrugged. "Some of our best memories were in that treehouse. I didn't want Akil and all the next generations to miss out on the fun."

But really, that was only half the reason. Sure, it had been a fort for Capture the Flag, a sleepover spot, and a secret hideaway from responsibilities as the next Alpha. But it had also been here that I'd kissed Nimue for the first time. Even at eight, I'd known then that I wanted her forever.

"Shall we go up?" Nimue asked, her smile turning mischievous as she grabbed the ladder rungs.

"After you." I nodded.

That was a mistake. I realized that right as I glanced up, ensuring the rungs were safe for her, and was greeted by the sight of her perfectly round ass above me.

I locked down the groan that wanted to work its way out of me, and turned to look out over the water. A beaver worked tirelessly on its dam across the lake, unbothered by the large raindrops plunking into the water around it.

"Coming up?" Nimue shouted down from above, drawing my attention back to her.

I glanced up at the sky, praying for self-control, then grabbed the rungs to follow her.

When I rebuilt the treehouse, I expanded it, making sure the height was tall enough for me to stand inside, but the space was still cozy.

"Glad we made it," Nimue said as I settled at her side, shivering at the thought of being out in the downpour.

I leaned back against the treehouse wall, trying to put distance between us, avoiding her intoxicating scent. Practically grinding the back of my head into the wood, I closed my eyes and tried to think of anything else but the demon in here with me.

Inventory at the shop.

Akil's latest YouTube video.

The terrifying portrait that Caedmon had shown me of Val naked in front of the lighthouse, glancing coquettishly back over his shoulder — my brain refused to unsee it.

Nim's mahogany hair.

Rosewater and rain.

The constellation of freckles over her left cheek that looked like Cassiopeia.

Shit.

"Kit." Her voice was somehow soft and sharp at the same time. "What happened?"

I didn't open my eyes, but I heard her moving closer. "Nothing happened. I don't know what you're talking about."

"*This!*" She didn't yell, but she might as well have the way the word slapped me. "Are we just going to pretend that you didn't drag me into a closet and pin me against a wall a few days ago? Did I do something? Or say something?"

Jaw clenching, I forced my eyes open. I didn't want her to think that, even if I couldn't tell her the truth. "No. You didn't do anything. I just —" lightning flashed outside at the same time her eyes did. "— I don't know. I shouldn't have done that. It was a mistake."

The words sounded cruel even before they left my lips, and false as well. Kissing her could never have been a mistake.

Her head jerked back as if I'd slapped her, eyes expanding with hurt. "What the fuck, Kit?"

Nimue practically never swore, so it cut like a knife when she did.

"Is this because you feel an impulse to want to have sex with me? Or an Alpha-shifter possessive thing?"

I choked on nothing. "What?"

She rolled her eyes. "Did you think you were hiding it?" She worked to suppress a smile at my expense. "It's no big deal, Kit. Do you know how often strangers on the street have the same urge? Friends, too, sometimes? It's fine. You don't have to be weird about it. We can still be friends."

If I could have felt my fox at that moment, he would

have fucking snarled at that, but my blood began to warm all the same. Who *else* wanted her? Were they in town? Could I find them? Could I fight them?

She laid a hand over my arm, and continued saying loathsome, infuriating things. "Really. Urge isn't the same as wanting to act on it, I promise. Not always. You should feel some of the impulses I sense in people; then, you'd know how hilarious and messed up people can be. I know you don't really *want* to —"

"See, this is the problem, Nim," I seethed through my teeth, unable to contain the words that spilled out of my mouth. "I want to be friends with you again. I really fucking do." Her eyes widened with hope at my words before I brought down the hammer to shatter it, my gut clenched in anticipation of what I was about to reveal. "But the problem is I also really *do* want you."

My fox would have hummed in approval if the bastard wasn't asleep, or locked up, or whatever was happening as I pushed off the wall and drew towards her. She took a step back in surprise, scanning my face as she processed what I'd just told her.

"What? You didn't sense that?" I took another step, the instinct to shadow her taking over as I backed her up against the side of the treehouse.

"You know I can only sense impulses," she said, a breathy quality to her voice I'd only heard once before — in the closet at the club when she'd asked me to promise to fuck her. "Not the reasons or thoughts behind them. And it's entirely possible you only *think* you want this, but it's just my magic making you feel the urge stronger than you would otherwise, and your brain is trying to assign reason to that, so —"

A soft exhale escaped her as she thumped into the wall, my hands coming up to rest on either side of her shoulders, caging her in. Even though she could quickly flicker out of here or push me away, she didn't. My eyes dropped to her neck, magnetizing me to lower my head there, graze her skin with my nose and lips, and once again inhale her scent the way I'd been thinking about for days.

Chapter Twenty-Three

NIMUE

"WELL, THEN, WHAT'S THE PROBLEM?" I tried to maintain some level of coherency to my thoughts, but it was difficult with the way he was caging me in like this, with his lips lighting up the nerves along my neck, my breaths growing heavier. "You want this. I want this."

His teeth skittered across my neck, sensitizing the skin there even further, and I shivered. "It's not that simple."

I reached out, running my hand across his chest as my demon impulses pumped harder, pushing for more, relishing the heat of his body so close to mine. He leaned into my palm ever so slightly, and I traced my fingers across the hard planes under his shirt. As I moved towards his abdomen, he suddenly caught my wrist, stilling its motion with a firm grip.

"Nim," he hissed, his lips still hovering just above my skin. "You don't understand. We can't do this."

Groaning, I shoved against his chest, but he didn't budge. "Explain it to me then, Kit, because you're driving me insane."

He drew back enough to look me in the eyes, and I sensed conflicting urges within him — one to tell me everything, whatever that entailed, and another to bolt out of the treehouse altogether. Though I was tempted to reach out, to coax the first impulse, I didn't. I just waited.

"I shouldn't tell you this." It came out as a whisper, his voice pained, more like he was talking to himself than to me. He turned his head away, and I couldn't help reaching out to cup the strong line of his jaw, though he wouldn't turn back. "You're my true mate."

I pulled back, my hand dropping from his face as I sank into the wall behind me, though there wasn't anywhere to go. Shock coursed through me as I struggled to comprehend those words. Demons didn't have mates. That was only a shifter thing.

Before I had any time to comprehend what this meant, Kit was pressing his entire body into me, seeming unable to stop as a shudder ran through him that I felt down to my bones.

"You're my mate," he whispered again, mouth at my ear, before he nipped the lobe, and pressed his lips into my neck.

"But —" I let out a breath of surprise as his hand found my hip, hauling me against him. "I'm not a shifter."

He laughed against my neck, the sound rumbling through both of us in a way that sent heat pooling between my legs. His laugh turned to a groan as he scented my need for him, and he pressed harder into me, the rough wood at my back digging into my skin.

"It seems my fox doesn't give a fuck." His hand slipped down, and I held my breath as he fingered the waist of my jeans. "Your soul is my match; he wants me to show you that you're mine."

Before I could figure out what *that* was all about, he claimed my lips with his, not even hesitating as his tongue invaded my mouth. The desperation flooding him fueled me, my demon magic on fire as he finally gave in to this impulse.

"Nim. If you want this to stop, I suggest you flicker out of here now."

I reached down, pressing my palm against his hard length, eliciting a low growl from him. "Why would I leave?"

"Fuck." He moved his leg, pushing it between mine, and my eyes fluttered closed at the friction. His lips slammed back down on mine, devouring my heart and soul with each passing second. Sliding his tongue against mine, his hand crept up my ribs until he reached my breast, his thumb tracing until a moan escaped my lips, heat pooling low in me. The sound had him pulling back, his eyes darkening as he took in my flushed state. "Turn around."

My lungs hitched at the steady order, and it took me a moment to realize he was moving back just enough to let me twist and face the wall. My demon urges rose to resist the command, so I leaned up to press my lips to the corner of his jaw before turning. When I complied, his hum of approval sent tingles down my spine.

"Palms up on the wall." I shot a glance back at him before I did so, then he reached around and unbuttoned my jeans, pulling them and my underwear down together, the stormy air around us cool against my skin. "Keep them there."

One palm slid along the curve of my ass, as his other hand braced on the wall beside my shoulder. Tantalizingly slow, he drew his fingers down until they lightly skated between my legs.

"You're so wet for me already." He nipped my shoulder in praise as he twirled his fingers around me. "Dripping for your mate. I can't wait to taste you, Nim." A whimper escaped me as I tried to push into his hand, needing more.

Too soon, his hand left, and a cry of frustration rose in my throat as the heat of his body against mine disappeared. Before I could turn to see why, any objection was cut off as his hands gripped my hips, pulling me out from the wall enough to lean forward slightly.

Kit lowered to his knees behind me, and a moment later, his tongue was on me. I moaned at the feel of him as my brain turned to mush. Kit Sayana, my childhood best friend, turned *much* more fun adult friend, was teasing and licking me while he kneaded my ass. I pushed back, willing him to give me more, and gasped when he did.

"Kit," I breathed, unable to think clearly enough to add anything else as his mouth moved on me. Panting, need coiled sharply within me while every nerve of my body was alight and firing, my demon blood screaming for more.

Right when I was about to see stars, he stopped, pulling back as I groaned. I heard him stand, then the metallic clink of his belt and zipper. Stepping forward until his body was flush with mine again. One hand rested possessively on my hip while he teased himself against me.

"Nim," his voice was guttural, barely controlled. "You're mine. You always have been. I am going to fuck you so hard you'll never even think of another male again."

I closed my eyes again, nearly whimpering with anticipation, more than ready for this. A moment passed, his breathing as heavy as mine, and my mind tried to catch up to why we were waiting.

Then I realized… he was waiting for me. This was the only way he could give up any control right now. The Alpha in him was battling against his rational, human urge to make sure I was ready for this; his shifter instincts wanted to go full steam ahead either way.

I nodded, panting heavily, but somehow managed to find the words. "I'm yours, Kit."

With another *Fuck* under his breath, he pushed inside me in one smooth motion, a gasp catching in my throat. He stilled, biting my neck again as he waited for me to adjust, though his entire body was shaking with the restraint.

When I pushed back on him again, a breath left him as he moved, yanking my hips towards him as he forced me to bend over further.

With each slap of skin on skin, my eyes shuttered, unable to stay open through the sensations of this finally happening. Kit pounded into me, and I delighted in it. My head dropped forward, leaning on my arm still braced against the wall as I fought for air.

"The way you take me," Kit growled as his hands gripped my ass. "Fuck. You were made for me, weren't you?"

I couldn't speak at that point, his movements so rough he stole my breath, but I nodded, and mumbled an *mmhmm*.

"How did I ever think I would be able to walk away from this?" he went on, kissing down my spine as his hands circled my waist. My skin was on fire everywhere he touched as something hummed deep inside me. "How could I ever walk away from you?"

As his fingers returned to my sensitive nerves, my body shivered beneath him. "That's it, Nim." His motions slowed slightly, hitting me just right. "You're going to come for me, aren't you?"

My mouth fell open in a silent scream as my body climbed higher than I'd ever felt before.

"That's right."

Never in my wildest dreams would I have thought Kit would talk like this, and I loved it. My body convulsed, legs shaking as I fought to keep my balance. His fingers swirled as he moved deep inside me, slamming into me with such force my body rocked into the wall. "*Now, Nim.*"

For once, my demon urges willingly gave in to a command, unable to control the overwhelming sensations racking my body. I cried out as I plunged into a downward spiral, my entire body buzzing as I fought to suck in air.

Kit swore again, his motions growing jerky until he groaned, pulsing right along with me.

My heart threatened to break free of my ribcage as Kit heaved breaths behind me, slumping his weight across my back. My knees wobbled, hardly able to support me any longer. Kit must have felt it because his hands wrapped around me, pulling me to standing as he left me empty and aching in all the best ways.

He held me upright as he spun me around, his gaze trailing over me as we both caught our breath. Once I was steady on my feet, Kit bent down, sliding my underwear and jeans back in place, and then fixed his own. When we were both dressed again, he pulled me to him and towards the wall, where we slid down, and cradled me to his chest.

"You're my mate, Nim," he said quietly as his lips touched my forehead, sounding more like he was talking to himself. My eyes drifted shut, exhaustion setting in. "You're mine."

Chapter Twenty-Four

KIT

I HAD difficulty letting go of Nimue, loving the feel of her body leaning heavily into mine. Closing my eyes, I felt down the skulk lines, trying to sense her addition. My forehead wrinkled in concentration, searching… but nothing had changed. The branch off of my own that would signify my mate was still as faint as before — more an impression of a soul than the solid presence it would be when we both accepted the bond.

Maybe it was because my fox was suppressed by whatever was going on with the magic in town, or perhaps it simply took time for some bonds to solidify. Nimue said she was mine, and I'd taken her fiercely. If she hadn't been moaning and squirming beneath me, I would have worried I'd scare her off. Her head nuzzled into my chest, ear resting right over my beating heart, and I let that mystery go while we listened to the rain patter outside the treehouse.

We rested, exchanging soft caresses and kisses much more tender than before until the rain seemed to slow, the sound of it fading away. Nimue's hearing was almost as good as mine, and we turned as one towards the window overlooking the pond.

"I'm going to go out and keep looking. Want to stay here, or come with?" In answer, Nimue pushed to her feet, dusting off her hands on her jeans, pacing towards the hole in the floor, and I smiled.

We padded through the forest on quick, quiet feet, just like we'd done so many times as kids. The rain had turned to a light mist, but Nimue ducked from tree to tree to avoid most of it. We were silent as we moved, and my mind spun with conversations we should probably have about the whole *true mate* thing. But with the skulk bonds acting strange, I wasn't sure where to start.

My skin itched with the need to shift, but my senses were still sharper than the average human's. Catching a scent, I crouched down to make sure it was who I suspected, searching for what the fox had rubbed against.

"It's Sophie. She's down this way." I focused all my senses on tracking my cousin down the game trail away from the pond, Nimue at my heels. I followed her scent until the path reached a stream, then lost it. She must have walked one way or the other in the water for a while.

In the middle of the day, especially when it was just downpouring, her fox instincts would have taken over — she'd be burrowed down somewhere. I walked, ducking low under dripping pine branches, searching for a hidey-hole.

Some ways downstream, I saw it; the perfect spot, buried beneath the roots of a fallen tree, far enough from the water that it wouldn't flood. If I were in my fox form, I'd hide there.

Forcing the Alpha energy I could still reach to the surface, I centered myself in my power, feeling the faint lines radiating from my skulk — so much duller than they should have been — and willed her to cooperate as I shoved my hand into the hole. My fingers sank into her soft fur, and she shrieked and writhed against my grip as I yanked her from the hiding spot to clutch her in my arms.

As I stood, Nimue sucked in a breath, Sophie still squealing and flailing. Several beats passed as Nimue checked out my body beneath my now damp t-shirt and flannel, and the Alpha in me purred in delight. *Mate*, my magic screamed at me, and a sly smile crossed my face.

But Nimue's gaze then moved to the small, light orange fox in my grasp, the black cross of fur stretching over her shoulders and down her spine a match for Nadir's markings. Sophie screamed at me while I held her by the scruff in one hand, supporting her back legs by pinning her between the crook of my elbow and waist.

"Can't communicate?" she asked, stepping towards me.

"Oh, no. She felt my command," I glared down at the fox, who continued to try to twist from my hold. "But she wanted to stay holed up, so we're doing this the hard way. I don't think she understands she's stuck like this right now."

"Where do we bring her?"

"She'll have to stay in the yard until the barrier around town is up."

All fox-shifter houses had large, well-fenced enclosures in their yards for the kits to scamper around before they learned how to control their shift, ensuring they stayed safe and close to home while in fox form.

Nimue nodded, retaking my arm, and flickered us to my uncle's house to safely drop the little fox home.

I quickly dropped Nimue's hand as we strode towards the cedar-shingled home next to my parents' farmhouse, Sophie under my arm. Nimue glanced at me, confused, but facing my family after the decisions I'd just made with her brought everything uncomfortably back into perspective.

My aunt Aubrey was in tears as we left Sophie in the fenced-in yard, hugging Nimue and me. "I am so thankful you found her," she sniffled as she gripped me tightly for the second time, clinging to me. Her eyes were tinged with pink against her sun-kissed skin, her skulk tattoos standing out in stark contrast on her arms as she turned around to embrace Nimue again. "And you, sweet Nimue, a demon in the rain. I know how your kind hates water, so I'm even more appreciative that you didn't give up on your search. I'm just so worried about everyone."

I fidgeted, rubbing a hand across the back of my neck as I stared at the ground. Nimue's brow drew down as she tried to read my body language, to understand my urges, as Aubrey stepped back. Right now, all I wanted was to get the fuck out of here.

"Really, Kit did most of it. I'm just glad we found her,," Nimue answered her kindly, as she always did. My aunt's gaze swung to her again, tears brimming in her eyes as she nodded.

After we said our final goodbyes, I stepped away from the houses a ways, and Nimue followed.

I felt down the skulk lines, turning towards her and hoping that this time I'd feel Nimue's solid presence there, showing her place at my side… but still, nothing. Just the same shadow of a presence that had been there since we kissed four years ago. But it didn't matter, since I could never ask Nimue to join our skulk as a non-shifter, and I doubted a demon would want to be so tied down anyway. My heart sank at my next words. "We can't do this right now. I shouldn't have…" I bit my lip, wincing and unable to put to words what we'd just done.

Her eyes narrowed slightly, seeking something in mine I couldn't give her. Clarity, probably, or honesty. "I started it as much as you," she offered finally.

"I should've put my foot down with my father and gone out there alone, avoided dragging you into all this. None of this is meant to be, Nimue."

She said nothing for several minutes, her gaze piercing me as my heart rate skyrocketed. "Oh. Right. Yeah. A shifter and a demon. I mean, this could never work."

Her words stung, no matter how true they were. I forced myself to calm down. Maybe this was safer. Seeing her here, with my people, just reminded me how different she was — how hard this would be for her. Nimue wouldn't want this; to be mine. Mated to a fox Alpha. "Exactly."

Before I could even think to say anything else, Nimue sniffed, her expression pained, and was gone.

Hearing their voices from the porch, I knew the others were back before I stepped foot inside my parents' house next door. I slipped off my shoes at the door and entered the living room.

Despite our family's status in the community, our home had always been humble. A portion of my parents' income came from the skulk, and my father never wanted to take more from them than he had to. As such, we had a small house on a plot of land we shared with my uncle and his family, and nothing in our home had ever been new or fancy. Nonetheless, our modest living room with its mismatched, well-loved furniture, my grandmother's rocking chair untouched next to her husband's armchair, had always been a comfort for me.

Akil sat cross-legged on the floor, intent on his phone. Emerson was deep in the corner of the sectional with his hood pulled over his head, and my parents were on either side of him. My grandfather was reading in his usual armchair, but he dropped his book when I entered. Wrinkles showed at the corners of his eyes and mouth as he studied me intently, and I straightened my damp shirt under his inspection.

"Were you successful, then?" he asked with a raised brow as he rested his hand on the empty chair next to him.

My mind stuttered momentarily, wondering if he knew about Nimue. Could he sense that I couldn't solidify my mate's bond with her?

"Find anyone?" Ma's eyes were hopeful as she patted the seat next to her for me to take, and it jogged my mind back to the present.

"I'm drenched, Ma," I indicated my dripping clothes

and leaned against the mantle instead. I was also aware that her nose was better than any in our skulk — while I'd been in the rain for quite a while, I was sure that if I sat next to her, she'd smell Nimue all over me. "But, yes. We found Sophie. What about you all?"

"We've accounted for all but three of the skulk now," Pa informed me, concern deeply etched on his face.

"Lily?"

My mother's body tensed. "Still no word."

I met Emerson's eye before sliding it to our father's. While *he* seemed to know about Lily running with the wolves, I wasn't sure Ma knew. Or if he wanted her to know.

"Have we asked her friends?" I asked instead, hoping he'd catch my drift.

A muscle twitched in Pa's jaw. "I haven't been able to get in touch with all of them yet."

So, Julian wasn't responding to his calls or texts. He was either out of range somewhere in the woods, or being very stupid to ignore an Alpha's call. Even if my father wasn't *his* Alpha, there was a code to these matters. Shifters all had to respect each other, or none of this would work.

"Who else?"

"Isla and Sayeed." Isla was of my parents' generation, but Sayeed was Akil's age.

"Shit," I muttered, but it was still loud enough for my mother to catch, and she *tsk*ed at me.

Akil laughed at me from behind his phone, and I reached down to pop it up from the bottom, sending it flying out of his hands to thunk down on the thin blue carpet a few feet away.

"*Boys*," came my mother's sharp admonishment as I resumed my position against the mantle.

"Do you want me to try to track down Lily's friends?" Though it had already been a tiring day, I wanted the distraction. Needed to keep moving to keep my mind off my other problems.

My father pointed at me with a nod, and I turned to head out, but my grandfather caught up to me at the door as I pulled my shoes back on, laying a hand on my shoulder.

"You know, even an Alpha doesn't get to make everyone's decisions for them."

I blinked, tilting my head. "You think Lily can take care of herself?"

He gave me a sympathetic grimace, squeezing my shoulder. "I'm not talking about Lily." With that cryptic message, he left me to my task.

I left my parents, running through the woods as fast as possible, searching for any places I thought Lily might hide. My muscles ached with the urge to shift, my body feeling heavy and awkward in my human form. Running as a fox was so much smoother.

Lily, out of all of us, was the wildest. Four years younger than me, she often ran with the wolf pack outside our land, away from the prying eyes of the stricter older generation. Everywhere I looked, though, nothing.

Julian was ignoring my calls, and the other wolves I knew Lily liked to hang out with were all occupied searching for their kin. I knew they'd bring her home if they found Lily along the way.

My phone buzzed at eleven o'clock, alerting me that the boundary had been put up — the one Devanna, Ryker, and Orion had strengthened — which meant that, for now, all the shifters that were in town were contained there. Along with the rest of us. But it also meant that we had nothing left we could do until we learned more from the witches, so I finally returned to my apartment above the shop. After my fruitless search, I couldn't bear to face my parents again tonight.

Sleep was nowhere to be found, though. I tossed and turned, my mind switching between worry for Lily and the lost shifters, to reliving every single breath Nimue had taken in my presence.

Nimue caused the pendulum of my heart to swing from the highest of highs, capturing her moans with my lips, to the lowest of lows, watching her expression shutter in pain at my words.

A huge part of every shifter's life was, naturally, their animal: shifting into them and the experience of the dual soul. But for an Alpha like me, it would take up an even greater presence in my life. Not being able to share that with her, not being able to shift together… it would be like an ache that never went away.

There was also the matter of our more animalistic side, even in human form: the skulk hierarchy; the body language we used without thinking; our instinctual urges, territoriality, and possessiveness. It wasn't fair to ask her to take all that on, to accept it, when she'd never truly understand it.

Nevermind the skulk itself. I wasn't sure how they would

respond to an Alpha's mate not being one of us. Would they see my loyalties as divided, with one foot out of our world? Would they only accept her in my presence, if at all? The thought of Nimue feeling like an outsider — never truly one of our skulk, but required to be at my side — pained me more than anything else.

Chapter Twenty-Five

NIMUE

WHY DID it have to be raining? And why had I insisted on a new form of self-torture by walking around in it for the last several hours, turning Kit's words over and over in my mind until I could barely see straight? The problem was, as upset as his words had made me about us not being meant to be, I knew he was right. A demon and a shifter could never work — the one species rarely capable of steady relationships, the other centering their entire life around them.

I threw open the door to my carriage house, drenched and angry. The house was exceedingly dark, with the sky outside not providing any light into the room, and I closed the door behind me, staring into the pitch black.

Water dripped off of me, puddling on my pretty wood floors, which finally pulled me from my funk. Instantly, I yanked my magic to the surface, and steam rose from my clothes as heat washed over them. That was one of my favorite tricks; Blaze had taught me when I was learning to control my magic. The only problem was it wreaked havoc on my hair.

The half-wet frizzy brown mess hung limp around me, no longer curling like when I left this morning. It was hard to fathom that then and now were the same day. Before —

"Are you going to turn the lights on, or just creep around in the dark?"

I jumped, clutching my chest as a burst of flames erupted from my palm, flashing the room in light.

"Good God, pull it together, Nims," Devanna said from where she sat on my living room couch, her blue hair piled on the top of her head in a messy bun, slightly more disheveled than usual.

"Why…" I cocked my head to the side, pausing as I stared at my friend, "are *you* sitting in the dark? In my living room?"

"Because I had a shitty day, and, for once, I can rant about it to my best friend that I've missed the fuck out of these last four years."

I flipped on the lights, and slipped off my shoes before I padded across the pink shag rug to where she sat on my couch. It was a buttery soft grey leather that had cost a fortune, but I'd promised to let Blaze be my favorite cousin forever if he bought it for me. Fortunately for him, he was already my favorite, and he had difficulty saying no to me. Althea, his grandmother, left us both a hefty fund for the house, and I loved the more luxurious lifestyle when it came to home goods.

"Hi, bestie." I dropped down beside her, throwing my feet up onto the velvet-tufted ottoman, leaning my head onto Dev's shoulder. "I've missed you, too."

"I hate Orion," she said on a sigh, and I bit my cheeks to rein in my smile.

"He's not *that* bad."

"Yes. He is," she responded quickly. "All he does is boss me around. Mr. Perfect. Everything is so buttoned-up, even when he's trying to fix a crisis that is about as damn far from perfect as they come. He even tried to tell *me* which crystals to use to harness the power of the new moon tonight. Like, are you fucking kidding me?"

I raised my eyebrows, trying to act surprised by this information, but I also knew my friend well enough to understand what really irked her was that she *also* liked to be in charge. Always. The two were like night and day together, but apparently, Mo's meddlesome ways had rubbed off on me, because I couldn't help but want to meddle some more.

"How was hunting with Kit?" she asked when I'd been quiet for too long. I froze, my pulse skipping erratically as I tried to come up with how to answer her. Dev knew me well enough to tell if I was lying, and I wasn't sure I was ready to admit what had happened.

"Weird." There. It was the truth, right?

"Mmhmm." Dev slid out from under me, and I caught myself right before I toppled face-first into the cushions. "I'm getting you some wine."

The next thing I knew, I was dressed in my pink-striped pajamas, standing on the couch with a glass of demon wine in one hand and a karaoke microphone in the other.

Kelly Clarkson's *Since U Been Gone* blared through the speakers under the TV as Dev and I danced around the room, singing off-key and enjoying every minute of it.

"I didn't agree to you two having this much fun without me," Selene yelled out over the noise from where she and Petra stood in the doorway. My eyes expanded as far as they could, a broad smile taking up residence on my face.

"Hi girls! What brings you by? Want to join our old-fashioned slumber party?" With a wave of my hand, a golden balloon banner appeared on the wall reading, *Girls Rule, Boys Drool.*

"What brings us by?" Selene laughed, glancing sideways at Petra. "You… texted us? I was about to head back to Boston, but you asked us to come over."

"Oh! I did?" I laughed entirely too loud and long, then gasped. "I did! Yes! So smart of me!" My voice dropped down an octave as I said, "I approve, Nimue," then went up again, "Me too! Good choices, Nimue."

Petra glanced at Selene hesitantly, then back at me where I stood on the sofa still, my smile downright goofy.

"Demon wine," Dev answered, and I laughed, taking another sip. "She gets a little loopy after that third glass."

Petra nodded, taking in the scene, and I sensed the urge in her to slowly back out the door and bolt. "Don't go!" I yelled, my ability to manage my volume wildly out of control. I dropped to the floor, stopping the wine from splashing out of my glass onto the carpet, sucking in a deep breath. "Sorry. Stay. Please."

There.

Normal. Serious.

I laughed.

Selene's eyes were alight with mischief as she glanced from me to Dev and back. "What happened to her today?"

"She went out hunting for the lost foxes," Dev answered.

All three of them, in unison, drew out a long, "Oh."

"Oh," I mimicked them, shaking my head as I drew it out even longer, sticking my tongue out at the end.

Selene finally stepped away from the door, heading into my kitchen as she opened and closed cabinets looking for something. Before I could ask what she was looking for, she stopped, her hands stilling on a jar of herbs in my cupboard I didn't recognize, and then bent to retrieve my gold teapot from under the counter, making herself right at home. Then, it clicked. I knew what she was doing.

"I don't want to be sober yet, Selene," I whined, plopping onto the couch dramatically. She paused in the kitchen, and all three girls spun, turning to me. With everyone's eyes on me, I slumped, my shoulders curling in, and a sob left me without my permission.

"Oh no." That was Dev, I thought, but I couldn't be sure.

"I'll make the tea." Selene, definitely.

"Is she okay?" Petra.

"He hates me." The words came out on a sob, and tears streamed freely down my cheeks.

No one said anything for a minute, and then Dev's light jasmine scent drifted next to me, pulling my head into her lap. "No one hates you."

"Yes, he does," I sobbed harder, unable to control my emotions. Why did I always forget the crash that came with too much demon wine? This was why I hardly ever had more than one glass.

"That's it." Dev flipped open a knife she'd conjured out

of nowhere. "No one makes my sweet baby Nims cry. I'm cutting his balls off."

"Just to be sure I'm not jumping to conclusions," Selene circled the ottoman, holding out a steaming mug. "Whose balls are we talking about?"

"The only balls that matter, Selene," I cried out, hearing how pathetic I sounded.

"Kit?" Selene whispered, and Dev confirmed. "Ah."

"Maybe you should go back to the beginning, Nims. What happened out there today?"

I dragged my hand across my nose, wiping the snot away, disgusted with my sloppiness, and sighed. "We were out in the forest looking for the other foxes, and it started to rain. I hate rain." They all hummed in confirmation. All demons hated rain. Blaze could only tolerate it more because he was half-witch. "So he suggested we go up in the treehouse to escape the worst part of the storm. Did you know he rebuilt it after the fire?"

Without waiting for anyone to answer, I continued, "Then we were stuck in this tiny treehouse together, staring at each other awkwardly, full of this tension that stretched on and on. Then I finally got him talking, and he pinned me up against the wall and *fucked* me so hard I could hardly stand." A chorus of gasps rang out around me, including one, "*oh shit,*" that was probably Dev. "But when we went to his parents' house after, he said it was a mistake and we would never work out."

"I'm getting my shovel," Dev hopped to her feet, storming towards the door, then scoffed at herself. "Never-mind. I'm a fucking witch, and we don't have time for that. I don't need a shovel. I'll levitate that fucker into the clouds, then let him drop. Can foxes swim? I heard a report of a kraken sighting past the lobster buoys near the lighthouse. Could land him right there."

"You can't kill him, Devanna! It might kill me! I don't know how true mate bonds work — demons don't *have* mates. Except I'm the worst demon ever because SURPRISE!" I waved a hand in the air. "I do."

At my exclamation, everyone in the room stilled, wide-eyed in disbelief.

"This might be a terrible time to have this question," Petra said matter-of-factly, "But *can* a mate bond kill you? Kit said it was something about your soulmate, more or less. Or is there more to it?"

"I don't know. He was too busy growling dirty words I'd *never* expected him to say to sit down and explain the bond to me. But there's a magical component, so who knows?"

Dev scoffed in disgust, running her hand over my hair soothingly. "That fox should be so lucky to have you as a mate, babe. The fuck is he thinking treating you like that?" Patting my head, she leaned a little closer to my ear. "Do you think I could hurt him... just a little bit?"

"Don't listen to her." Selene gave Dev an exasperated glare. "Drink this." As Dev muttered, *"Well, I'm slashing his tires,"* under her breath, Selene shoved the mug into my hand. "You'll regret it if you let the anger come in next. The tears sucked, but I know how much you hate the next phase."

I held it up to my lips, letting the God-awful stench waft up my nostrils as I cringed away from it. "I can't. Too gross."

"Do you *want* to rip a hole in the wall like you did that

one time?" A soft whine, maybe even a whimper, rose out of me, and I pinched my nose. "You love this wallpaper. You'd be mad if you ruined it."

She was right. I did love it, the pretty art deco-style scallops. With that, I squeezed my eyes shut, and gulped back the tea.

Chapter Twenty-Six

NIMUE

I HATED DEMON WINE.

Well. That wasn't entirely true. At the moment, with just one glass, I loved it. The anxiety I constantly felt over ensuring everyone's happiness dissipated, and I focused solely on my own. That was a lovely, freeing feeling.

But the crash. God, I hated the crash.

I woke up the next morning after our girls' night not only physically exhausted from the late night — not to mention what Kit and I had done in that treehouse — but also emotionally wrung out.

I moped around my house the entire day, not even opening the blinds: just me and the darkness. I didn't have any more tears to cry over him, because I didn't understand anything that had happened. But still…

I hurt.

His words were hurtful. His actions were confusing. His kisses were dizzying. And still, I wanted more, even as I could feel him pushing me away. This was a special kind of stupid.

The worst part was that he was probably right to push me away. Demons couldn't do relationships; we weren't wired that way. Blaze could probably only manage it because he was half-witch. But me? Full demon? I would just end up hurting Kit in the end, and then I would hate myself even more.

The night passed, and I ignored all my phone calls and messages, wallowing in my swirling confusion and self-pity. I fell asleep on the couch, and decided to stay there.

The following day, I lay sprawled in the living room watching *The Princess Diaries* — the ultimate comfort movie — for the thousandth time, my mouth only catching about every tenth piece of popcorn I threw in the air. It lay scattered across the floor, and I didn't even care.

Blaze barged in, not bothering to knock before he zapped the lock and pushed the door open. "Wanna come — uh oh." He glanced at the TV, then at the popcorn on the floor, then back to me. "*The Princess Diaries?* Nevermind. Not a question. Get up. We've got work to do."

I didn't move, though — still moping, and now glaring at my cousin.

"Petey said you hit the sauce hard." He smiled broadly, and I hated him a little bit. "From the looks of this, you didn't quit before the happiness gave way to the sadness. But do I have holes to patch in the drywall? Please say no." He paused, waiting for me to respond or acknowledge him, but my eyes stayed glued to the screen, watching Paolo try to subdue Mia's frizzy hair. "Be thankful we don't get hangovers. I've heard from Petra and Dev that they suck once you're in your 30s. They're no longer a morning-after slump and more of a very begrudging week-long affair where you get to sit back and regret all your decisions."

Deciding not to answer, because hangover or not, that was precisely what I'd done for a whole day, I threw the popcorn in my hand at him. Blaze ducked, incinerating it in the air as it sailed right by.

"Now my whole house is going to smell like burnt popcorn," I whined.

"You and Orion can commiserate together," Blaze grinned, and I stared at him, confused. "Guess you had to be there. On your feet, soldier. You're coming with me."

"To do what?"

"Your job as Second."

I side-eyed him. "You still haven't explained to me what that entails."

Blaze shrugged. "It's more of a learn-as-you-go type position."

"So you have no idea either, then."

"You're overthinking it, Nimmie. Now, get up. I'm in charge. As Head Demon." He couldn't even keep a straight face as he said it, and we both chuckled at the absurdity of Blaze being in charge of anything.

I threw my blanket to the side, popcorn scattering across the floor until I curled my fingers, sweeping it all into the air and back into the bowl. Carrying it to the trash, I dumped it, then brushed the crumbs from my leggings and sweatshirt.

"You look like shit, by the way." I whipped my head up at Blaze, feeling the heat of my demon blood fuming at his words, but he only smirked. "Anger is better than sadness, as long as I don't have to patch the drywall later. Let's go."

Flames licked across my hands as I trudged across the Haunted Meadow through the overgrown grass, looking for any signs of recent activity. We'd flickered up to the site, meeting with Mo and the coven where they'd been searching the area for anything unusual. They paused their search to chat with Blaze when we arrived, but, not feeling up to socializing myself, I continued to scan and circle the area while they talked. The air was still cold, a blanket of clouds blocking the mid-morning sun, and a low fog clung to the field, holding onto the dampness of the night before. I hated it.

"Hi, baby," Mo said as she finally separated from the group and jogged over to me. She'd opted for a black and white floral kimono today, as subdued as her wardrobe allowed, in light of the severity of events. I paused, waiting for her to fall in step with me, and then continued circling again, looking for God only knew what.

I couldn't remember a time before Mo adopted me; she raised me in a loving home, just us two girls. I loved her beyond comprehension, but she was also a meddlesome woman who insisted on sticking herself into my life — and everyone else's. Right now, I didn't want to hear it. Her fingers circled my wrist, reading my aura, and I had to fight not to yank my hand away.

"Have they found anything?" I nodded to where the rest of the coven huddled with Blaze, hoping to distract her with whatever was going on here rather than my issues. Mo glanced in their direction, concern etched into her features.

"Something happened here, that much we can tell." She bit her lip. "The aura is not how it should feel, but aside from a bit of ash, there's nothing physically out of the ordinary. We want to do an imprint reading."

I nodded slowly, and we both began to make our way back to the main group. Growing up with Mo, I'd become well-versed in most things *Witch*, even if I didn't need their rituals and talismans to work magic the way they did. An imprint reading would let them view in their minds' eyes what had occurred here, but they could only see, at most, seventy-two hours into the past. We had to hope whatever had happened here was that recent.

Before we reached the others, Mo held out a hand to stop me. "Honey, I know something is bothering you. You don't have to say anything, but I want you to know that I'm here for you if or when you need to talk about it. Just like always." With sympathetic eyes and a gentle pat on my shoulder, she went to rejoin the other witches just as Blaze was stepping back, coming to my side.

I felt guilty that I'd hurt her feelings — that hadn't been my intention, but I needed time.

The witches formed a circle, one of them placing several items from her bag on a stone between them — a large citrine crystal for enhancing memory, a bundle with amaranth and dandelion root for summoning spirits, and butcher's broom to boost their psychic powers. She lit the bundle of herbs and placed that on the stone in the center, the aromatic smoke drifting between them and up into the sky. A column started to form, spinning like a gentle, cylindrical tornado, and the witches joined hands. They mumbled low words under their breaths, and Blaze and I could only wait while their magic worked.

"So," Blaze drew out the word, keeping his voice low so as not to interrupt the witches. "Ready to tell me what's eating you yet? Actually, that sounded dirty, and as your br-ousin, I do not want to know the answer."

I rolled my eyes.

"Is it about Kit?"

"You're as bad as Mo. You know that?" He gasped and swatted my arm.

"He's not a bad guy… for a fox." Blaze shrugged. "His pranks could use a little more ingenuity, but the skulk always seems to get away with it, which as a fellow deviant, I find admirable."

"Wow. What shining accolades. He will be so proud."

"More importantly, he's been mooning after you since you could torch a marshmallow." I glanced out of the side of my eye towards Blaze but said nothing. "I do like that about him."

I internally scoffed at that. Even if Kit did think we were mates, I had no future with him. And I deserved better than his mind games, even if they were unintentional on his part.

Just then, the witches seemed to fall out of the reverie of their spell, dropping their hands and shooting each other anxious glances.

Blaze stepped forward. "What is it?"

Pulling away from the group to join us, Mo only said, "We need another meeting. This may be worse than we thought."

Chapter Twenty-Seven

KIT

I MUST HAVE PICKED up my phone a hundred times since Nimue left my parents' house, flipping it open to call her before reason overcame the haze of the mate bond, and I snapped it shut again. After staring at my ceiling for hours, I gave up on sleep entirely before the sun rose the next morning. I needed to distract myself from two things: the constant, building necessity to shift that ached like a muscle cramp; and the problem of Nimue.

Lucky for me, I got a text shortly after I entered the tea shop with just the thing to distract me — another emergency meeting.

Immediately upon entering Town Hall, I could tell the tension had kicked up a notch from the last meeting to this one. Several days had passed that the shifters were stuck, unable to change between forms. For those trapped as humans, it was uncomfortable, bordering on pain when our emotions were up. But for those in their animal forms? With the limited concept of time, past or present? Every hour they remained, they would lose a little more contact with the human side of their soul. Already, we were seeing changes in the behavior of those like Sophie, who we at least knew were safe and cared for.

But what of the ones still unaccounted for, lost and fending for themselves? How long before the tether to their human soul snapped? Even though half our souls were asleep and our connections more muted than usual, the rest of us could still feel their branches fading from our bonds.

The witches muttered furiously amongst themselves, a whole group of them here this time instead of just Ostara and Lysander.

Even though a seat was open beside Nimue, I opted to stand, leaning against the far wall instead. I didn't trust myself to get too close to her, especially in a public forum like this. I was terrified of reacting to her scent and proclaiming her my true mate right here in the middle of the town hall.

"Still no nymphs, then?" Ostara cast a haughty glance around the room, nodding to the two empty seats left for the sea nymphs, who rarely came to the mainland if they could help it.

"Ronan probably couldn't find a shirt," Ryker muttered.

"What have you found?" Orion's voice called over the scattered conversations, bringing them all to a close as our gazes swung simultaneously to Ostara.

With a regal wave of her hand, she invited a group of witches to approach the table to relay their story, Morgaine among them. Morgaine kept shooting me glances like she knew exactly what was on my mind, or what had happened with Nimue.

"At the Haunted Meadow yesterday," Castor, one of

Devanna's friends, began, twisting one of the many rings on his light sand-toned fingers. "We sensed a disturbance to the aura, but didn't see any obvious physical evidence of what had occurred, so we performed an imprint reading."

He paused nervously, and the witches looked between each other for a moment before Morgaine took over, her voice lacking its usual sunny surety.

"We don't know the exact spell they performed, but a group of witches completed a ritual in that field within the past three days. The spell drew significant power from the ley lines, and required a human sacrifice." Gasps erupted from around the room, but quieted back down quickly when they saw Morgaine had more to say. "But there were more than witches out in that meadow. There was also —" she broke off, making eye contact with Blaze a few seats down the table. "There was a demon with them. Contributing magic to the spell."

Winona, the local bear Alpha, leaned forward, her brow furrowed. "Demon fire?"

"No," Dev answered. "A demon, wielding witch magic."

All eyes swung to Blaze, the only demon-witch combo in the area, but he looked as shocked as the rest of us.

"It wasn't Blaze," Morgaine added hastily. "But, honey," her face turned sympathetic as she met Blaze's eyes. "I think it was Errakal. It's been a long time since I've seen him, of course, but..."

Blaze's eyes shuttered at the mention of his brother's name, and he nodded slowly. A heavy silence filled the room, all of us contemplating the ramifications of witches working with a demon. Adding his considerable magic to theirs. A half-demon/half-witch was simultaneously the most powerful witch, and one of the least powerful demons.

"Anything else?" Orion finally cut through the tension.

"Yes," Morgaine admitted. "The witches knew not only to use the Meadow, but also the exact historical location of the pyres." Behind her thick teal glasses frames, her eyes found Orion's. "At least one of the witches has to be a local. No one else knows those coordinates but those in our coven." Her voice was laced with pain and betrayal; the sentiment also reflected on the other witches in the room.

Just when we thought that was the worst of it, she proved us wrong. "The last thing we saw was the witches returning the next night, but they didn't perform another spell, only stood around talking. We're worried they reached the same conclusions we did — that the pull on the ley line's power was so intense, it affected the shifters' connection to their soul magic. If they're trying to increase their power with each ritual..." she cleared her throat, eyes searching the room around her. "So, the next logical step for them would be..." her voice broke, her words trailing off as she was unable to speak them, but Castor came to her rescue.

"The next logical step would be for them to increase the power of the spell by changing their sacrifice," he said grimly. "They need power from the sacrifice itself, as well as the ley lines. Any one of our missing shifters would do the trick, and amplify their spell in the process."

Another wave of gasps swept through the room, and my father swiveled in his chair to look back at me, the same thought going through our minds.

Lily.

As everyone stood to leave after the meeting, I stepped into my father's path.

"Let me." I raised a hand to stop him from chasing down Julian. As Darius' Second, Julian would be used to only taking orders from his own Alpha, and probably would not respond favorably to my father's interrogation. With me being another Second, there was a chance I could get him to open up more.

His jaw hardened, his whiskey eyes trailing Julian as the wolf swept from the room, but Pa nodded. All the same, his voice was laced with authority as he snapped at me, *"Find her."*

I hurried out of the hall, jogging to catch up to Julian before he loped off into the woods of his territory.

"Julian."

He slowed his steps but didn't stop, turning his head only slightly. Dropping into step beside him, I was reminded once again of the overwhelming might of power that emanated from the wolves. Shifted, they were larger and stronger than us, but we always outsmarted them — brain over brawn.

His messy, light brown hair was half in a loose knot, the rest hanging just past his shoulders. The sleeves of his button-down were rolled up, displaying his numerous geometric pack tattoos. He didn't even bother to slide his eyes to me as I joined him, and I bristled at the insult, but forced myself to push it aside. This wasn't about me.

"I need to talk to you about Lily."

His cavalier, controlled gait never wavered. "Can't control your own, little fox?"

"This isn't a joke, Julian. You heard them in there." I waved back towards the town hall. "They could be hunting shifters for sacrifice next. Was she with you that night? Or with someone else from your pack? Noah, maybe?"

Bullseye.

Julian stopped in his tracks, swinging around to face me. I knew by insinuating Lily would choose a lower-ranking wolf such as Noah over him, it would sting his ego and get him to pay attention. A low blow, but effective. We had reached the edge of the forest, Julian now only a few steps away from wolf territory, where I would be stupid to follow him with so many shifted wolves right now.

His unblinking green eyes leveled on me, but I stood my ground.

"You foxes think you're so clever, like we can't see right through you. But fine, not that I think you want to hear this, but yes, your sister was with me that night." He paused, gauging my reaction before adding, "Why do you think we were both unshifted? We were busy enjoying each other's human forms."

A muscle in my jaw ticked at his implication. I wanted to punch this douche in the face for talking about my sister that way, but again, I had to push past it. This was progress, and I needed more information. "And then what? Where is she now? If she's still with you, fine. Just have her contact us so we know she's safe."

"Wait, what do you —" Julian paused, the color draining from his face. "She's missing?" I nodded as he stared me down, then scrubbed a hand across his jaw. "She was there that night — she'd left her phone somewhere, I think, she didn't have it — but then she was gone. I assumed she'd gone home. *Shit.*"

My pulse rose, both in anger at Julian and in fear for my sister, knowing she truly was missing, not just hiding out with the wolves. "And the thousand calls from my father that you ignored? What did you think all those were about?"

"I thought he just wanted to chew me out for spending time with his only daughter. But she's an adult. She can make her own decisions. And I have a lot of shit on my plate right now."

I scowled at him, sure that day was coming soon, but focused instead on what was most important. "You're acting as Alpha, Julian. Not accepting another Alpha's call was a stupid move, no matter your reason. You're in charge of your people, and he's in charge of his, but the responsibility still falls on us. Don't ignore phone calls again."

Julian's jaw worked, feeling the command in my words and fighting against them, but I didn't break eye contact. Whether Julian knew it or not, I was stronger than him, even though he was larger than me.

"I'm not here for a power struggle, Julian," I finally said, and Julian dropped his eyes, "I just want to find my sister."

Chapter Twenty-Eight

NIMUE

I COULD TELL Blaze was more upset about the news of his brother's involvement than he was letting on. Their relationship was a complicated one — Errakal was a few decades older than Blaze, and hadn't had Mo to fall back on when their mother died. Kal had chosen to follow their father, Nergal, instead, even though the male had never expressed any interest in his progeny and was a deplorable parent all around.

Kal had visited the Cove a few times over the years, but Blaze never let him anywhere near me. I got the sense that Kal might have earned his *demon* moniker a bit more honestly than Blaze or I had. Or dishonestly, I supposed.

Despite his behavior, Blaze had always been oddly protective of Kal, making excuses for his behavior while never really explaining what that behavior was. No matter how much time had passed, Blaze always tried to see the good in his brother, even if, at least from what Mo said, there wasn't much good to see.

As the others filed out of the room, I approached Blaze

where he stood from his seat at the main oval table and spoke in a low voice with Mo. She wrapped an arm around my waist as I reached them.

"What do you think Kal wants?" I rested my chin on Mo's shoulder.

Blaze scratched at his trim beard. "I wish I knew."

"Are you going after him? Could you find him?"

Catching my eye, he opened his mouth to respond, but Mo beat him to it, stiffening beside me. "I don't think that's a good idea."

Stepping out of her hold so I could see her better, I frowned as Blaze asked the question on my mind.

"Why not?"

"It's clear they're trying to amplify their power. They already have one half-demon — what greater damage could they wreak with two?"

The minute Blaze and I cleared the eyesight of the town hall, he grabbed my arm and flickered us back to the house, landing in the backyard.

The inevitable conclusion was in both our minds.

"You're going after him."

"Obviously."

That decided, the next step would be to figure out how to find him.

"Locator spell?" I offered as we stepped onto the deck and settled onto the red Adirondack chairs, but Blaze sighed.

"I don't have anything of his to tether to him. Pictures,

mostly. A few things that reminded me of him, but nothing of his that would work for a spell."

We stared across the lawn, lost in thought as we both pondered how to solve this until I slipped my phone out of my pocket.

"What are you doing?" His tone was an accusation.

"Texting Dev. Maybe she knows another way."

Suddenly my phone was zapped out of my hand, flying through the air to Blaze, who caught it easily.

"Nope."

I stared at him. "Give me one good reason why not." When he wouldn't respond, I reached out with my magic, letting it skirt across him, sensing his impulse. I coughed a laugh in surprise at the simplicity of the solution that Blaze was fighting the urge to suggest. "Oh my God."

He winced. "*No.*"

"Boz, I'm a grown-up now, okay?" I rolled my eyes. He was being an irrational, over-protective *br-ousin* again.

He needed my help — my demon powers — to amplify his, but he didn't want to get me involved. I thought through his idea, wondering if our powers together could track Kal simply through the lure of more demon magic. Like magnets, we were drawn to each other. Demons cast a sort of aura about them, and the greater our numbers, the greater the strength of it. The two of us together might be able to reach into our combined power to help pinpoint where Kal was holed up, especially if Blaze amplified it with a witch locator spell at the same time. All of which Dev would undoubtedly know.

My brows dipped as I glared at Blaze. "If I want to help you find your wayward, *murdering* brother by putting our powers together, there's nothing you can do to stop me. There are shifters missing whose lives could be at stake, Blaze. If we can stop this now, we have to try."

I yanked my phone back with my own burst of magic, and he groaned.

"Fine. But here's the deal: you can help me locate him, but the second we find him, you're getting the fuck out of there. Understood?"

The fire in my veins tingled at the order as I laughed. "Doubtful."

If there were future sacrifice victims with Kal, I wasn't leaving without them.

Pushing to his feet, I heard Blaze mutter something that sounded like *"impossible, foolish demon"* as he headed into the house, with me following along close behind.

We called Devanna in to help with the locator spell since Blaze's witch magic wasn't equal to a full witch's. She brought an assortment of items from her stock to assist, but insisted we meet in my carriage house rather than the main house to avoid any possible interaction with a certain someone *else*.

"What do you need me to do?" I asked as she knelt, arranging items on the floor around her. A bundle of wormwood to increase the divining nature of the spell, a chunk of obsidian to enhance scrying and our intuition, and a blackbird feather to aid the psychic connection to our magic.

"You stand there," Dev sat back on her heels and

pointed to one corner of the pentagram she'd made with salt. "And Blaze, you there."

We assumed our positions and waited for further instructions as Dev lit a candle.

"This stuffed bunny was Kal's?" Dev asked skeptically as she lifted a tattered stuffed animal that was so far past its prime, I was shocked it hadn't disintegrated. I bit my cheeks to keep from laughing at Blaze for having an emotional support *bunny*.

"Well," Blaze said as he glared daggers at me, daring me to say anything. "No. It was mine. But he gave it to me when I was five."

"A hundred and forty-two years ago," Dev deadpanned. Her eyes momentarily flicked to the bunny she held by one ear, pinched between two fingers. Just then, a button eye came loose, dropping loudly to the floor as it spun in place. The three of us stood mesmerized by the sight, waiting until it settled.

"Yeah. No." Dev dropped the bunny, and Blaze flickered the distance to catch it before it hit the floor, cradling it to his chest like a newborn baby. "That's not going to work. The two of you need to reach into all the demon magic you can. I'm essentially going to be using *it* as the tethered object — even though it's not an object, but no way are we attempting to use that *literal* dust bunny — to locate like-magic in the area. The spell will find Nox and any other local demons first, theoretically, so we want to wait until it reaches further than that. Blaze, since you know Kal and what his magic should feel like the most, you should be able to sense when we've tracked to him."

Blaze nodded, but I still sensed his hesitancy. He wanted to shut this all down as much as he wanted to keep going.

When Dev gave the signal, I closed my eyes to wrap myself in my magic, feeling it rise to the forefront of my mind and body. With a mental shove, I pushed it out into the ether, casting it out like a net magnetized to haul in other demon magic. I didn't know what Dev had to do for the spell, but I knew the pulsing lure of our magic would flood her, and I sent out a silent apology. Dev did *not* like feeling out of control, and I knew our combined magic would be making any impulses she might hold in her mind feel almost impossible to resist right now.

"That's Nox," Blaze said after a few moments, and I nodded, eyes still shut. Dev hummed in agreement, all of us recognizing the signature of his magic within the town lines.

"Endymion," I added a moment later. The demon who ran the general store —when he felt like opening it.

We also recognized a few others — some that had been in town for the festival and remained trapped within the border. Then we fell silent for several minutes, our nets inching nearer to the town lines.

"There," Blaze said at the exact moment I said, "That has to be him."

He felt almost like Blaze — not quite the same as other demons, not quite a witch either — but he reeked of greater darkness than my mostly-harmless cousin. An involuntary shudder ran through me, and for the first time, I thought I understood why Blaze always kept me from meeting him.

"Catch on to his magic. Try to get an impression of

where he is," Dev coached. "You might be able to see him in your mind's eye, or see what he sees, so look for landmarks."

Taking a deep breath, we both tugged on Kal's magical signature. I envisioned a rope ascending into the ether that I latched onto, descending hand over hand as I followed it down to the male at its origin.

With a gasp, my eyes shot open, and I immediately found Blaze's, his expression as startled as mine.

"Did it work?" Dev blew out the candle and pulled herself to her feet, gaze darting between us.

I nodded. "It worked. He's —"

But, sensing a change in Blaze, I stopped mid-sentence, lurching across the pentagram to grab onto him just before he flickered away, forcing him to take me with him.

Chapter Twenty-Nine

ONCE IT WAS clear that Julian didn't know where Lily was, we decided to split up. He was going to get the pack involved — they still had people out looking for their own, so he had them sniff a shirt she had left at his place. Upon hearing that, I had to subdue the growl that rose in my chest, but I reminded myself, *again*, that Lily was 25. If she wanted to spend time with someone — even a *wolf* — she could. Maybe if I said it to myself enough, I'd start to believe it.

Our differences aside, it was still reassuring to know more shifters were looking for her. I texted my family and friends to update them of the new plan, then flipped up my hood as I headed back across town somewhat aimlessly — I had no leads on where to go next. As a last hope, I decided to go back to skulk lands, thinking I could attempt to pull on the power of the bonds within us — stronger on our territory — to see if I sensed anything there.

I passed Scallywags, lost in my thoughts, when a brown hand thumped into my chest, stopping me in my tracks.

"What —" I looked into Devanna's accusing brown eyes behind her glasses, blue hair wavy in the humidity.

"Just the shifter I need," she said, but her lip curled in disdain as she gave me a once-over. Even with the Alpha blood strumming in my veins, I fought a wince, trying not to show weakness in front of this powerful female, but the image of her scowling across the club still stuck in my head. Her eyes narrowed, head tilted as though debating what she wanted to say, before she sighed. "Look. I'm telling you this as a friend, and because I know you're missing shifters. I just helped with a locator spell for Blaze's brother Kal."

I blinked, my senses sharpening as I sensed a hunt. "Did it work? Where is he?"

Her hands went up as she shrugged, and my muscles tensed. "But it made me think. Normally, a shifter like you," Dev grimaced, "an *Alpha*," the word caused her to pause, swallowing exaggeratedly as if she couldn't stand the taste of it in her mouth, "wouldn't need help locating those in your pack."

"Skulk," I corrected on reflex, and her expression grew darker, but I didn't care. I had bigger things to deal with — namely, finding my sister and getting her away from murderers. "Continue."

Dev breathed deeply through her nose. "Don't make me take back the *friend* comment from earlier. But your sister is missing, and I know Nim's your mate—"

My chest tightened just hearing someone else say the words, and I wasn't sure if it was in pride, anguish, possessiveness, or joy. Maybe all of them. Also, in shock that Nimue had told anyone about it after the way we left things. "Did she tell you —"

"Oh yes." Dev's eyes flashed dangerously. "She told us about your little treehouse tryst, fox boy." I flinched. Fuck, I hoped Nimue hadn't gotten too graphic about that.

"And let me tell you something, as *Nim's* best friend now." Dev stepped closer, jabbing her pointer finger sharply into my chest. I fought not to take a step back. "She wouldn't want me to tell you this, but if you make my girl cry *one* more time, you can say goodbye to those peanuts you call balls. I'll hex you so bad you'll *wish* I'd just cut them off instead. I've been thinking of the perfect spell for *days*."

I had to resist protectively cupping myself, but I was not about to show weakness to Dev, an Alpha in her own right, especially not while she was glowering at me with that slightly maniacal *Make my day* gleam in her eye. Besides, there was something more important that she'd just revealed, enough to make me temporarily push aside the urgent need to hunt down any witch that might be hurting Nimue. "Nim was crying?"

Dev groaned and made a strangling motion towards me, her gold bangles jangling in emphasis. "Oh, my *God. Males.*" The way she said it, it was a curse. "I'm going to give you *one* chance to make this right with her, or you know what happens next. Got it?" She raised her eyebrows and pointed sharply down towards the aforementioned goods.

"But that's not why I stopped you. The tracking spell had me wondering." Dev reached into the bag slung over her shoulder, and withdrew a large amethyst crystal that glowed like pale moonlight. "This is charged with the power of the last full moon. I'm hoping that between this and your *Alpha*-ness," she waved her hand dismissively over my whole body, "you refuse to acknowledge, you'll be able to summon enough power from the pa—" she stopped, "*skulk* to find Lily. Nims too, through the mate bond," Dev finished, still all but glaring at me.

"Wait," I said, my mind snagged on the last part as my pulse raced. "Why do I need to find Nimue? Where is she?"

"Oh." Dev's brows rose as she glanced at my confused expression, then over my shoulder across town. "Uh. Well. Best be finding her quickly because she flickered out with Blaze when they got a lock on Kal's location. She's already there." She gave me one last searing glare before striding past me, heading back towards the center of town and her shop.

"How do I use this crystal with my magic?" I called after her, panic rising within me.

"I can't do everything for you, Sayana," she shot back. "That's your shit. Figure it out."

Knowing that both Nimue and Lily were potentially in harm's way, I ran the rest of the way to my SUV, dropped the amethyst on the passenger seat, and threw the car in gear as soon as the ignition clicked over. With our magic weakened, my best bet to access our skulk bonds would be on our lands, so I floored it, counting on my fast reflexes.

Fortunately, the roads were empty as I sped out of town, grinding my teeth as I drove. Images swirled through my mind as acid flooded my stomach, of Nimue and Lily being held or hurt or worse by faceless dark witches, and the gas pedal hit the floor. As my tires skidded over the dirt road leading back into our land, I pulled *hard* on the skulk power, feeling what was left of it surging under my skin. Every single member would know it was me who had done this, and it was my first true show of dominance for the skulk as a whole.

After this, there would be no denying that I was a higher-level Alpha than my father. He would be forced to step down, or fight me for control now that I'd exposed the extent of my power. But I didn't have time to think about that. That was a problem for a later day.

Right now, my sister, and my *mate*, mattered more than any power struggle. If it meant I'd have to step into my role as Alpha today to find them, I'd do it.

What if it was already too late?

In front of my parents' house, I shoved my SUV into park, threw open the door on creaking hinges, grabbed the crystal, and stepped onto the land. With my fox still locked down, I sank to my hands and knees, clutching the crystal in my locked fingers, needing the power of our land. I slammed my other palm into the ground, yanking on the bonds. One by one, I felt my skulk emerging from the homes around the property, coming towards me.

"Where the fuck are you?" I growled in frustration as I sifted through the bonds, waiting to feel someone who wasn't here.

One by one, soul lines reached out to me, feeding me strength.

"Kit," my father's voice drifted into my consciousness, hesitant as he stood nearby.

"Not now, Pa," I ground out, shaking my head as the cut edges of the crystal warmed under my palm. "I have to find her."

He said nothing, only kneeling next to me, placing his

palm between my shoulder blades where I still hovered above the ground. "Take from me."

My eyes flew open, sitting back on my heels with the crystal in my lap to search his face, knowing what this would mean for our family. But we didn't have a moment to lose, so with a nod, his hand gripped mine, and my magic exploded. I sucked in a breath as the Alpha ties to our skulk transferred to me, my father relinquishing control completely.

Immediately, the faint lines of our spiderweb of power glowed brighter, illuminated in red in my mind's eye as they traced between me and each of the skulkmates around me.

My mother. My brothers. My cousins. My family. My friends. All of them. All of their magic tied directly back to me in the center of it all.

My eyes closed as my father's hand lifted from mine, and I sucked in a deep breath, examining the bonds. Searching.

There, next to me in the center of the web, was a shadow of a bond, not fully lit up like those around me. The others glowed with life. My heart sank at this further reminder that my mate bond wasn't sealed yet. Somehow, Nimue was still not fully a part of the skulk.

Before I could sink into my frustration, another bond caught my attention, further out than those around me. "Where are you, Lily?" I said aloud, and my mother began whispering a prayer.

Several hands all lay across my skin, and without opening my eyes, I knew that my whole skulk was acknowledging me, as my father had moments before.

Again, my power surged, and my bonds seemed to zoom in on the life under my protection that was furthest from me.

A sly smile spread across my face. "Found you."

Chapter Thirty

NIMUE

MY FEET SLAMMED into the ground under the cover of the trees, swaying ominously in the breeze of the storm rolling in over town. The pink sun sinking behind the treeline ahead of us was the opposite of the dark clouds looming at our backs.

"Dammit, Nimmie," Blaze spun on me, his gaze furious. "You weren't supposed to come with me."

I said nothing, only raised a brow at him.

"Yeah, yeah." He rolled his eyes. "I would have done the same thing. I know."

"I'm not letting you go by yourself to face him, Boz." Without even thinking, I reached my hand forward to brush his. "I know how hard all of this is for you. Always is, when Kal is involved. And," I paused, trying to weigh my words carefully to be the least hurtful, "I thought you might need my powers. Just in case."

Fortunately, pride wasn't one of Blaze's flaws, and he nodded thoughtfully. "Can't hurt," he shrugged. "But if you put yourself in danger, just know I'll kill you. Then bring you back, so you have to watch Mo kill me. It'll be a whole bloody family affair fit for the demons we are."

With that, I spun away from the trees behind us, looking out over the clearing. "It's been a long time since I've been out here," I said as I scanned the area for movement.

"Well, I can tell you that The Last Resort is just as shitty and rundown as the last time you were here, too. You haven't missed much."

"Is it open?" I scrunched my nose as I took in the sloping roofline, the cracked pavement, and the weeds growing straight out of the concrete as if even they were clawing their way away from the dilapidated building. Its white siding was peeling, several windows were cracked or boarded up, and a section of gutter hung down in the middle — right over where the entire structure appeared to be sinking slightly into the earth. Unlike the rest of the town, The Last Resort wasn't glamoured to look run-down — it was just this bad.

"Ferron still owns it, and has a listing up on websites," Blaze shrugged. "Petra tried to stay here her first night in town, but it was flooded."

"Did you sense Ferron out here when searching through the demons in town before? Is he helping them?"

Blaze shook his head. "After the flooding in August, he closed up and left for the season. Last I heard, he was in Nevada."

We stood quietly for a few moments, and I took the opportunity to take in the space around us. Now that we'd searched for Kal, I could feel his nearness in my blood. Technically, Blaze was the demon in charge in town, but I was more powerful than he was, as a full-blooded demon.

With the three of us together nearby, I could already feel the current of gathering power.

"I hate to ask this, but do you have a plan?" I glanced sideways at Blaze.

He scoffed, and met my gaze, but said nothing.

"Yeah, I didn't think so. Bust in or scope it out?" I held up a hand as he opened his mouth. "Before you jump to 'bust in,' remember you have a very human girlfriend back in town who might be upset if you get hurt. Or killed. Never mind the rest of us."

"Fine! Scope it out." Blaze pointed to the right side of the building for me to take while he started for the left.

Heading to the right, I tried to keep out of the line of sight of the windows as I crept closer, not knowing where Kal and any of his other minions might be. Reaching the edge of the building, I started peeking into each room as I inched along the perimeter, looking for any signs of life within.

While I had participated in many pranks over the years with Blaze, this whole creeping around thing was not me. The closest I'd ever come was sneaking out with Kit, but even then, it had usually just been to play in the forest, or prank the wolves along with Kit's friends. Nothing like this, with life and death at stake.

Anxiety seeped into me as I ducked from one window bay to the next, peeking through the dirty glass where it wasn't boarded up. Worry for Blaze and how he would feel after seeing Kal again. Worry for Kit and his skulk. If Kal and the witches had taken Lily — if something had happened to her — it would break him. The first raindrops splashed across my face, and I suppressed a hiss as I glanced up at the sky. Any minute now, those clouds would open up.

With that, I picked up my pace. "Come on, you piece of crap. Where are you?"

"Did you just call him a piece of crap?" Blaze asked as he rejoined me, and I jumped at the nearness of his voice. "After all these years, you *still* don't swear?"

"I do." Why I felt defensive over this fact was beyond me. "Occasionally."

"Oh, yeah? Say one. Right now. I dare you."

I opened my mouth and closed it again before retorting, "You, of all people, should know not to give me a command. I'll *say* one when the moment *calls* for one."

"Who knew that a goody-two-shoes demon existed in the world?" Blaze bumped my shoulder, and peered through the window we both huddled under. "Balances out the *crap* the rest of us do. Like this asshat right there." He pointed, and I followed his gaze.

There, in the middle of the room, stood Kal.

I'd never met the male before, but there was no mistaking that was who it was. It was easy to tell that he and Blaze were related. Same dark hair, although Kal wore his longer, trimmed just above his shoulders, hanging straight and loose. Same olive skin. Same black irises, though that could be said about all demons. Thanks to how demons aged, even though technically Kal was about thirty years older than Blaze, he only looked a handful of years older. For most of our lives, we looked to be in our mid-thirties.

"What do we —"

Before I could even come up with the end of my thought, four witches walked into the room with a girl slung between them. Her long dark hair hung down over her face, blocking my view, but my pulse sped up as worry raced through me.

The largest of the witches — a male, if I was guessing based on his stature — shoved the girl towards Kal. She fell to her knees, catching herself at the last minute before her face hit the ground. As she pushed back upright and onto her heels, her eyes met mine for the briefest moment, and my breath caught in my throat.

"Shit." Yep. This called for swearing.

It was Lily. Though I'd heard she was at Blaze's Halloween party, I hadn't seen her in four years. She'd changed a lot between the ages of 21 and 25, but she still had the same defiant expression, amber eyes like Kit's, and the tell-tale skulk tattoos down her warm bronze arms.

"We have to get in there," I murmured to Blaze, and he nodded. "Before they hurt her, or —" I broke off, unable to say it, but we both knew.

"Now you're on board with bust in?" He raised his eyebrows, and I bit my lip.

Peering back into the room, I tried to scan the space beyond them that I could see through the doorway. There weren't any shadows of movement — it seemed empty.

"Let's flicker to the far room." I pointed through the doorway we could see. "Try to eavesdrop? Maybe we can figure out what all these attacks have been about. But if we hear *anything* that could put Lily in danger, I'm flickering in, grabbing her, and getting out of here."

"And I'll deal with Kal," Blaze agreed.

With a blink, we both vanished into the ether, reappearing in the dimly lit hallway outside the room where the four witches and Kal kept Lily. We held our breaths as their voices drifted out to us.

"Did you bring everything I need?" It was a male's voice.

"It's all here, Brennan," a female voice answered him. "And isn't it everything *we* need?"

A scoff sounded from within, but Brennan didn't answer.

"You truly think this will amplify the power?" A second woman's voice spoke.

"The shifters are highly attuned to the ley lines. We should have thought of it from the start." Brennan again.

"You're making a mistake." Hearing Lily's voice, my heart sank, and I shut my eyes. "Every skulk *and* pack member in this region will hunt you down if you kill me."

Chest tightening at the ferocity of her words, I had to admire her fight. Then I stifled a gasp as I heard a sharp slap. Blaze gripped my shoulder, in case I tried to barge in there. There was still a chance to learn more.

"Are we sure about this?" the second woman's voice again. "Humans are one thing, but shifters are our own —"

"You think we're the same as shifters, Ligeia?" another male voice jeered. "They're fucking animals. Do you want this power or not? Let's get on with it."

Before Ligeia or any others could respond, another voice cut in; this time, it was unmistakably Kal. He sounded eerily similar to Blaze, only where Blaze usually spoke in an amused and teasing tone, Kal's sounded slick. Dangerous. A snake hiding in the brush.

"Take it into the next room and get set up. I'll be right there."

With some murmuring amongst themselves, the witches heeded Kal's command, the sound of items being gathered up and feet shuffling reaching us. Lily's complaints were loud and clear as they yanked her to her feet and pulled her along.

A few moments later, the noise died down, and a door clicked shut.

"Miss me, baby brother?"

We whipped around at the sound of Kal's voice behind us, his black gaze scanning first Blaze, then myself.

"Aw, is this little Nimue?" A wicked grin crept up his face as he extended a hand to me. "A pleasure to meet you, cousin. Sabazios never did want me to introduce myself."

Before I even considered shaking his hand, Blaze reached out and slapped it down. Kal frowned at him.

"I sensed the minute you two flickered outside the building," Kal continued, turning back to Blaze. "Hear everything you needed to?"

"What's going on here, Kal?" Blaze ground out at him. "What are you doing hanging around a bunch of dark witches?"

A sympathetic grimace formed on Kal's face. "Oh, Sabazios. So simple-minded." He patted Blaze's head before Blaze could duck out of his reach, glaring at him. "*They're* hanging around with *me*. But the *why* is none of your concern. For now. So, you can flicker right back out of here, or you can stay and watch that little vixen get sacrificed. The choice is yours."

With that, Kal disappeared, presumably flickering into the other room with the witches. Rage boiled in Blaze's eyes, sparks flashing at his fingertips, but a small smile crept up my face.

"What?" Blaze's brow furrowed in concern when he glanced in my direction. "Why are you smiling? Have you gone crazy?"

"Call Orion, Boz. Tell him we caught the witches," I said, one of my brows lifting. "I think your brother has forgotten the difference in power between a half-demon and a full. And he's underestimated me." I smiled at him reassuringly, and even as he opened his mouth to speak, I flickered out, hoping he would do as I asked. I might be more powerful than Kal thought, but it didn't mean my power was infinite.

Flickering into the room where the others had gone, I popped in directly outside the salt circle they'd spread around the chalk pentagram on the ground. Items were scattered along its lines — crystals, bones, bundles of herbs, piles of dirt and salt, vials of water, and others of what I feared were blood — and the witches and Kal each stood at one of its points. Lily knelt, bound, in the middle.

As one, all heads turned to me when they heard me appear, but my magic was already working.

"Who are you —" one of them shouted, but I ignored them.

Using the salt they had conveniently prepared for me, I pulled on my magic, and flipped their power against them as I turned that ring into a veritable jail for them. Confusion washed over their faces as they looked between Kal and me.

Kal narrowed his eyes, sensing what I was doing. The shield wall I created from the salt to hold the witches in place until Orion could get here probably wouldn't work against him, being half-demon, but he might not know that yet.

"Boz!" I shouted, and Blaze appeared beside me right on time, shoving his phone back in his pocket. Suddenly, Kal lurched over to us, the salt only slowing him down before he burst over it. The witches tried to follow, but were rebuffed by my invisible wall. Kal made to come for me, but I flickered out of his grasp and into the center of the pentagram behind me.

Faster than he could turn around, I grabbed Lily.

"Close your eyes." Lily's amber eyes met mine, blinking only once before she listened, and squeezed them shut.

The sound of a fist cracking into a skull was all I heard as I flickered Lily to safety.

Chapter Thirty-One

KIT

LEAPING BACK INTO MY CAR, I barely had the key in the ignition when the passenger and back doors opened. Nadir filled in beside me, and Emerson, Casey, and Asher piled into the back. My chest tightened at their unquestioning support, but then I turned and saw Akil approaching the SUV as well.

"No," I told him bluntly through the open window.

His dark eyebrows rose indignantly. "She's my sister, too."

"You haven't even come into your full powers, even if you *could* shift. You're staying here." I laced the last words with enough of an Alpha command that he flinched and took a step back, eyes dropping down, but at least he wouldn't be going anywhere tonight. Starting the car, we took off back towards town, blood pounding in my ears.

Were they all right?

How many witches could a full-demon stand against? Two or three? Surely not four. Or five. Did Errakal count as one? As more than one?

"Someone needs to contact Julian," I told the others as we turned back onto Ocean Avenue and headed south along the shore. I swallowed, shaking my head to clear out its stupid, insistent pride as Nadir instantly reached for his phone. "Tell him I think Lily is at The Last Resort, and he should bring whatever wolves he has."

Four sets of eyes swung on me as they processed that we were asking the wolves for help, but none of them questioned my judgment. Movement from the corner of my eye told me Nadir was texting furiously.

The urge to shift grated along every nerve as we tore across town towards the rundown motel where I'd sensed my sister. The flood of Alpha magic from my father still coursed through me and left all my senses heightened. If they'd hurt even one hair on Lily's head, I was ready to tear them all to shreds, human form or not.

What felt like hours later, but was only minutes, we pulled off the main road onto the winding drive that led out to The Last Resort. The dilapidated motel was more or less how I remembered — roof practically caving in and all — but none of that was what caught my eye. In a blink, Nimue appeared at the treeline of the property, my sister Lily clasped in her hand. A breath whooshed out of me at seeing both of them there — alive and safe.

Slamming on the brakes and throwing the vehicle into park, I tossed the keys to Nadir and jumped out of the car, running over to them.

Nimue took a step back as I approached, dropping her hand from Lily as I grasped my sister's shoulders, looking her over for signs of injury.

"Are you hurt?" I asked. Lily's eyes widened as Alpha

power flowed through my words — unintentionally, but there was still so much of it freshly pulsing through me, I couldn't help it.

"I'm not hurt," Lily answered, unable to resist, and blinked. "What, you're Alpha now?" she snapped next, and I let out another breath. Lily was just fine, except for the light bruise forming on the side of her face and the nick on her cheekbone.

"Who hit you?" My thumb skimmed over the mark, a growl rising in my chest.

She rolled her eyes. "Kit, I'm *fine* —" She tried to push my hand away, but I snatched her wrist, needing to know who did this to her so I could make sure I killed the right witch.

"Hold still."

Lily froze, though her eyes glared daggers at my chin, unable to meet my eyes with this much dominance rippling off me, as I brought her wrist to my nose. I then moved to her arms, then that bruised cheekbone, scenting any witch who had touched her. Luckily, there were five signatures on her, so I had some fun ahead of me.

Satisfied that Lily was relatively unharmed, I dropped my hands from her, though I didn't lift the command on Lily to stay put, and I finally transferred my attention over to my mate.

Pulling Nimue to me roughly, my hands grazed over her body, searching for any signs that anyone had dared to lay a hand on her, and she shivered at my touch.

"I'm fine," she whispered, echoing Lily's words of a moment before, but my eyes still scanned her body. I knew she wasn't easily harmed with her demon magic, but I needed to see it myself.

"Can you flicker her out of here? Get her home?" I asked, my voice full of barely-suppressed rage that anyone would kidnap and harm a member of *my* skulk. Because it was *mine* now, and the Alpha in me was fucking livid.

Nimue shook her head. "I have to stay nearby. My magic is holding the witches until Orion gets here, and I have to get back in there. Blaze is going up against Kal as we speak—"

My fingers dug into her waist where I still gripped her. "You're not going back in there."

Lily winced at the power behind my words, her head ducking automatically, but Nimue merely raised a brow. Fuck, how could I forget you couldn't tell demons what to do?

"You got her?" was all Nimue said, indicating Lily. Before I could respond, she slipped out of my hold and disappeared.

My pulse skyrocketed, the need to follow her inside burning in my soul. To protect my mate. But there was also the need — stronger than ever now that I was officially Alpha — to assert my dominance, claim her as mine, and show her whose orders she would be listening to from now on.

Nadir, Emerson, Asher, and Casey prowled over then, having given me space to handle Lily first. Lily crossed her arms over her chest, glowering at me for still not letting her move, while the others assessed her, their gazes catching on the cut on her cheek as well. I felt their indignation rise along our bonds, echoing my own.

"Emerson and Casey, take Lily back home. Asher and Nadir, come with me."

"I'm coming with you, too," Emerson shot back, and I turned to face him. He met my stare, challenging me in a way I'd never seen from him, though his entire body shook from the effort of resisting my orders.

"I need Lily safe. I don't have time for this, Emerson." I took a step closer as Casey touched his shoulder, trying to nudge him out of this stand-off.

"I'll take her," a voice called behind us, and my eyes lifted from Emerson to see Julian and a handful of his pack approaching, all of them large, strong males ready for a fight. We all were — the inability to shift grating on all of us.

"Julian!" Lily's tone held a relieved joy I didn't want to examine too closely, her face lighting up as she saw him, then turning back to a scowl as she faced me. "Kit, let me go with him."

Julian stopped a few paces away, taking me in anew as he no doubt sensed the change in status.

"*You're* Alpha now?" he coughed, then waved a hand, dismissing the issue for another day. "Sayana, you know she'll be safe with me. I'll bring her home to your parents. I swear it."

My jaw clenched at the mere thought of not only letting Lily out of my sight again so soon, but to let her go with a *wolf*. But I did believe he would see her home safely, and I had to get into the motel. I had to find my mate and be at her side — or better yet, *between* her and any threats. Or even better than that, dragging her the fuck out of there. I leveled a stare at him.

"Fine. Lily, Julian can drive you home." I turned back to

Lily, grabbing the back of her neck to force her to meet my eyes, making sure the full force of my Alpha command carried through my words. She tried to wrestle out of my hold, not wanting to be ordered like the rebellious female she was, but I was stronger. "Check in with Pa, then stay in the house." I dropped my hand, and she backed away, rolling her eyes at me again as she stepped over to Julian.

Exchanging another look with Julian, he nodded at me, tacitly agreeing to follow my terms, even if I couldn't order him. He raised his arm to throw it around Lily's shoulders, but when all of my skulk tensed at the sight, he wisely dropped it, only jerking his head at her back towards his car. I heard him issue orders to the other pack members who had come with him, but we were already rushing for the motel by then.

Chapter Thirty-Two

NIMUE

FLICKERING BACK INSIDE THE MOTEL, I arrived just in time to see Blaze flying across the room and slamming into a dresser, shattering the wood under his weight. Whether he'd been thrown by magic or hands, I couldn't say, and Kal turned to me at my reappearance.

"Ah, Nimue, maybe you can help him make the right choice," Kal jeered. The next thing I knew, his hand was a vice around my arm.

The four witches trapped by my magic were muttering together, likely trying to find a way to undo the jail I'd put them in, but I had to stay focused on Kal. Even though he was only half-demon, he could still do much more damage to me than the four of them put together.

I met Kal's black eyes to keep his gaze on my own instead of on his hand, which I slowly but surely began to burn. He smelled the smoke before he felt the pain, then dropped his hand with a hiss. It wouldn't kill him, but even to another demon, our fire stung like a thousand fire ants.

My lips tipped up in a smirk. He kept underestimating

me. But it was fine, as long as it worked to our advantage. "You bitch," he seethed.

"That's rude." I scrunched my nose at his insult. My response caught him momentarily off-guard before his power flipped on me, searing heat into every nerve of my body. Heat sizzled along my skin from his power, more than I'd anticipated, but nothing compared to mine. I clenched my jaw, fighting the pain surging through my body by reminding myself that his focus was still on me, not Blaze. "Is that all you've got?"

Kal roared, and blasted me with everything he had. Flames licked at my skin, singeing my clothes, but still not touching me. I sneered back, battling between the need to push against him and still holding the witches in place.

Blaze flickered to my side, pushing with every ounce of his powers against Kal until the surge against me stuttered to a halt, and I sagged in relief.

Whatever Kal was doing to amass more power for himself was working. A half-demon should *not* have been that strong.

"Aren't you tired of being the weakest in the room, Sabazios?" Kal called out, standing straighter as he sent Blaze skittering across the room once more. I jolted forward to distract him again, and found myself weightless. Kal's magic levitated me before he tossed me across the room as well, wood splintering into my skin as I skidded across the floor. My head snapped into the wall when I reached it, dazing me, pinpricks of darkness in my vision. I blinked, breathing while my body healed, then scrambled to my feet. "So much power here with the ley lines. With our witch's blood, we can call it to us, amassing it like the witches can't, and wielding it as demons can."

Blaze charged him, resorting to physical strength, and landed his shoulder right at Kal's waist. They both crashed to the ground, and I glanced around the room.

Smoke billowed around us as the furniture caught fire, blazing bright. Still, the four witches at the center chanted, but a sense of panic filled their voices, their movements turning jerky as they watched the flames.

Demons couldn't burn, but witches could.

"Aren't you tired of never being enough? Of watching others have what you cannot?" Kal's voice reached me from where he and Blaze wrestled, flames licking across their skin. "Don't you want *more?* Join us, Sabazios."

"I already have *more* than I could ever dream of, Errakal."

Indecision racked me as I fought for what to do next. We just needed to keep Kal here and the witches trapped until Orion could arrive. I guessed it had been ten minutes since Blaze would have contacted him — surely he'd be here soon. Hopefully, before Kit and the others came in and tried to tear the witches apart.

But right then, I heard the outer motel door burst open, and the five foxes from outside, along with a few wolves that hadn't been out there before, skidded into the room. My gaze found Kit's automatically, drawn to him like a magnet, his amber eyes burning as they raked over me before flicking to the trapped witches.

He lurched towards them, but I stepped into his path, pressing a palm to his chest. Kit's head tilted as he looked from my hand back up to my face. Though his magic was different than mine, rooted in the soul rather than in fire, I could still somehow sense a deeper current of power flowing through him. His eyes locked on mine, and I could *feel* his new powers, just as I'd seen him wield them with his skulk outside. Kit was now Alpha, and pride for him simmered in my veins.

"We might need them to undo whatever they did to lock up your powers," I reminded him urgently. I mentally pleaded with him to look past the frenzied impulse to retaliate against the witches, to remember the bigger picture.

The other members of his skulk came up behind him, a silent formation waiting for his order, Nadir to his right and Emerson to his left, though their eyes were trained on the witches.

Suddenly, a thunderous power knocked through all of us, the witches toppling to the ground, and the rest of us nearly lost our footing as well. I tripped forward into Kit, who wrapped an arm around my waist on reflex.

A moment later, Orion swept into the room, lightning flashing through his storm gray eyes as he folded his white wings tight against his back and took in the scene.

"Get hi —" I shot my hand out to point to Kal, but before I could finish, he'd flickered out.

"FUCK," Blaze and Orion shouted simultaneously. They shared a glance, then Orion turned to the witches while Blaze and I pulled the fire from the room.

"No more of that," Orion called over to the witches and stole their magic away in a heartbeat. They gasped, fear widening their eyes as they felt what he'd done.

"You can't do that —" one of the males shouted.

Orion merely raised a brow, because he could. Angels

had the ability and authority to confiscate magical power as they saw fit for the safety of our community.

Out of the corner of my eye, Emerson took a step forward, and Orion swung on him.

"Stay back," he ordered. Though his voice was calm and steady, power thrummed through the words that brokered no argument. "These witches must face trial."

The witches exchanged glances again. No one in their right mind wanted to face the court and judgment of the angels.

"Pascar will be here soon to take them away," Orion continued, probably referring to another angel from head-quarters. "Until then…"

He approached the salt ring, stepping over it effortlessly. The witches backed as far away from him as they could before bumping into the other arc of the circle. Orion grabbed one of the males by the shoulder with one hand, and when the witch tried to jerk back out of his hold, he swept a whisper of magic over him. The male's eyes went wide as he froze, unable to move in the grip of Orion's magic. Orion pressed his other hand to the male's forehead, and closed his eyes.

When he opened them again and released the male, the witch seethed at him, gaze narrowed and teeth bared, but Orion paid him no mind. He pulled his phone out of his pocket as he casually stepped back out of the salt circle.

"Ostara, come to The Last Resort, and bring a few witches with you. I know how to reverse the spell."

Chapter Thirty-Three

WE WAITED at The Last Resort for at least a half hour for the town witches to show, and the whole time, I couldn't let go of Nimue now that I had her in my arms.

Once Orion had the situation under control — even if Errakal had escaped — some of the tension in the room eased. More so when he announced he'd taken the information from the witch's mind for how to undo the spell that had trapped the shifters. The sleeping soul within me had roused slightly hearing that, impatient to be let loose again.

The others sat with their backs leaning against the wall or on spare chairs they found scattered around the place, but I couldn't sit, still too on edge.

Usually, when Alpha powers transferred, there was a skulk ceremony, including a shifted run or hunt. The new Alpha would lead the run to demonstrate their dominance and give the skulk a chance to accept the new order, but also to help siphon off the surge of magic. There hadn't been time yet, and the power thrumming in my veins itched for a release.

Finally, Ostara showed up with Lysander and some other town witches. Despite the emergency, Ostara looked as intimidating and regal as ever in a high-collared, floor-length plum dress and her short white hair neatly styled. Even if Lys's skin had matched hers perfectly instead of being several shades lighter, it was hard to picture them as mother and son. Lys typically looked, as he did now in his ripped jeans and unbuttoned flannel, one second away from stepping on stage with his band. They went up to Orion to begin questioning the bound witches, get the details they needed, and decide on a course of action.

"Hey."

I started, pulled from my thoughts to the demon in my arms, her black eyes searching mine.

"I'm fine," she continued, tapping my arm around her waist. "I'm not going anywhere. You can let go."

I was about to ignore her, or maybe tell her that I'd let go when I damn well pleased and not a moment earlier, but Ostara turned to me then.

"We'll need one of you," she said, and it had to be me. I forced my arms from my mate as I stepped over to the witches, following Ostara's signal to stand in a circle of salt and soil.

Several others joined us from Ostara's coven, including Aurora, a young blond witch who worked at the police station; Devanna and her friend Castor, both clad head-to-toe in black; the exotic pet-shop owner Beverly, her bright clothes out of place in the grimy motel and glaringly bright against her nearly translucently-pale skin; and Zale, a middle-aged male witch who rarely came into town and looked like he came straight from the office in a blazer and chinos.

Together with Lys and Ostara, the seven of them circled me. I glanced from Lys to Dev, the two witches I knew best, and they both gave me reassuring nods as Ostara conjured a knife and held her palm out for mine. I offered my hand, and she pricked my finger, then directed my arm to allow drops of blood to fall at seven points in the circle of salt and earth around me.

Next, Castor took a handful of amethyst he'd gathered from the items they had brought in. With a murmur under his breath, his magic pulverized them into a fine powder that he spread around the circle at my feet.

"To help bring back awareness of your shifter spirits," Dev explained as I watched.

Beverly performed the same routine next, but with a handful of fluorite. I raised my eyebrows, wondering what this one was for, and Lys answered my unasked question.

"Increases mental abilities. It should strengthen your ability to communicate with your fox."

Zale came forward next, a bundle of clover in his hand that, with a whisper, began to smolder at its tips as he trailed a circle of smoke around me. "To summon your animals," he explained, and I nodded.

As they moved back to form a circle around me, the witches began chanting in unison while magic hummed under my skin. Their tempo increased, and I tilted my head back in relief, feeling the magic trapping the other half of my soul starting to shatter.

Like breaking through the surface after being underwater just a touch too long, magic streamed back into me, my fox coming alive once again. The force of it reawakening to its new status as Alpha was blinding — or maybe that was my eyes shifting uncontrollably between human and fox and back again. Every muscle twitched, pushing me to shift and let my fox take the reins after being locked down.

Which was what every other shifter in the room was doing, sounds of relief sweeping through the room. Unable to resist any longer after having been denied that part of themselves for so long, the other shifters were already halfway out of their clothes, not giving a damn that anyone else was in the room. A moment later, the wolves trotted from the building. I gave my skulk members a nod, and soon after, they were gone.

"You can go with them." Nimue was tapping my arm again, having approached me while the magic flooded back into my system. "I can bring all your stuff home." She indicated the piles of clothes left behind.

But my eyes snagged on her fingers on my arm, blinking as my eyes kept shifting. Her rosewater scent filled every corner of my thoughts until only one was left, my fox chanting it at me emphatically.

Mine.

Witches and angels and half-demons forgotten, I grabbed her arm, pulling her out of the room with me. Even as I winced at the memory of when I'd done practically the same thing at the club and lived to regret it, I couldn't help myself.

And I didn't stop until we were outside, in the fresh, clean air after the rain, far enough from the front door that we'd have some privacy.

"Kit." My name from her lips was a spell, and I tightened my grip as I spun her around to face me. "Really, I'm fine. It all worked out."

But it *wasn't* fine. Didn't she get that? Couldn't she see?

Mine, mine, mine.

"I couldn't find you," I managed to get out.

Her brows drew together. "But, you *did* find me."

"*No.*" I shook my head, jaw tight. "I found *Lily.*"

"Oh." Understatement of the century. "Well, still — you found *us*, so it's okay —"

A bitter laugh escaped me. "Nim, I fucking *panicked* when Dev told me you'd gone after these murderers, when I reached into our bonds, and yours was too faint to follow. What if Lily hadn't been with you? And I hadn't had any way to get to you? It's *not. Fine.*" I took a deep breath, her black eyes searching mine. "You were in danger today, and I couldn't find you."

"I wasn't really in *danger* —"

"You can't be sure of that," I growled, frustrated at her for not understanding. "How many witches can you take, Nim? And Errakal?"

She closed her mouth and swallowed, unable to answer me because I was right. We didn't really know.

"I've been in love with you since I knew what it meant," I continued, her eyes widening at my words. "And I've known you were my mate for four years. Today, Nim, I could have lost you because our mate bond isn't solid."

"But we..." her eyes tracked from mine, to my lips, to my hand still around her wrist.

"It takes more than sex." I scented a change in her at the word, at the memory it brought up, and I had to fight to stay in control. The human-me. "You don't understand what it means."

Annoyance flashed through her. "Well, tell me, then."

"It's not like deciding to date. This is not a, *Let's try it out and see what happens*. If we accept this bond, it's permanent. No backing out. It means you are mine," my fox shivered at the word, relishing the sound of it in my mouth, "and I'm yours."

"Kit —" Nimue reached for me, but I wasn't done.

"And now that I'm Alpha? You would have always had to become part of the skulk to be my mate, but as Alpha… Nim, I can't have a mate who won't — or can't — follow my orders. That's not how it works for shifters. We have a hierarchy that must be followed to maintain order, balance, and peace." I willed her to comprehend something that she never possibly could.

"What if I could?"

"What?"

"What if I could follow your orders?"

My mouth dropped open as her words went straight to my dick. *Fuck yes.*

"But, you can't. You're a demon —"

Her hand came up, cupping my jaw and forcing me to look down at her. "Kit, I've loved you for years, too." My focus fell to her lips, begging her to close the distance. "And if that's what it takes, I'm sure there's a way around the demon magic so I don't… disturb the peace."

A desperate, shaky laugh left me. "Nim, accepting the mate bond, it's like saying we're getting married. Right now. Skipping the proposal and wedding and all of it."

She quirked a brow at me, a smile tilting up the corner

of her mouth. "If you asked me to marry you right now, I'd say yes to that, too. I love you."

Unable to resist any longer, I crushed my lips to hers, pushing her back against the post of the motel sign.

"There's so much you'll never understand —" I breathed against her lips.

Her fingers trailed across my abdomen under my shirt, and I groaned. "You'll explain it. You can teach me. I'll learn," she said, punctuating each statement with a kiss along my neck. "I want this." She pulled away enough to search my eyes again. "Do you?"

My fox screamed at me, and for once, I listened. "You're all I ever wanted, Nim."

With a grin that nearly burst my chest, she grabbed my hand and flickered us away.

Chapter Thirty-Four

NIMUE

LANDING BACK in my carriage house — conveniently in the bedroom — we wasted no time. I reached for Kit's flannel, tearing it off him in my hurry and tossing it across the room. But when I went for the hem of the t-shirt underneath, he stepped back, head tilted, eyes calculating.

"You first," he said, a challenge flashing in his gaze. He was testing me, feeling out whether I'd have any ability to follow directions. I had to admit, it wasn't easy; my magic was already tingling, and he hadn't technically given any orders yet.

"Take off your clothes."

I blinked, my magic flashing, but I worked to redirect it. I *wanted* to do this, I reminded myself. My own impulses should be able to cancel out the magic. Theoretically.

"Nim." His voice held a note of warning as his eyes darkened. "I don't give orders twice."

Heat pooled at the dominance in his tone, a shiver of excitement running through me. Reaching for my zipper, I dropped my eyes and heard a rumble of approval.

Right. Body language. That would be big for him; I'd have to remember that.

I stepped out of my jeans and went for my shirt, risking a look up at him as I did so. His eyes were sporadically shifting again, from his usual deep amber to his fox's slightly lighter, sharper gold as he studied me. A hunter waiting for the perfect moment to strike.

When the last of my clothes dropped away, Kit circled behind me, sweeping my hair over my shoulder to kiss my neck. Goosebumps rose all along my body at the sensation, electricity shooting through me and straight to my core. Fingers trailed across my hip, then up my side, while his other hand found my breast, teasing me as I arched into his touch.

"You're so fucking beautiful, Nim," Kit's breath grazed my neck. His tongue slid across the sensitive skin as he laid kiss after kiss there, torturing me with the slow movement. My eyes closed as I reveled in the feeling, tilting my head back onto his shoulder behind me. "I love how your body responds to me." The hand at my side slid forward until he pressed gently against my lower abdomen.

I turned my head to try to find his lips. "Kit — *more* —"

Suddenly, both hands dropped, and he stepped back so quickly that I nearly lost my balance. I shivered at the loss of body heat behind me, which was ridiculous, considering I was a demon.

"What —"

He came around in front of me, tilting my chin up between his thumb and fingers. "There might be a day when you can give *me* orders." His thumb brushed over my lower lip. "But not today." He stilled, head tilted, waiting to see what I had to say about that.

Through our bond — more solid than before, but still somewhat faint — I could feel the overwhelming Alpha magic in him, and knew what he was trying to tell me. This wasn't a request, but a *need* for him. His power demanded this, to be in control tonight, to assert his claim as part of his new status in the hierarchy. I could also feel, through my own magic, the strength of his urge to make sure I was okay. That I wanted this as much as he did.

And boy, did I.

I gave him a sly smile, licking my lips as I nodded.

His amber eyes sparkled with my acceptance, and he lifted his belt buckle. My eyes slid down to watch, wanting to reach out and feel the smooth leather slip between my fingers, to peel the fabric from his body, but I didn't move.

As if testing my ability to listen, Kit undressed slowly, the sound of his clothes sliding off his body the only thing filling the room besides my heavy breathing. The sight of his beautiful bronze skin on display for me had me rubbing my thighs together, needing anything to take away the building ache he caused even when he wasn't touching me.

With a glance to his side, he threw his clothes on top of mine and closed the distance between us. The soft feel of his lips on mine after the slow tease drew a moan from deep inside me, and my hands came up to rest on his lean, muscled chest.

Suddenly, Kit's hands were on my waist, and we were moving towards the bed. My eyes cracked open in confusion right as he spun us. He laid with his back flat across the mattress, and let go of me only long enough to turn me around. His fingers dug into my waist as he pulled me onto the bed backwards, situating my hips over his shoulders.

I gasped in surprise when I suddenly felt his lips on my inner thigh.

"Fuck, you smell amazing, Nim." His voice grew rougher with every word. "Put your mouth on me."

Kit's voice rumbled through my skin, and I dove towards him, ready for it. Right as my tongue licked across his skin, his own descended on me. I gasped as his hands dug into my ass, kneading as he greedily sucked and licked.

"Oh, my God," I moaned. Then he slapped me hard, my ass tingling as I jerked forwards on him, the sting replaced by the soothing touch of his fingers.

"What did I tell you?" he growled, and I nodded, remembering what I was supposed to be doing. He slid across my tongue, and I sucked him into my mouth, in time with his own movements.

His tongue moved just right, and I jolted forward, the sensation almost too much. His hands gripped the tops of my thighs to hold me in place for him while he continued to lick me with expert precision.

How many years could we have been doing this? I wondered as my skin warmed, my muscles coiling with each second that ticked by. A breathy moan escaped me as he hit just the right spot, and he jerked his hips up, forcing himself deeper into my mouth at the same moment.

My body shook with the release until he pushed against my hips, sliding me forward over his torso. My mouth came free of him with a pop, and his hands gripped my hips as he slid me off him to the side.

Instantly, I was on my back, and Kit rose above me.

"You're fucking perfect, Nim," he growled, lining himself up with me as he lifted one of my knees to press into my chest. "And the best part is—" he slammed into me so hard and fast I whimpered, "you're mine."

He didn't wait for me to adjust, not that I needed to. I was as ready for this as he was, his fullness finally righting my emptiness, and I met him thrust for thrust, lifting my hips as he ground into me.

"You taste amazing, you know that? I could never get sick of it." He leaned down, kissing me and forcing me to taste myself on his lips.

His momentum increased, driving into me somehow harder than he had at the treehouse. Our breathing grew ragged, my entire body coiling. When he felt me begin to flutter around him, he leaned down, sucking along my breasts as he pressed against my core, and I moaned out his name, giving in to the ecstasy he made me feel.

His lips found mine as he continued his pace, his tongue pushing into my mouth with the same relentlessness as the rest of him.

"Say it."

My muscles were tightening, and my brain was short-circuiting, but I knew what he wanted.

"I'm yours, Kit. I'm your mate." A low growl of pleasure rumbled in his chest, and I raised my fingers to his skin to trace the sound. "And you're mine, too."

"Fuck."

His tongue was in my mouth again, claiming every moan from the second round of pleasure that shot through my body, and then with a groan of his own, he drove into me deeper, pulsing as his movements slowed.

Pressing his forehead to mine, we lay entwined, his eyes the deep amber of his human soul I knew so well as he gazed into mine. He kissed my cheek tenderly, then took a breath and closed his eyes.

"What are you doing?"

He tapped my nose. "Just wait."

A moment passed, then another, and suddenly I felt an awareness spread through me. My lips parted as I realized, impossibly, I was feeling his magic — *shifter magic* — pulling on my own. It shouldn't have been possible, but there it was. And I realized I felt…

"You're part of the skulk now," he said, opening his eyes and grinning at me, the first full smile I'd seen on him in years. "I can feel you in the skulk lines."

"I…" I closed my mouth again and swallowed, unsure how to say this and suddenly almost *shy*, which was unusual for me. "I can feel you, too, and the others. I didn't know how powerful you are."

His grin took on a smug twist as he kissed my jaw again. "All to find you, Nim."

KIT

THE MATING BOND nestling under my skin pulled something deep and primal out of me, and all night, Nimue met me head-on. It was as if the years I'd — *we'd* — spent denying these feelings surfaced, and consumed us both.

Fortunately, my fox settled some, and my vision stopped flickering between his and my own. But the need to take Nimue, to make her wear my scent, to feel her skin on mine, did not.

It was a frenzy. And I fucking loved it.

She moaned beneath me while I finished, my hands on her hips as sweat dripped off my forehead and onto her back beneath me. Like this, my fox was happiest.

I slumped down across her back, finally feeling the animal inside me curl up to rest, and I slid to my side on Nimue's bed, pulling her with me.

"Kit," she said on a heavy exhale. "This is insane."

I chuckled, but my eyes were already drifting shut as exhaustion settled over me. Sleepily, I brushed a kiss across her shoulder blade, running my hands across her bare torso. "Rest for a minute, and then I'll help you get cleaned up."

She turned in my arms, placing a kiss gently on my lips, and shimmied from under my hold. "A girl's got needs," she tossed back over her shoulder, and my eyes tracked her naked ass as she paced to the bathroom. The door snicked shut behind her, and I groaned at the half-hard status already happening downstairs for me.

The last four years without Nimue, knowing she was my mate, had been torture. Even before then, I'd known I was in love with her; my feelings extended far past *friendly* since that first kiss in the treehouse when we were eight. Without knowing then what I was feeling, I recognized it easily now. The memory of a game and hide and seek that found us both trapped in the small interior of the treehouse on my land surfaced, and it was as if I could still feel the tingly zing that shot through my skin just as it had that day.

A lifetime ago.

And now? It was hard to believe this was all happening.

Mine, my fox sang inside me, and I couldn't help but smile. Nimue was mine, forever. I wasn't sure how that would work yet, but we had a lifetime to figure it out.

She slid back into bed minutes later, and I pulled her into me, her face resting on my chest. Nimue's porcelain skin contrasted my bronze as my hands stroked over her back mindlessly, just needing to feel her.

"I love you," she whispered sleepily a while later, and I kissed her forehead.

"I love you, too."

Sun leaked through the blinds of Nimue's carriage house the next morning, and I yawned, stretching languidly across her luxuriously soft sheets. Nimue moved in her sleep, her face relaxed, brown hair sprawled around her, long dark eyelashes laid across her freckled skin. She was gorgeous in an almost painful way, and my fox thumped his tail in possessive approval.

I could have stared at her for hours, but the sound of my phone vibrating from somewhere on the floor drew my attention back to the present. Sliding across the bed, I dropped my feet to the floor and reached for my jeans. My phone was still in the back pocket where I'd left it the night before, and I flicked it open.

Several texts from the skulk filled the screen, but the most recent was a missed call from my father. Glancing back towards the bed, I walked out of the room and into the hall.

My nerves surfaced as the phone rang, waiting for him to answer. The entire skulk would have felt Nimue slide into place in our skulk bonds last night, but they might not necessarily know *who* had filled that spot.

"Son." My father's deep baritone immediately had me standing straighter. "Seems like congratulations are in order. Yesterday was quite the day for you."

I hesitated for only a moment, before replying quickly, "Thank you."

"I know how hard of an ask this is, but I do need you to resurface from the, ah," my father paused, and I could hear him scrubbing his hand over his face, "*mating,* and come formalize some things as Alpha."

"I know," I agreed, trying to avoid extending the whole, *Hey, Pa. We both know I just had crazy sex all night, and it will be all I can think about for the foreseeable future,* conversation. "We'll be there later this morning."

"Good." He hung up abruptly, and I stared down at my blank phone screen.

I'd just agreed to bring Nimue with me to my parents. As my mate.

"Who was that?" Nimue's sleep-heavy voice came from behind me, and I turned to see her leaning against the doorway, wrapped in only a sheet. Immediately, my pupils dilated, inhaling the smell of her, and my hands were on her before I could even comprehend what she'd said.

"Good morning to you, too," she said between kisses. "*Mate.* Or is it husband?" At that, she paused, pulling back. "Crap. Are we married?"

"Not yet," I kissed her neck. "But I'd marry you today if you want to."

A light laugh, high and musical, left her lips, and I memorized the sound, pulling her body tighter to mine. "Is that what you want?"

I focused intently on her face, ensuring she understood what came next. "Nimue. I want anything you want to give me, but only if it is what makes *you* happy."

Her eyes moved between mine, sensing the honesty through our bond. With a light nod, she said, "I'll think about it. I don't think demons usually get married. Do shifters?"

"Not always, but what about our situation is typical?" I answered as my hands and mouth roved her body.

"True." Nimue nodded, her fingers sinking into my hair as I closed my mouth over her skin. "Is it always like this? Insatiable need?"

"It'll slow eventually," I breathed out as I pulled her on top of me on the bed, feeling her skin rest perfectly against mine. "Maybe. But you are the answer to a craving I've had for over a decade, Nimue. We have lost time to make up for."

So we did.

Sometime later, my more responsible human side surfaced, and reminded me of my duties to the skulk. I pulled Nimue into the shower with me, and fought to restrain myself from exploring her yet again. No amount of time would ever be enough, it seemed.

After we were both clean, I towel-dried her hair for her, watching her in the foggy mirror over her shoulder.

"I have to go deal with some Alpha responsibilities." I gently kissed her shoulder, afraid to let my touch linger any longer than necessary. "Without asking you, I mentioned I'd be bringing you. I hope that's okay."

"What, you're not going to *order* me to join you?" Nimue's brows rose in a teasing manner.

"In this, no," I replied, and dropped the towel from her hair. "To be with me, you will be a part of the skulk, but no. I will not push you today if you're not ready. I know this has been very sudden."

At my words, she spun, her delicate fingers laced along my jaw. "Kit. Here's *my* order — I want you to listen to me right now as I don't want to say it again." My eyes snapped to hers, and my Alpha powers hummed at the command in her voice, but I let it slide. "I choose you — every time. As mates, lovers, or husband and wife, I choose *you*, and all that comes with you. Just as I am yours, you are mine, and that starts right now."

She pulled my face to hers, slamming her lips onto mine in a possessive move, and I growled into her mouth.

Yes, my fox hummed, and I agreed. *Mine.*

Chapter Thirty-Six

NIMUE

AFTER ASKING Kit whether we needed to dress up — to which he'd thrown a bewildered look my way and scoffed, *"We're not businessmen"* — I'd dressed casually in jeans, sneakers, and a sweatshirt, and Kit had pulled on his clothes from the day before. I flickered us out to The Last Resort to fetch Kit's SUV, and we climbed inside. Capital Cities' *Safe and Sound* came on as the engine turned over, and my pulse ratcheted higher as we pulled out onto the main road.

The skulk was a tight-knit group, and while I knew all of Kit's generation, it wasn't just *them* he was Alpha over now. He was now the leader of *all* of the foxes. His parents. His family. His friends…

"They already love you." Kit's hand reached across the dash and brushed his thumb across the top of my hand.

"Can you read my mind?" I asked as I tilted my head towards him. "Is that part of the mate bond thing? Or the skulk ties?"

Kit laughed, but shook his head. "I can feel your presence,

and to some extent, your emotions. But no, I can't hear your thoughts." He lifted my hand and kissed the back of it tenderly. "Right now, I can tell you're nervous, and even though I can't read your mind, I *know* you. Better than anyone."

With that, I pulled my hand from his grip, shoving it under my legs to put as much distance between us as possible, lest I demand he pull over. "I'm not walking into your mother's house smelling like I just banged you in the car on the way here, so hands to yourself."

Kit's eyes lit with mischief at my words, but he smiled. "If you insist."

Turning to glance out the window, I watched as the tall pines and the skeletons of trees that had already dropped their leaves drifted by on our way out to the skulk lands northwest of town. Soon, we pulled off the main road and onto the dirt path leading back to their property. I forced my breaths to even out as we grew closer.

"Will we have to move out here?"

Kit glanced my way hesitantly, and the car slowed. "Yes, eventually. Are you—"

"Stop," I flipped my hand up, placing it over his mouth, which was a mistake. He kissed and nipped the inside of my palm, and I moaned, pulling it back. "Don't even say it. Where you go, I go."

Adjusting his grip on the steering wheel, he licked his lips. "You're sure you're okay to move back here and everything, though? I know you have a career and a whole setup in Colorado."

I lifted a shoulder. "I can flicker to any job I take, so it's not that big of a deal. And to be honest, I've wanted to move home for a while." I swallowed. "I never really wanted to leave; it just sort of… happened."

Kit nodded in understanding, shooting me a heated glance and probably remembering for himself the kiss that had changed everything four years ago, then cleared his throat. "We can build something out here together. Something you'd love to call home, and that will work for the skulk. I want you to be happy here."

"Out by Bear Pond? Where we can see the treehouse?" I suggested eagerly, remembering the peace and serenity I'd felt out there, not to mention its *other* memories.

The corner of Kit's mouth twitched, and I felt a warmth of feeling from him through our bond. "I'll build you whatever you want, wherever you want it, Nim."

With that, I grinned. "You mean, you'll let me decorate? Design the whole thing?" He nodded again, and I let out a gleeful giggle, clapping my hands in delight. "Okay. Yes. I like this plan. It will need to be a big space, with lots of room for everyone. Blaze will help, I'm sure. While Althea wasn't *technically* my grandmother, the only thing he loves more than me, Mo, and Petra — and his car — is a good construction project. There will be no stopping him. And I could set up my own photography studio. OH!" I gasped. "I want a dark room."

Kit chuckled. "No problem."

I melted a little at his words. "Gosh, I love you."

"I only have one request," Kit said as he parked in front of his parents' house.

"I'm listening."

"I want a view of that treehouse from our bedroom window. I want to wake up every morning next to you, and see the spot where I fell in love with you when we were kids. When I knew I'd love you for the rest of my life." He leaned over, wrapping a hand around my neck as he brought his lips to my ear. "And where I finally got to be inside you for the first time."

Unable to contain myself any longer, I unbuckled and threw myself across the car, sealing my lips to his in a quick but heated kiss. "Done."

Pulling away, I settled back in my seat as we stared at the white farmhouse in front of us.

"So," I started, then swallowed. "Do they know *I'm* your mate? Or just that you have *a* mate?"

Kit glanced sideways at me briefly, but said nothing as he shoved open the car door. I made to do the same, but he was at my side opening it for me before I could move. His hand slid down my arm, settling his fingers between mine as he pulled me from the car.

"Doesn't matter, right?" Kit smiled, now the one reassuring me. "We're in this together."

Before I could hesitate further, Kit's parents emerged on their front porch, followed by several other skulk members.

"Called it," Akil said as he held his hand out to Lily standing nearby. A bill changed hands as Lily rolled her eyes, but Akil beamed at us.

"Hey, sis," he called over as he descended the stairs. He lowered his voice to a whisper as he slipped something into my hand. I glanced down to see a sticker that said *Beats by Akil* over a logo with bright pink hair above thick turquoise headphones. "Does this mean I have a permanent spot as DJ for all of Blaze's parties now?"

Kit bopped his little brother upside the head, but I

chuckled, squeezing Kit's hand in mine. "I'll make sure I put in a good word for you."

"Nice." Akil grinned, the pink tips of his hair swaying as he bobbed his head and drew out the word.

Kit's mom headed towards us next, her arms open as tears gathered in her eyes. She wore her dark brown hair down like usual, her bright eyes taking me in with her characteristic mix of warmth and perception.

"*Beti*," her arms laced around my neck, crushing me to her chest, before she pulled back and planted a kiss on my cheek. "I should have known."

Her soft fingers laid across my cheeks as she appraised me lovingly, and my heart soared at the acceptance radiating from her. Kit had always wanted to keep the extent of our escapades under wraps from his parents, so I wasn't as close with them as I was with his friends, but I'd still grown up frequenting their house and joining them for meals. It meant the world to have her welcome me so quickly.

"And you, *jaan*." She dropped her hands from me and turned to Kit. With a light slap to his chest, she said, "How long did you know about this and not tell us?"

Without allowing him time to answer, she pulled him into a hug and planted kisses on his face. "My boy." She sniffed, holding back a flood of happy tears, and I couldn't help but smile.

Kit gave her a quick smile before his gaze snapped to his father standing stoically on the porch. Lily stood at her father's side, watching his reaction carefully, not a usual expression from the restless, free-spirited only-daughter in this family. I exchanged a glance with her, and she gave me a slight nod and tentative smile — I was glad to see she was doing all right since the whole witch fiasco.

"Pa," Kit said, his grip tightening on mine.

Mahit switched his gaze from his son to me, then back, still silent, before quietly nodding. "A good match. Alpha." He ducked his head in a slight bow to his son, and a breath left Kit in a swift exhale. I smiled over at my mate, squeezing his hand again, as Mahit and Lily came down the porch steps to join us.

Kit dropped my hand only to pull Lily into a fierce hug, and she gripped him back just as much.

"That wolf brought you home after all, then?" He pulled back, immediately reaching for my hand again, and Lily rolled her eyes at him.

A whole gaggle of chittering aunts, cousins, and skulk mates swarmed us, emerging from both houses on the cul-de-sac. Several others joined us from other properties nearby, circling us in hugs, and showering us with congratulations. Joy radiated from the skulk, and I felt it through the bond powers as it hummed alongside my demon fire.

"About time." Nadir clapped Kit on the shoulder and grinned at me. "I won't hug you because I'd prefer not to be mauled by your mate here, but welcome, Nimue. We're glad to have you."

The rest of Kit's generation — my friends for years — echoed his sentiment, and tears gathered in my eyes yet again.

"Seriously," Casey said, approaching and slinging an arm around Kit's shoulders. "Maybe he'll finally lighten up a bit."

"Oh yeah." Cole nodded, his arm around Skylar's waist.

"Mating can help with that a *lot*." Skylar coughed, jabbing him hard in the ribs, but she met my eyes with a blush as we exchanged smiles.

Hesitating only a moment, even Lily pulled me into her arms.

"I always wanted you to be my *actual* sister," she whispered, before breaking away and flicking Kit's ear. "And *that's* for letting me get fucking *kidnapped. Alpha.*"

Before he could retaliate, she turned and sauntered off, the rest of the group around us laughing at her retreat and the astonished look on Kit's face.

"That one's going to give you a run for your money, Alpha," Casey chimed in astutely, crossing his arms.

I turned to Kit. "I had no idea. I don't think she's said anything nice to me before, ever."

"That's sort of how she shows her love," Emerson confirmed, arms folded over his chest. "She should have been a cat shifter."

Mo and Blaze had always made up for any lack of family I'd missed out on, filling my life with love and support. But this, here, felt like home in a different way.

Sensing my emotions, Kit pulled me to his side, and kissed the top of my head.

Chapter Thirty-Seven

KIT

WATCHING Nimue smile as she chatted with each of the members of my skulk, fitting in as easily here as she always had, had my heart racing. She was perfect for me in every way, and I had been too stupid to see it all along.

My father caught my eye with a tilt of his chin, and I walked to his side.

"Well done," Pa said as we watched the skulk talk excitedly, crooning over Lily's return, the witch's lock lifted from our shifter powers, and now, Nimue. "She will be good for you."

I chuckled, glancing at him briefly, and crossed my arms.

"It's good to be challenged every once in a while as an Alpha," he continued.

At that, I outright laughed. "Your favorite pastime, right, Pa?"

"You and Lily are about as much as I can handle," he smiled, glancing my way. "Your mother is no docile vixen either, but you are not me. Your fox is the strongest I've ever seen, Kit."

My hands dropped to my sides, and I turned on my father. "What do you mean?"

"I've known you would surpass me since you were a boy," he sighed. "But it's not just about power, *jaan*. There's more to being an Alpha than just issuing commands. These people — our skulk — are yours to protect. You cannot let your worries get in the way of your duty to them, no matter what they think of you, or how they react."

His words hit like a slap, because that was precisely why I had held back from so much. From Nimue. From taking my role as Alpha.

But no longer.

"I hear you, Pa," I answered after a moment, allowing his words to sink in. "And I'm thankful to have your wisdom. Are you planning on staying? Or is this where you retire and leave us for good?"

"Please," Pa chuckled, pointing out over the crowd. "You want to tell me that with you, newly mated, and your sister, probably following in your footsteps, I could pry your mother away from here? It's more likely that Orion would pass an ordinance to allow shifters to walk naked through town than it is for me to get your mother to leave with the promise of the next generation of kits on the horizon."

I tried my best not to react to how he'd casually mentioned Lily and a mate, but he elbowed me. "I may be old, but I am far from stupid. I know Lily loves that wolf. I only hope this unfortunate incident with the witches teaches him a valuable lesson. Responsibility as a leader extends beyond our own skulk or pack."

"I'll keep an eye on him," I nodded in agreement, and sent my power down the lines of our skulk, searching for my sister. Next to her was a faint shadow of a bond, but it was far from solidified. "They're young still."

"Indeed."

"How is Sophie doing? Cole and Skylar? The others who were shifted?" I should have checked in on them right away, I mentally chastised myself, and shot Pa an apologetic look, but he waved it off. After all, he knew what it was like to be swept up in the mate bond.

"They're all right." He nodded to where Sophie stood. "But it will take them some time, I think, to be fully back to themselves."

I studied my younger cousin, Lily's shadow in every way since they were cubs. She'd always been a bit secretive, more like our wilder sides that way, but I could see a definite change in her mannerisms. Standing a little too still, her gaze was too intense to seem fully human as she watched more than mingled. I made a mental note to check in regularly with all those who had been stuck to ensure they were adjusting and see if I could help them.

We watched the gathered skulk for a few minutes more before he turned and clapped a hand on my shoulder.

"Ready to do this?"

I met his steady gaze with a nod. A warm feeling of pride spread from him through our skulk bonds as he returned my nod and took a step out from my side, his hand falling from my shoulder.

Closing my eyes, I sank into the skulk lines, drawing every member to me that wasn't already present and turning the attention of everyone who was already here my way.

In peaceful Alpha transitions, it was tradition for the

outgoing Alpha to hand off leadership to the incoming one, so I waited for my father to speak first.

"Yesterday, I bestowed the role of Alpha of the Arrowwood skulk to my eldest son, Kit," he began, his deep voice reaching even those standing farthest back. A few others trickled in from surrounding properties as they heeded my call and came to witness. Nimue reached my side again, and she twined her fingers with mine. I squeezed her hand at her support.

"As I'm sure most of you know and have felt by now, Kit possesses an immense well of Alpha power." His words were only interrupted by a few of my idiot friends joking quietly amongst themselves about how bossy I'd become since coming into my power, but my father ignored them. "So I know he will be a strong and thoughtful leader for our skulk, and I am proud to pass him this responsibility."

He turned to me, arm outstretched, and I stepped forward, dropping Nimue's hand. In respect and submission, I ducked my head and allowed him to wrap his fingers around the back of my neck — probably for the last time. I felt a bittersweet pang from my mother, and out of the corner of my eye, I saw Akil and Lily sidle up to her on either side, each taking one of her hands.

His following words were directed to me, though he still spoke loud enough for everyone, especially with our supernaturally gifted hearing.

"We've discussed this before, son, so I know you take this role seriously. But today, I remind you that, yes, your skulk owes you their loyalty, respect, trust, and obedience — but only while you give them your protection, guidance, wisdom, and love. From now on, your first thought every morning will be of your skulk, of what they need and how you can help them, and your last thought every night will be to wonder if you have done enough, and what you can do better. Their success is your success, and yours is theirs as well." His hand moved from my neck to my shoulder, allowing me to lift my head and meet his eyes. "You are lucky you have already found your mate to help you with what is both a privilege and an immense responsibility."

Our gazes held for another moment until he stepped back, leaving me to speak with the skulk for myself. I wasn't the biggest fan of public speaking — but this was my family.

"Arrowwoods," I began, and immediately had to halt my speech due to the whooping calls and cheers issuing from the left. I suppressed a smile as my eyes flitted over to see the twins, Nadir, Asher, Mikaela, and a handful of my generation there, grinning back at me. "I humbly accept this responsibility from my father to look after you, to see to your needs, listen to your concerns, and help and protect you in any way I can. If there ever comes a time when any of you feels I am not fulfilling my duty, I trust you to seek me out and tell me to my face so I can make it right. If even that fails to solve the issue, every single member of this skulk has the right to challenge me should they see fit, but I hope it never comes to that. I'm taking this role much earlier than I thought, but rest assured, my father will be here to offer me his guidance when I need it."

Moments like this, the whole skulk joined in common feeling, it felt as though our souls synchronized. Water droplets in a bucket, temporarily becoming one.

I looked to my father, and he nodded again. I spared Nim a brief glance before I shifted my nails into claws and made a nick on my thumb, immediately shifting them human again.

Letting my blood drop onto the soil, I continued with our traditional words. "This land was the Arrowwood skulk's home long before my family arrived here, and will be Arrowwood long after all of us here today are gone. But this soil is in my blood, and my blood is now in this soil, and I will protect this land and our family with my life."

A series of cheers swept through the crowd, many of them my close friends and relatives who had known they would one day witness this, even if they hadn't known when.

My father stepped up to me again, pulling a ring out of his pocket. It was a tarnished bronze, handed down through generations of Alphas, but the magic reset with each new appointment.

He bent down, pinched soil between his fingers, and then stood to his full height again. The ring had a cover that he flipped open, and under it, a tiny compartment where he dropped in the grains of soil.

"The soil of our land," he said and held out a hand to me. I reached out my own, and he held it, pressing my thumb against the compartment. "And the blood of our Alpha."

The entire skulk seemed to be holding its breath as he closed the cover, sealing soil and blood together with a click. I saw the familiar design on its cover as he held it out to me.

Two crossed arrows forming an A for the name of our skulk.

Accepting the ring, a wave of power swept over me

again as I slid it onto my finger, the magic giving me an even deeper connection to our land and my skulk.

"Alpha Kit!" Nadir was the first to call out, grinning. The others repeated his chant as wave after wave of their warmth, acceptance, and good wishes washed over me.

After the first part of the ceremony was done, we moved on to the second part. I had accepted responsibility as Alpha, and now each of the skulk needed to accept and acknowledge my authority. To a non-shifter, this might have seemed awkward. They had to approach me and display respect and submission the same way I had with my father — ducking their head and allowing me to place my hand on the back of their neck. When I moved my hand to their shoulder, they would meet my eyes in a moment of mutual recognition.

Per tradition, my father went first, and then his Second, my uncle Jay, who looked like a younger, wirier version of my father. He turned to Nimue after my hands dropped from him, placing a hand on her shoulder.

"I never got to thank you for helping to find my daughter and bringing her home safe," he said, my light-hearted uncle unusually solemn, swallowing heavily as he turned to include me in his thanks. "I hate to imagine what might have happened to Sophie if she hadn't been found."

After them came my Second, Nadir, and then the others formed a line. I tried to get through them quickly without making anyone feel like I had rushed them.

"Oh, *jaan*," my mother said as she came up, dabbing at the corners of her eyes. "You're all grown up."

"Ma, please," I chided under my breath lest anyone else hear, but I smiled at her.

She moved off after, and Cole took her place.

"Our baby boy," he said with a sniffle, and I clapped him over the ear before gripping his neck.

"Hurry up. I need to gaze into those sweet amber eyes, too," Casey teased from behind him, and Cole aimed a kick that didn't even come close.

"You guys are idiots," I muttered as I traded twins.

This part of the ceremony took a while, but Nimue never left my side, instead taking this opportunity to greet those she knew and introduce herself to those she didn't. My chest tightened with pride for my mate, and I couldn't wait to show her how much it meant to me to have her here, with us, at this ceremony, on my land.

Maybe we needed a quick intermission to the treehouse.

Chapter Thirty-Eight

NIMUE

WHEN KIT MENTIONED we were heading out to his parents' house this morning, I had no idea what to expect. I'd thought his family might be more hesitant, but they had readily embraced me. Maybe it had something to do with the skulk bonds, now that I was officially part of them. I understood it would take time to get used to my presence among them, but overall I hadn't sensed anything but kindness and curiosity.

Still, I was exhausted from the battering my emotions had taken. While the Alpha ceremony took longer than I thought, it was also sweeter than I'd ever imagined. I knew how much responsibility went into being an Alpha, but had never understood it the way I did after today. Rites like these weren't things most shifters let outsiders observe, but then again… I was no longer an outsider.

We left shortly after the ceremony, and I breathed easier once we were on the road. Kit reached across the console and grabbed my hand, pulling it to his lips as he drove us back towards town. "Tell me what you're feeling."

"Overwhelmed." I was shocked at my honesty, but it had always been easier for me to let my guard down around Kit than anyone else. "Sorry."

"For what?" Kit shook his head lightly. "Honestly, me too. Not about you, though. You, I've waited my entire life for."

Tears gathered in my eyes at his words, feeling the honesty radiating off of him.

"It just all happened at once," Kit continued. "The shifters. The witches. The mate bond. The Alpha ceremony. It's a lot."

I nodded in agreement, and we rode in contented silence. Trees blocked most of the water from view as we drove back towards town, and I pulled in a deep breath, trying to center myself for everything we still had in front of us.

"So, Morgaine's?" Kit glanced my way.

"Yeah. Let's do it."

Kit slowed the car, pulling over to the side momentarily, and pushed it into park, glancing my way. "If you've had enough for today, we can be done. We can go back to your house, and I'll worship your body as I've been dreaming for the last several hours. We have an entire lifetime ahead of us, so tell me right now if you're done for today, and I'll deal with everyone else."

My breaths came heavier at his words, knowing he'd read my emotions through our bond, and had sensed my unease. But that he knew me well enough to understand the *why* behind that unease emphasized how real this was. How *right*.

I leaned across the seat, delicately placing a kiss on his

lips. As badly as I wanted to skip back to the carriage house, I knew we couldn't.

"Thank you," I said as I pulled back slightly, but Kit grabbed onto my chin, pulling me back to him again. Our kisses grew more desperate, and I moaned as I broke away again. "Hey, stop making this difficult." I laughed lightly, shaking my head to clear the fog of sexual energy.

"Doesn't have to be," Kit smirked, and glanced behind us at the backseat.

"No," I shook my head again. "Mo's first. Then home. Let's get it over with so I can have this behind me."

"Well, don't sound too excited," Kit replied, but sarcasm laced his words. He knew me well enough to know my attitude had nothing to do with my feelings for him, and everything to do with my feelings for everyone *else*. My mother included. Which reminded me…

"You'd better call her Mo now," I informed him. "Since you're basically her son-in-law, or whatever. She'll be insulted otherwise."

Fifteen minutes later, we pulled into the drive of Mo's bright magenta house, the same color as the sunset over the water. Kit parked and turned off the car, pausing as he looked at the house.

"You nervous?" I asked, reading his emotions just as he had mine earlier.

"Kind of," he shrugged. "I feel like I should have called and asked for her blessing, but that also seems like an archaic tradition. You don't need anyone's permission to make your own decisions."

"I promise you; she'll see it that way, too." I smiled at him, unbuckling my seatbelt and grabbing the door handle. "You ready?"

Before we had time to think twice, Blaze was suddenly at Kit's door, yanking it open.

"You." Blaze scowled at Kit, and I ducked my head to glance at him. "I have a bone to pick with you."

Kit stammered briefly, and I glanced behind Blaze to see Petra on the steps behind him. "I promise, it all just happened. We were on our way here next to tell you all the good news."

"No one messes with —" Blaze paused, his shoulders relaxing slightly as he glanced at me, then back at Kit. "Wait. Good news?"

"So, the thing is, Nimue," Petra grimaced behind Blaze, inching towards the car. "When we didn't know where you guys had disappeared off to after The Last Resort show-down, Devanna told him about the whole mate bond disaster."

Blaze's eyes tracked over us, noting the way Kit still held my hand across the center console, and then met mine. "What am I missing? You two look awfully cozy now."

"Surprise!" I forced a smile onto my face as I fought to combat the awkwardness that hung in the air. "Mate bond works just fine now."

Kit brought my hand back to his mouth again, gently kissing my knuckles before glancing back at Blaze. "We were on our way here to tell you and Morg — Mo."

"Tell me what?" Mo called across the lawn as she joined the party.

At that, I finally peeled my hand away from Kit and opened the car door. As my feet touched the ground, Mo paced towards me, then skidded to a halt. Her eyes expanded behind her thick glasses — pink frames today — as a smile crept up her face. "It happened."

Kit stepped around the car, gently lacing his arm around my waist.

Mo squealed in delight, throwing her arms wide as her leopard-and-floral-print kimono slid down her arms. Instantly, she held us both firmly, hugged tight to her chest.

"I always knew it," she whispered in my ear, kissing me softly on the cheek. "Kit would be the one to bring my baby back to me."

I kissed her cheek back, settling into her warmth, feeling the love radiating off her.

"I never really left *you*," I said with a smile, "but yeah. I'm coming home."

Chapter Thirty-Nine

BEFORE I COULD COMPLETELY UNDERSTAND what had happened, Mo's spindly fingers wrapped around my wrist, and she pulled Nimue and me through her hallway, into the living room. She ushered us onto the couch, and then dropped into her floral wingback, sighing contentedly as she glanced between Nimue and me.

"I'm just so happy," she beamed, and Nimue laughed.

"Really, Mo?" Her eyebrows raised as she looked at her mother.

"You don't understand." Mo shook her head lightly as Blaze settled into the other wingback chair, and pulled Petra into his lap. "Both of my children, grown, and in love. It makes my heart happy. The only thing that would make me happier —"

"A party!" Blaze's eyes went wide as he swung his gaze towards us. "Please? It's been like four weeks since my last party. It's time."

Nimue glanced my way, trying to read my expression before answering. I could feel her hesitancy through our bond, but I didn't know if it was for a party or because she could sense my nervousness. In this, though, I took the lead and turned towards Blaze.

"Only a small one. Family only."

"Right, right," Blaze nodded, his gaze far off, and instantly I knew my request would be denied. "At Scally-wags. Wait, no. My house."

"*I'm* hosting the party," Mo cut in, and Blaze eyed her hesitantly. "Blaze, you can be in charge of the entertainment and the food, but it's *my* daughter we're celebrating. I'm hosting. That's what they do for weddings, right, Petra?"

"Uh," Petra stuttered, her eyes focused heavily on Nimue at my side, searching for any hint for how we wanted her to answer. "Yeah. The bride's family usually hosts the reception, but many people don't follow those traditions anymore. I mean, marriage isn't even essential if you don't feel the need for labels."

"I bet Kit wants all the labels." Blaze glanced my way, and I smirked. He wasn't wrong.

"We've gotten ahead of ourselves here, everyone." As one, the room went silent, and they all turned towards me. "This is all a little much, and so fast."

"Oh." Nimue nodded, and began to pull her hand free of mine. "No, you're —"

Before she could continue down whatever train of thought she was on, I scooted off the couch, and slid to one knee, turning towards her.

"Nimue Fitzpatrick, will you marry me? Be my mate for the rest of my life? Stand by my side as we lead our skulk together? Grow old with me?"

Mo began weeping loudly, lost to emotion, as she

watched me kneel in front of her daughter. "My heart," she cried, clutching her chest as tears streamed down her face.

But I couldn't look away to glance behind me at the woman who loudly blew her nose. My eyes were glued to Nimue in front of me.

Her mouth hung slightly open in shock as her black eyes glanced between mine, trying to read my emotions, my urges… all of it.

"Are you sure?" she whispered.

"Whether you say yes today, or tomorrow, or two years from now, or never, I know that I will love you until the day I die, Nim. Whether that's as my mate, wife, or partner… that's up to you. But I want anything you're willing to give me."

Nimue's eyes drifted from my face to glance around the room, taking in Blaze and Petra to our left, and Mo to our right, still trumpeting into a handkerchief.

"They don't matter." I reached up, tilting her chin back towards me. "Only you. You and me."

A tear trailed down Nimue's cheek, and I swiped it away before it could fall.

"Yes." She nodded. "I'll marry you."

I pushed up off my knee, pulling her face down into mine as I kissed her. It didn't matter that her mother and cousin sat only feet away; I had dreamt of this moment for over twenty years.

"OH!" Mo called out, then began clapping her hands together excitedly, and I pulled back. Nim's eyes focused on me, not glancing behind us to where Mo had rushed from the room.

"What is she doing?" Petra turned to Blaze.

"Fuck if I know," Blaze replied, and I held back a chuckle. Nimue's family was wild and chaotic — the opposite of the rigid structure in mine. But just as she'd now share in my family, I would be a part of hers as well.

"You can't get married without a ring," Mo said as she jogged back to our side, her kimono swishing behind her as she skidded across the wood floor in her socks.

In her hand was a large emerald-cut pink diamond set into a gold band. Nimue finally broke our eye contact as she turned to Mo, then gasped as her eyes widened.

"That's from Eddie." Nimue nearly panted as she eyed the diamond. "I can't take that."

Even as she said it, though, I could feel through our bond how badly she wanted it. Nimue had expensive taste in just about everything.

"Yes, Eddie gave me this many years ago." Petra's eyes were wide as she took in the size of the rock, and Mo shot her a wink. "A railroad man," she grinned before turning back to Nimue.

"Child, I was happily married to that sweet human for 62 years." Mo smiled at Nimue, pulling my mate's hand into her own. "We always dreamt of what it would be like to have a child, but that was never in the cards for me. Not until you." Tears leaked down both Mo's and Nimue's cheeks as they shared this moment. "There is nothing I could ever want more than to gift this to you. Eddie would agree if he were still here."

With that, Mo turned to me and handed me the ring. I took it gently from her, realizing I would never be able to afford anything like this, and thankful for Mo's generosity.

Nimue's left hand shook as she held it out in front of her,

and I grasped it lightly, placing a gentle kiss on her hand before sliding the ring onto her finger.

Light sparkled off the diamond, casting a rainbow of glittering light on the walls around us, and Nimue glowed as bright as the stone.

I stood, pulling her to her feet, and circled my arms around her waist as I kissed her deeply.

Without hesitation, she flickered us home.

Chapter Forty

NIMUE

WE SPENT the next several nights wrapped up in each other, giving in to all the mate bond demanded. As I snuggled into Kit's arms, my heart felt lighter. It had been an emotional rollercoaster of a week between the Alpha ceremony, meeting the skulk as Kit's *mate*, and his proposal in front of my family.

While my body and mind were tired, I had never been happier. Kit kissed my shoulder lightly, pulling my back into his front before his breathing evened and sleep took hold of us.

It had been years now that I'd been on the road, running from all I'd left behind here, but I was delighted to be back home. Right where I needed to be.

A phone vibrating across the nightstand woke me the following day, jerking me back awake. Sunlight leaked through the blinds, early morning light casting a warm glow over Kit's face, where he slept next to me.

I reached across the bed to grab my phone, and my movement woke Kit.

"Good morning," he said in a sleep-heavy voice that was entirely too sexy. "This week has been the best I've slept in years."

I smiled as I swiped across my screen, glancing down to see what I'd missed.

"That's weird," I muttered as my brow scrunched.

Kit sat up, the sheets falling to expose his bare chest. The bond between us snapped tight as I fought to focus on my phone instead of his lean muscles next to me.

"What's going on?" he asked as he leaned into my arm, peeking down at my phone.

"Blaze called me." I showed him my missed call log. "At 7:30 in the morning. On a Tuesday."

Kit's eyebrows raised, understanding that a demon awake *that* early was a bad sign. "That can't be good."

He reached across me for his phone, his skin brushing across mine tantalizingly slowly, and I almost moaned. "This is the sweetest torture."

Kit laughed, kissing me lightly as he drew back onto the bed, flipping open his phone.

"Shit."

I turned, but Kit already held the phone up to his ear, ringing on the other end.

"Nadir," Kit answered brusquely, "what's going on?" He pulled the phone down, and switched it to speaker phone so I could also hear.

"Ready for your first big job as the boss?" Nadir's voice

sounded strained, and I listened intently. "Even if you're not, it's go-time. Orion has called for the witch trials today. All leaders and seconds are required to attend. Begins in an hour."

"Crap," I muttered, swiping my screen again and texting Blaze that I'd heard the news.

Kit hung up a moment later, and we both rose from the bed.

"I don't think I have the willpower to shower with you," Kit nipped my shoulder, and I squeezed my thighs together. "Not with the sudden time crunch. Take your time, and I'll rinse when you're done."

With that, I rushed into the bathroom, and flipped the water to cold.

An hour later, we were crossing the square to Town Hall. For once, the aqua and white VW coffee van was right where it should be — maybe Val and Caedmon had heard about the meeting and taken pity on us — so we joined the line of the other leaders and Seconds to grab coffee and breakfast before heading in.

"Well, well," a voice came from behind us, and I turned to see Devanna giving Kit a steely once-over, her gaze settling on our clasped hands for a minute before raising a brow at me. Wordlessly, she handed me a large cup, steam billowing out of it that carried the signature notes of Pumpkin Spice. "He stopped being an idiot?"

Kit cleared his throat, furrowing his brow, but waited for me to answer.

"Yes, Dev." I smiled at Kit, squeezing his hand. "You can put your shovel away."

"Not a chance," she scoffed, but the slight glimmer in her eye told me she was happy for me. Probably. Pointing a dagger of a finger at Kit, she warned him, "You're on probation."

"I'm — what?"

"You heard me, fox." She crossed her arms, squaring up, and I had to press my lips together to stop from smiling at her tiny form — albeit augmented in her black platform boots — challenging my Alpha like this. Her head barely reached his shoulders.

"All right," he let out an exasperated sigh, but I could tell he was trying not to laugh. "For how long?"

Dev tilted her head. "As long as I see fit." And with that, she stepped around him to steal the spinach and feta crois-sant Caedmon had just placed on the counter. "Charge the fox for it, C.".

Crumbs tumbled from her lips as she bit into the warm pastry, strolling across the square without another glance. Kit raised his eyebrows at me behind her, and we shared a shrug. Dev would cool down in time.

She was far from the last to comment on our new situa-tion, though everyone else's reception was much warmer since they weren't my self-assigned personal assassin. As we moved into the town hall, several eyes shot our way, but it wasn't only because of our new relationship status.

"You're Alpha now?" Lysander said, noting that Mahit and Jay were nowhere to be seen. "When did that happen?"

Kit gave him a tight smile that was more of a grimace. "It's been a busy few days."

Lys nodded slowly, then extended his hand. "Well, congratulations."

A sharp bark from his mother Ostara had Lys grimacing as he moved off. Some other Alphas came forward to greet us and recognize Kit's new status, including the wolf Alpha, Darius, looking as un-policeman-like as ever with his casual jeans, Timberland boots, and a light grey sweatshirt that offset his rich brown skin. He seemed more twitchy than usual, having been stuck as a wolf, but he'd readjust in time. Winona, head of the local bears, offered a motherly smile that creased her sun-worn and freckled face as she wrapped us in a warm hug. Ryker merely gave Kit a nod from across the room, unable to be bothered to move from his seat.

We approached the oval table to take our place next to Blaze, Nadir arriving a few minutes later and taking the seat next to Kit. Looking around the table, Orion was at the end, wings ruffling with impatience, but we weren't sure what we were waiting for.

"Isn't this everyone?" Blaze called over bluntly, voicing all of our thoughts.

Orion let out a deep sigh, pinching the bridge of his nose. "Not quite."

Just then, the doors to the conference room banged open, and everyone around the table snapped our heads to see who it was.

"Oh, my God."

Many others shared my sentiment around the room as Ronan, the king of the sea nymphs, strutted into the room, his sun-tanned chest on full display. He wore loose-fitting sand-colored linen pants and nothing else. No shirt, no shoes. Definitely not weather-appropriate for late November in Maine, where we were likely to get snow any day. His scant clothing did nothing to hide his tall, trim form and lean muscles — the swimmer's build that all sea nymphs possessed. His dirty blond hair was sun-bleached and windswept, hanging around his shoulders, framing the ink running across his chest.

On top of that, I couldn't remember the last time Ronan had set foot on actual soil. Usually, the nymphs preferred to keep to their own, underwater or offshore. Similar to shifters, the nymphs could take human form, but where shifters could only change into one type of animal, the nymphs could change into several. In fact, I wasn't sure anyone knew the extent of their powers, and they wanted to keep it that way.

His Second, Xuma, walked in behind him and at least had the decency to wear a shirt. Still, he too had weather-inappropriate clothes — white linen pants and a coral shirt, the buttons undone halfway down his chest and the color contrasting his deep brown skin. His waist-length locs were tied back loosely, revealing several studs and rings in each ear as he ran a sharp eye over everyone in the room.

Orion coughed pointedly, and Ronan raised a brow as his piercing blue eyes met Orion's grey ones. Orion nodded his head at the sign on the wall to Ronan's left. Ronan turned, scoffed, pulled it down, and tore it into pieces.

The sign had said *Shirt and Shoes Required.*

Not anymore, apparently.

Some muttering and uncertain chuckles made their way around the table, but silence fell once Ronan and Xuma took their seats directly across from Orion, whose lips were in such a tight line, they were white.

"Where are the witches?" Ronan boomed from his end of the table like we were all hard of hearing.

Taking a deep breath, Orion ignored him and addressed the rest of us. "In a moment, we will call the witches in for questioning. Inquisitor Pascar will render them unable to lie, and she will then take them back to headquarters for judgment and sentencing. Shifters," he leveled a look at each of the Alphas in the room. "This was very personal for you. If you cannot conduct your questioning in a levelheaded fashion, you will be asked to leave. Any questions before we bring them in?"

"Why are the angels taking them?" Ronan butted in immediately, leaning his elbows on the table. "These witches tampered with our magic. We can execute them today."

"They still deserve a trial," Lys retorted before his mother shot him a sharp look.

"My son speaks out of turn, but he is correct. They are still witches, and as such, protected by our coven laws," she answered, her dark hands folded calmly on top of a red, leatherbound notebook on the table in front of her. "They will have a trial and be dealt with accordingly." Her tone turned icier as she continued, "And I may remind you, Ronan, that *none* of our sentences result in execution anymore."

"Maybe *your* sentences," he jeered, lip curling. "You land-dwellers have gone soft. In my realm —"

"I'll remind you, we're *not* in your realm," Orion bit out at him. "We must follow our *universal* supernatural laws."

They stared off for a moment, the rest of us swinging our gazes back and forth between them and wondering who would break first. Ronan's jaw worked overtime before he finally waved a supercilious hand.

"Proceed, then."

Eyes narrowing slightly, Orion hit a button on the intercom before him. A moment later, four witches in iron handcuffs were led into the room by Cove police, and seated in a row facing the conference table. As the police escorts were leaving, an angel entered with a level of power that had the static in the room drawing tight.

"Inquisitor Pascar, welcome," Orion greeted her. Though her gleaming eyes never left the witches, she nodded stiffly.

Like all angels, she had silvery hair, which she had tied back in a thick braid, grey eyes, and her lustrous white wings draped elegantly behind her. Her dark purple, nearly black lipstick only highlighted how pale her skin was, and her black-painted fingernails were sharpened into points. In a skin-tight black dress, black leather jacket, and motorcycle boots, she was not what I would have expected from a head angel.

Nearing the witches, the entire room held their breath as she trailed a black talon along each of their temples. She uttered no words, the only sound the slight ruffling of her feathers as she walked and the quiet gasps from each witch as she enchanted them.

Finishing with the last one, she stood behind him, arm resting casually on the witch's shoulder. "There. Ask your questions. They'll tell you no lies," she said in a hauntingly sing-songy voice that told me she might enjoy her job a little too much. The witch under her flinched as she squeezed his shoulder before moving off to sit at the table.

"You're — staying to watch?" Orion asked her, forehead wrinkling.

"Oh, yes," she responded breezily, but her smile could have cut diamonds. "I can't wait to see how the leaders of this town operate. The ministers instructed me to bring back a *full* report."

Silent glances were exchanged between Seconds and leaders around the room, my gaze meeting first Kit's and then Blaze's.

Whatever that meant, it couldn't be good.

Chapter Forty-One

KIT

IT DIDN'T TAKE LONG for a few of the shifters to get themselves kicked out of the meeting. One of the witches, a smug bastard named Brennan who fancied himself their leader, shot a taunting jab at Darius, who had been stuck as a wolf for four days. He lost it, with the bear Second, Jenna, backing him up. Orion jumped to his feet, intercepting the two shifters, and ordered them out immediately. Brennan looked only too pleased with himself with the result, but the other three witches around him appeared uneasy, rightfully nervous about how this would play out.

"What was the purpose of your spell?" Ostara asked, bringing us back to the point of this interrogation.

Brennan opened his mouth to jeer again, but Pascar pointed a snow-white finger at him, and a shimmer of magic shot between them. "I think we've heard enough of you," she purred.

Though he tried to speak, no sound came out. A wicked smirk tipped her lips as Brennan's eyes widened, and the witch to his side cleared her throat.

"To draw power," the witch said, and Brennan kicked at her feet. "Enough," she hissed at him. "I'd rather tell them *here* than —" she broke off, swallowing heavily, and Pascar's grin widened, her tongue tracing her teeth.

"You're a smart one," the angel crooned appreciatively. "Shasta, was it?"

"We were trying to harness the power from the ley lines and lock it into amulets," Shasta continued, looking to Orion.

"With Errakal?" Blaze asked.

"Yes," she confirmed. "It was his idea, initially. He came to us for help with the spell."

"Why put the energy into the amulets?" Lysander asked, and Ostara *tsk*ed loudly at him to be silent.

"Errakal had an idea that if we were able to perform the correct spell, and lock the power into the talismans, then witches might be able to perform magic the same way demons and angels do. Without needing spells, incantations, ingredients, potions, or any of that. That we'd be able to use it instantaneously."

A heavy silence fell as the room considered the implications of that, until it was interrupted by Blaze's coughed laugh.

"Why the fuck would Errakal care about that?" he said, glancing over to Orion. "He can already use magic that way."

Orion nodded his agreement with the sentiment. "What did he tell you?" he directed at the witches.

"I asked him that once," said the other female witch. "He only said it was none of our concern, and we could take his help or not."

Blaze and Orion shared another long look before Ostara spoke up again.

"So, were you successful? Are you able to use magic like demons and angels?"

The other male witch shook his head. "We never completed the cycle. We had to perform spells on sequential moon cycles at each nexus point. First, we were interrupted at the Hanging Tree —" he shot Ryker a wary glance. The dragon merely cocked a brow at him, his giant arms crossed over his chest. "So, we had to start over. After our spell on the October full moon —"

"Wait, nothing happened on that full moon." Blaze leaned forward, glancing between the other leaders for corroboration. "We checked all the sites."

The witch opened his mouth again, but closed it as he shot a glance at Ronan. The nymph was glaring daggers at him.

As one, the leaders' heads swung to the end of the table.

"Ronan? What's the meaning of this? What happened on the full moon?" Orion called over.

Ronan leaned back in his chair, running a hand along the strong line of his jaw.

"The night of the full moon," he began slowly. "We began to experience some anomalies."

Orion narrowed his eyes. "Explain."

Waving a hand, Ronan scoffed. "No." The lights crackled above, but Ronan ignored it. "Suffice it to say, we sent some males out to investigate. They found a corpse. Human. Clear signs of ritual sacrifice."

Silence descended again, barely controlled anger beginning to simmer from the other end of the table.

"If you had informed me of this at the time," Orion tapped a finger on the table, "we might have been able to avoid all of the other events."

"It didn't seem relevant. How was I to know there was anything similar going on above-water?"

"*If* you could follow the guidelines set forth by the treaty, and maintain regular contact with the mainland, then —" Orion was practically seething, but Blaze interrupted him.

"So you found a body," he said, his tone much calmer than Orion's. "And you won't tell us what effects you experienced. Have you fixed all of them now?"

Ronan stared at him until Ostara's tinkling laugh filtered through.

"Of course, they haven't," she said. "They'd need a witch. And unless someone else in the coven is hiding things from me, they haven't requested one yet."

His frown deepened, but Ronan grunted something in the affirmative to her assertion.

"Well?" she turned to him, sitting up straighter and giving him a mockingly expectant smirk. "Is this you asking for my help? It's polite to say *please*."

Ronan sneered at her, lip curling. "The day I ask for your help is the day my sea dries up, crone."

She barked out a bitter laugh, not seeming surprised in the slightest.

"I'll go," Lys offered, leaning forward to look around his mother.

Ostara wrapped a hand around his shoulder and pushed

him back in his seat. "You will not. If they want our help, they can damn well ask for it like civilized people."

"Ostara, Ronan, enough." Orion pressed a finger into his temple, done with their bickering. "Do we have any further questions for the accused?"

"I do," I leaned forward, and Orion nodded to me. "Where do we find Errakal now?"

The witches exchanged glances before Shasta spoke up again. "I don't know. He could be anywhere. We were staying outside Spring Harbor —"

Even amid the trial, the mere name of the odious, well-to-do town to the north sent a series of grumblings around the room.

"— But I doubt he'd still be there, knowing that's the first place you'd look."

Beside me, Nimue nudged Blaze. "Could we try the spell again?"

Blaze tilted his head. "We could, but I bet he's moved farther out — I doubt we'll be able to reach him that way."

Nimue's shoulders sank, but she nodded. I reached over, placing my hand on her knee and squeezing gently, and she leaned into me.

"So, where does that leave us?" Julian asked, once again assuming the role of wolf leader with Darius kicked out of the room. "We know Errakal is behind this, but we don't know his true purpose, where he is, if he'll try again with other witches, or in another town with concentrated nexus points?"

Everyone at the table exchanged glances, but Julian was right. That was about the scope of it.

Letting out a heavy breath, Orion turned to Ryker beside him. "I think I have another job for you."

Chapter Forty-Two

NIMUE

RYKER GRUNTED his agreement with Orion's assignment to start hunting down Errakal. Immediately, he stood and strode from the room, ready to start on his new task.

"Done with them?" Pascar asked Orion, jumping lightly to her feet with a glint in her eye.

Looking around the table one last time to see if anyone else had other questions, he nodded at her. "All yours, Inquisitor."

A fiendish smile appeared on her face as she sauntered over to the witches.

"Hear that?" she hummed. "All *mine*." With a twist of her fingers, she yanked them all to their feet with her magic and began to march them out of the room, singing, "*Hush, little witchlings, don't cry or yell; angel's gonna find you a witchling cell.*"

As soon as they had cleared the room, I turned on Orion. "*That* was a head angel?"

"Inquisitor."

"Still, she doesn't seem quite all *there*." I moved forward in my seat. "Can we trust that she'll —"

"She'll see them safely to headquarters," Orion assured me, but I was unconvinced. That the angels had someone potentially unhinged working in this capacity, it almost made me wonder what the rest of their organization looked like. The supernatural community trusted the angels to oversee us and maintain law and order, but had *they* ever been questioned?

"Inquisitors do not make judgment or sentencing decisions," Orion continued like he could tell I wasn't on board yet.

When I met his eye, Kit tightened his grip on my knee again and offered me a half-shrug.

Blaze pushed away from the table and rose to his feet. "Well," his gaze swung around the room, "it's been real. It's been fun. But it hasn't been real fun, and I have a party to plan."

Orion sighed so heavily that his wings moved in the wind. "Can you take *nothing* seriously?"

"Plenty," Blaze scoffed. "I take wedding planning *very* seriously."

Orion's head jerked up, his hand dropping down to the wooden table. "You're getting married?"

"Not me." Blaze slapped his hand down on my shoulder, yanking me forward. "Nimmie and Kit finally noticed they're in love. It only took their lives to see what everyone else already knew."

Orion arched a brow but didn't argue the point. "I suppose congratulations are in order, then." He smiled over at us. "When is the wedding?"

" Saturday!" Blaze clapped, rubbing his hands together. "I've got a lot to do."

Without another word, Blaze flickered out of the room.

"How wonderful," Ostara said, startling me as I hadn't noticed her approach. She yanked my hand forward to inspect my ring. "What a beautiful ring. Hand-cut stone. One of a kind, just like you, Nimue. No power in it, but beautiful nonetheless."

I gently pulled my hand back from her, trying my hardest not to wipe my palm on my jeans. Ostara was one of the most intense people I'd ever met, and she always gave me the creeps.

"The Coven will be delighted to hear the news about the party." She smiled, flashing her teeth in an almost predatory way.

My eyes widened suddenly at her words. Kit opened his mouth to respond, surely to tell her she wasn't invited, but I clamped my hand down on his, tugging hard. The only way out of inviting the Coven — which meant inviting the whole town — was through a slew of hurt feelings, and I didn't need that weighing down on me.

"Lovely!" I forced a smile, leaning heavily on Kit. I could feel his gaze practically burning a hole through my cheek, but I didn't flinch. "We can't wait to celebrate with you all. Blaze will be in touch with the details."

With Kit's hand firmly in mine, I flickered us out, and back to my house.

"Did you just intentionally invite the whole town to the wedding?" Kit asked as soon as we landed back in the carriage house.

I groaned, dropping my head into my hands. "I

panicked. The thought of disappointing anyone was so crippling that I did the only thing I could think of."

Kit tilted my head back up towards his, and I slowly lifted my eyes. "If that's not what you truly want, then say the word, and I'll cancel the whole fucking thing."

"What?" I pulled back. "No. I mean, not unless you're having second thoughts."

"Nim. When it comes to you, there *are* no second thoughts. I have wanted to spend my life at your side since the moment I met you. But if you want it to be small — just family — I'll cancel on everyone in town and have no regrets."

My eyes searched his momentarily, trying to read his urges and emotions simultaneously. "When did you become so confrontational?"

Kit grinned, raising one brow. "All part of the Alpha package. And when it comes to protecting you — and that includes protecting you from *yourself* in times like these — I'll gladly put my foot down. I don't care who I have to pick a fight with."

Heart racing at his words, I gently kissed his lips, wrapping my arms around his neck as I thought through my next words. What did I *really* want?

"Let's have a party. Everyone will turn out, and maybe it will give our town the opportunity to gawk at us for a day and get it out of their system. Plus, it'll give the shifters a chance to let loose and celebrate now that everything is back to normal," I rambled, thinking through any positives I could to distract myself from the overwhelming thought of being the center of attention in a few days. "What do I need to know about your traditions? Is there anything special you want to happen in terms of honoring shifters or your family?"

At my words, Kit moved his mouth to kiss along my arm. "I love how thoughtful you are, Nim." Another kiss, quickly becoming distracting, which maybe was his intention. "If you're sure, then I'll call my mother. She would love to help."

I nodded, smiling up at him, and he closed the distance, pulling me into his chest. "I'm sure."

Chapter Forty-Three

NIMUE

I SPENT the rest of the week tangled with Kit every night. During the day, he was busy handling skulk business, running the tea shop, and checking in with the shifters who had been stuck as animals.

Meanwhile, I hounded Blaze, Petra, and Mo for wedding details. None of them answered my calls, and any time I managed to track one of them down, I got nothing. Blaze refused to share any of the details with me, and Mo only flashed me a most disturbing evil grin. Petra shrugged and offered, semi-sympathetically, "I would tell you, but Mo said she'd stop working her hangover cure into my movie night drinks if I gave anything away. Frankly, I don't think I could handle her recipes without it."

Saturday morning was a flurry of activity. Nadir and the skulk came and captured Kit shortly after dawn, and not long later, there was a knock on my door.

"Open up!" Devanna called as she banged again impatiently. I threw on my pink robe and flickered downstairs quickly, unlocking it for her.

"Took you long enough," she said as she pushed through the door with her arms full of supplies — makeup, hair tools, and demon wine.

Before I could even acknowledge that I didn't think today was the day for day-drinking, Aditi, Lily, Kit's aunt Aubrey, and his cousin Sophie came up the path with a large tote, followed by Petra and Selene armed with snacks. Last in line, looking as wild as ever in an oversized pale pink hoodie and zebra-print leggings, was Mo.

Tears gathered in the corners of my eyes as I scanned over the group. "What are you all doing here?"

"Celebrating!" Selene pulled me into a hug. "It's not every day that the Cove has a wedding!"

"We thought we could help get you ready." Petra held up a tray full of coffees.

"Lily and I have some traditions we'd love to share." Aditi placed her palm lovingly on my cheek. "If you're interested."

"Of course." My lip wobbled as my eyes roved over the women gathered around me.

"I love you more than words, my baby." Mo pulled me down to kiss my cheek. "And to be married on the full moon! Today is a good day."

Once we were settled inside, Aditi called us to attention. "While not everyone in our skulk chooses to marry, we highly cherish the tradition when they do." She ducked down, pulling several items from the tote she'd brought in, including a beautiful red- and gold-beaded cloth, and stood to pace around the table where we all sat.

"*Beti*, sweet Nimue." Her eyes filled with emotion as she delicately lifted the fabric, draping it over my head. "This is far from a typical *Chunni* ceremony, and time didn't allow for some of our other traditions with how much the skulk had going on this week, but Lily, Sophie, Aubrey, and I are here to welcome you into our family."

"Oh." Mo sniffed loudly from next to me, and I turned, feeling the silken fabric slip across my shoulders. "This is just too wonderful."

Mo rose to her feet and pulled Aditi into a hug, the two women sharing in their overwhelming emotions.

"This is adorable," Dev said in an almost angry tone. "I need a drink."

Cyndi Lauper's *Girls Just Want to Have Fun* blasted in the background while I sat in one of my plush pink armchairs, Dev tackling my hair and Lily and Sophie applying henna in intricate swirls to my hands and feet.

"Usually, this would sit for at least a day," Aditi told me, indicating the henna with a nod of her head. "But Morgaine has offered to speed up the process for us."

"Oh, Adi, we're family now," Mo said, plopping a tray of peach bellinis on the ottoman and passing one to Aditi. "Call me Mo."

Lily and Sophie exchanged an amused expression as Aditi took the glass. Lily's eyes met mine with a raise of her eyebrows. "Watch out," she mouthed, and the cousins laughed together.

I eyed Sophie when she first arrived, trying to be subtle, but with that almost sixth sense of awareness all shifters seemed to have, she caught me out. Offering me a reassuring smile, she did seem improved from the last time I'd seen her at the Alpha ceremony. I relaxed a bit, relieved she was recovering from her time stuck as a fox.

Mo splashed a little demon wine in one of the bellinis and passed it to me, which I took with a thanks.

"What are the guys doing all day?" I asked, assuming Kit wasn't receiving the same spa treatment.

"Not drinking too much if they know what's good for them," Aditi muttered into her glass. Sophie pressed her lips together, and Lily rolled her eyes.

"Nadir said something about a run," Sophie offered. "They haven't had time to shift together since the Alpha ceremony."

I nodded, a smile coming to my lips as I pictured the group cavorting in the woods; it was good they would have some time together today.

"What's the agenda for later?" I looked to Petra, who would know the most about Blaze's plans.

She flipped open a notebook, scanning her messily scrawled bullet points on the grid paper. "At four, we'll head over to the town square — we had to move the location from Mo's, now that practically the whole town is coming." She paused, meeting my eye for confirmation that that was okay, and I nodded, encouraging her to continue. "Val offered to lead the ceremony, so Kit's uncle Jay is over with him and Caedmon to work through some details."

I looked to Aubrey, her thumbs flying furiously over her phone until she glanced up and smiled at me, waving her phone. "Just making sure he's got all the bases covered."

"Blaze somehow wrangled a last-minute caterer, so they'll set up on the other side of the square," Petra continued, reaching the end of her list. "Akil volunteered to DJ, so after food, it's just dancing until your feet fall off."

She made it all sound so simple to throw together a wedding in less than a week, but Blaze had it down to a science. The male could run a party in his sleep.

Four o'clock came too quickly, my nerves building as the moment drew closer. Not because I was nervous about officially marrying Kit, but at the thought of how many people would be there watching.

Selene ran upstairs to grab the dress I described to her, and while she was gone, Mo performed a charm on the henna to set it. Reappearing in the room, Selene whirled the dress around to show it to everyone. It was a rose pink midi dress with fluttery cap sleeves and a flowing chiffon skirt. I was lucky I was an impulse buyer — at least for things in my favorite color — as I'd had this in my closet for years, but never had a reason to wear it until now.

Once I was dressed, Aditi drew a wooden box out of her tote and placed it on the ottoman in front of me.

"Hope you like gold," Lily teased as Aditi opened it. Together, they began sliding gold and white bangles up my arms, necklaces around my neck, and gold earrings into my ears. Dev eyed them too — my lion-hearted witch had a taste for gold jewelry — and Aditi laughed warmly.

"Yes, go ahead, Devanna," she gestured to the box. "Everyone wears bangles today."

Once everyone was dressed and ready to go, we headed for the door when Petra caught my elbow and pulled me aside.

"I know you don't know your biological family," she said, holding out a small envelope. "But I figured 'Fitzpatrick'... you've got to be Irish somewhere, right?"

I opened the envelope, bringing out a small silver coin.

"There's an old Irish tradition to place a sixpence in your shoe for good luck," she said. "If you want to."

Warmth bloomed in my chest for my friend's thoughtfulness, and I hugged her, chuckling at her startled *"Uhh,"* before she hesitantly returned the embrace. Petra was not a hugger, but today, she was getting one, whether she wanted it or not.

"Thank you, Petra," I said sincerely, drawing back and slipping my shoe off to drop it inside. "I love it."

Chapter Forty-Four

RUNNING with my skulk in the fresh air was just the distraction I needed before our big night. I clapped Nadir on the back in thanks for setting it up as we loped up the porch stairs to head in and get ready.

Thirty minutes later, we were showered, dressed, mostly sober, and heading to the town square, where the wedding had been relocated.

"Nervous?" Nadir asked from the driver's seat, glancing over at me.

"What should he be nervous about?" Casey said from the back. "Nim's going to take one look at you in that and fucking swoon." He plucked gently at my ivory and gold sherwani, and I batted his hand away.

The truth was, I was a bit nervous, but not for myself — for Nimue, knowing that she never liked to be the center of attention but never wanted to let anyone down. Luckily, I'd always been good at reading her, now even more so thanks to the mate bond, so I'd keep a sharp eye on her emotions for when she'd had enough.

Arriving in the square, Blaze motioned for us to wait in a white tent off one side of the green. We could already smell the food cooking from the other side of the square; the scents of ginger, cardamom, clove, and coriander wafted over to us, and my heart warmed that Blaze had considered my family's traditions and culture.

The tent had a selection of light appetizers that we nibbled on while waiting for the rest of the guests and the bridal party to arrive. Soaking up the last of the alcohol, I had just polished off some cheese and crackers and was reaching for a plate of roti when Blaze called out for everyone to find their seats.

The guys looked immediately at me, dropping their snacks, and Nadir shot me a grin.

"Showtime, Alpha," he chuckled, throwing an arm around my shoulder. Together, we walked out of the tent.

The gazebo was beautifully decorated with orange and pink roses, wildly out of season, but in times like these it was helpful to have green witches aplenty in town. They wouldn't bloom for more than a day, but I was positive that Nimue would be delighted with them. White swaths of gauzy fabric flowed in the cool coastal breeze, dancing where they draped from the posts of the gazebo, and between rods framing the aisle. Tea lights glistened from the tree branches around us, only adding to the ethereal vibe. How Blaze had managed to pull this together in a week blew my mind, but I was happy Nimue had so many people in her life that loved her.

I stood on the gazebo steps as plucked notes from an acoustic guitar began. Lysander was perched on a stool off to the right as he began to play an instrumental version of Dashboard Confessional's *Heart Beat Here*.

Since we weren't following a traditional Western ceremony, Nimue's friends were already seated at the front. I smiled at Selene and Devanna in their bangles, even if Dev cocked a threatening brow at me in return.

The guests turned around as Nimue appeared at the back of the aisle, a bonfire behind her. The flames framing her were a perfect vision of *Demon*, and I couldn't help but grin at the imagery. My chest swelled with emotion when she began to move, her flowy pink dress bringing out the warmth in her skin, accentuating her beauty in all the best ways. Her eyes trailed over me as well, and with a smirk, I sensed the same heat from her as I felt.

Val cleared his throat to let me know we were beginning, looking more official than I had ever seen him in his baby blue pin-striped suit. Usually, he and Caedmon dressed in board shorts and Hawaiian shirts, living their best beach town life while they worked from their coffee van. Then I spotted Caedmon wearing the matching suit in orange, and had to wonder if they'd purchased them from a menswear store or costume retailer, the resemblance to *Dumb and Dumber* hinting towards the latter.

Mo walked to Nimue's side, where she paused at the back of the aisle, and everyone rose to their feet. Arm in arm, the two women paced towards me, and my breathing grew shallow even as my grin spread wide. Still, I felt a pang of uneasiness down our bond as every single eye in the square tracked her every move, and I couldn't help myself from making my way down the gazebo steps to meet her.

I kissed Mo on the cheek, and then gathered Nimue's hands in mine. "You look incredible, mate," I whispered in her ear, and pink rose to her cheeks.

"You clean up pretty well yourself," she teased back, her eyes fluttering up at me before we both walked up the steps to Val.

"Good afternoon. I'd like to welcome all of you to the marriage of Kit Sayana and Nimue Fitzpatrick," Val began with his megawatt smile, and a loud sniffle already rang through the crowd. A few chuckles followed, and we turned to see Mo dabbing at her eyes from the front row, beaming at us.

"We've all watched Kit and Nimue grow up," Val continued. "We've seen them scampering around together since they were children. We've all pretended to be oblivious to their sneaking out together at night —" I shot a glance at Nimue before half-turning to find my parents out of the corner of my eye. My mother's jaw had dropped, and my father was frowning. *Great.* "— running around, breaking and entering while Nimue practiced her fire and photography, and Kit shifted to scurry after her. We've all let them dance out this ludicrous *will-they-won't-they* while they were too silly to realize what was *right* in front of them while we *all* knew —"

I cleared my throat, raising my eyebrows for him to possibly skip this part.

"Right." Val smiled again, taking the signal in stride. "As this is anything but a traditional situation — I mean, a shifter and a *demon*, of all things —" I caught his eye again.

"— Our ceremony will reflect the blended nature of the situation. Instead of saying your personal vows here, they will be later as part of the *mangal phere*, where you will each take a turn leading each other around the fire." He nodded to the bonfire in the back.

"For now, we will start with the handfasting, which closely resembles shifter and witch traditions." Val leaned forward to whisper to Nim, "Nimue, dear, I know you're not *really* a witch, but I figured, raised by Mo —"

Nim raised a hand to cut him off, smiling. "I love it, Val."

He beamed at her, and got started.

When a red woven rope was laced around our hands, we had officially tied the knot, fully hand-fasted. The square cheered for us, Mo clapping as she shot to her feet and came up to the front, whipping a broom out of nowhere and placing it on the ground at the bottom of the stairs. She motioned us down, and we met her in front of the broom.

"Centuries of witches have jumped the broom as part of their wedding ceremony," Mo explained to the crowd, at least half of which were shifters who might not be familiar with the tradition. "It symbolizes a sweeping away of the past and new beginnings," she continued, eyes only for Nimue and me now.

She motioned for us to hold hands, then stepped back. Locking eyes on my mate, we counted down and then leaped over the broom together.

More cheers sounded, especially from the coven

members in the crowd. As they quieted down, my uncle Jay took over.

"Lastly, let's move to the fire," he said, escorting us down the aisle again as the crowd stood to turn towards the bonfire.

"In the *mangal phere*, the couple will circle the fire seven times. The first three times, Nimue will lead; then, Kit will lead for the remaining four. As they complete each circuit, they will say part of their vows."

My eyes met my parents' again before we started, and tears of joy glistened in my mother's, fierce pride in my father's. Looking at my grandfather, he gave me a nod as Nimue took my hand, and we began our first round.

We circled the fire, declaring our love for each other in front of the town. Nimue beamed at me, practically glowing, as we finished the final round, and I clasped her hands.

"Today is the best day of my life, tying my soul to yours, Nimue. Today is also the first time a non-shifter has been brought into the Arrowwood skulk — and I'm so glad it's you. I am beyond honored to share my life with you, Nimue." I stopped in front of her, leaning down to grab her hands. "My mate in every way. And now, my wife."

When I kissed her, Nimue's body melted into mine. Cheers filled the air again, and I smiled down at her. "I love you."

She nodded, tears gathered in her eyes, "I love you, too."

With how many people came up to congratulate us, we barely had time to eat anything, though all the food smelled amazing. In addition to the tandoori chicken, rotis, and sauce varieties, there were lobster rolls, grilled scallops, seasonal steamed vegetables, and clam chowder. At one point, Mo swept by, a lobster roll in one hand, and dropped a plate of scallops down in front of Nim with the other.

"Have a lassi with the scallops," she said conspiratorially. "Sounds strange, but *trust me*."

We chuckled as she moved away, making room for the next round of well-wishers, but I did ask Nadir to snag us some lassis the next time we saw him. Maybe she was onto something.

We made our rounds after that, and even though I could tell Nimue was getting tired, she kept an authentic, warm smile on her face.

My mate might have been the sweetest person in the world.

Mate and *wife*, my fox reminded me, and fuck if I didn't like the sound of that.

As expected, Akil kept the dance floor — which was the street in front of Immortali-Tea — hopping all night with a wide variety of songs. As dusk faded into the evening, some of the older guests bade us farewell and took off for the night, leaving a crowd of mostly younger residents to keep the party going.

"Son," Pa had his arm around my mother as she beamed at us. "We're going to get going so you all can, ah —" he adjusted the collar of his black and silver sherwani, "— enjoy yourselves."

"Congratulations, *jaan*." Ma leaned over to kiss my cheek before turning to give her well wishes to Nimue.

"Sneaking out and breaking and entering, hm?" Pa said under his breath to me, but there was a glimmer in his eye.

I pressed my lips together, giving a half-shrug. "When your mate wants you to do something with her..." I trailed off, and smirked.

"You damn well do it," he finished with a nod. "Don't I know it." He glanced at Ma as she returned to his side, his eyes softening as they met hers. And then hardened right back up when he looked back at me. "Not too much drinking. You don't want to make a fool of yourself at your own ceremony."

As he turned to go, Ma stepped closer and whispered with a wink, "He only says that because he speaks from experience."

Pa choked out a gasp of shock and pulled her closer to him. "You promised you'd never say anything," he muttered as she laughed, and the two of them wandered out of the square and back to their car to head home.

"Took you long enough." A palm smacked the back of my head, and I blinked to see my grandfather had come over to us, but he was smiling at Nimue, the corners of his eyes crinkling. "Be patient with our boy here? At least he got there in the end." He raised a brow at me while Nimue chuckled.

She squeezed my hand. "He's not so bad."

He pressed a hand to her shoulder, then waved in the direction my parents went. "Can't miss my ride, but —" he cleared his throat as his gaze moved to me. "Your grandmother would have been so happy to see you two finally figured it out." My heart swelled yet again at his words, and I nodded at him before he moved off, trailing after my parents.

Realizing the formalities were over for the night, Nimue sighed as she leaned back in her chair, tension beginning to ease off her shoulders.

"Well, we did it," she said, a contented smile rising to her lips as she looked around the rest of our friends left in the square, most of whom were out on the dance floor.

"Not quite." I stood and offered her my hand. "Let's dance."

Chapter Forty-Five

NIMUE

DID I know Kit could dance? No, I freaking did not. Maybe it was those graceful shifter genes, or perhaps he and the boys had secret dance parties I'd never been privy to. So many questions.

Akil started up *Don't Stop Believin'*, and I couldn't remember the last time I'd laughed so hard or smiled so wide as I sang and danced with my friends.

Selene, Devanna, and Petra pulled me away from Kit to dance just with them for a few songs, and my heart felt so full it could burst. Between the way they'd pampered me this morning, and stayed at my side now, I had my own *skulk* aside from my husband's.

"You and Petra *almost* make me think I should find an actual relationship one of these days," Selene called out over the music. "I'm getting tired of first dates."

"As long as you let me vet them first," Dev said, downing another glass of champagne before setting it on a passing tray. She nodded at Petra and me. "It's too late for these two, but I can still save *you* from yourself."

Petra and I exchanged glances, my red-headed friend rolling her eyes as I pressed my lips together to keep from laughing.

We spent the rest of the night on the dance floor — the entire skulk loved to dance, and they tore it up with us into the wee hours of the morning. Finally, the last of our friends had to call it a night, and I was about to collapse.

"I'll take care of everything else," Blaze said, wrapping me in a bear hug. "Congratulations, Nimmie. You finally opened your damn eyes." He was grinning as he pulled back to look at me, and I rolled my eyes at him with a smile in return.

"Thanks for putting this all together, Boz. How did you manage to pull it all off so quickly?"

Blaze scoffed, "So little faith." Then he waved his hands through the air. "*Magic.*"

I couldn't help but laugh at him. "Now you'll always be my favorite brother," I teased, and he punched me lightly in the shoulder.

"Time to go, wife-mate," Kit said, lacing our fingers together. "You look like you're about to pass out from exhaustion, and we can't have that."

Blaze moved off, leaving us to it, as I quirked a brow at Kit. "Wife-mate?"

"I like them both," he shrugged before pulling me into him. I caught a glint of his eyes flashing gold before he leaned closer to whisper in my ear, "And we're going to need to catch a second wind because our night is *far* from over."

His words sent a tingling shiver down my spine as he pulled back, his meaning clear in his eyes. I glanced around the practically empty square, and bit my lip to halt my grin.

Flickering us out to the carriage house, I suddenly found a whole new burst of energy.

THE END

NIMUE

Epilogue

This next scene takes place after the end of *Karma is a Witch* and contains spoilers. If you have not read the entire series, we suggest coming back later!

Two Years Later

"KIT!" I called from the twins' nursery, trying to pin down a very wiggly Phoenix as he thrashed to escape his diaper change. Ember watched on from her crib, biting the railing as she held herself upright. Tiny teeth marks dotted the wood from my feral children, wild from the day they were born a year ago. "We're going to be late to their party if you don't come help me get Phoenix dressed!"

Kit came around the corner, hair wet from the shower, towel wrapped around his waist. Without hesitating, he stepped up to the changing table, leaning down over our son. "Hey little dude. What did I tell you about being nice to your mom?" He reached forward, tattooed and tanned arms tickling Phoenix's belly until he giggled, and I almost moaned.

The chemistry between Kit and I had always been off the charts, but something about seeing him as a dad was that much hotter.

His amber eyes flicked to mine, glowing golden for a beat. "Careful, mate, or I'll think you're ready for number three."

Was I?

Probably not. The last year with not one, but two, babies had been a lot. I couldn't remember the last time I'd slept through the night, but as I reached into Ember's crib, picking her up, I kissed her little cheeks and knew it was all worth it. "Why did you have to grow up so fast?"

Squealing drew my eyes back to the changing table where Kit executed a complicated maneuver, but finally got Phoenix's squirming body into his white onesie and jeans, dressed and ready for the twin's big day.

Tomorrow they turned one, and that felt like a huge milestone.

"We kept them alive for a whole year," I said with a wistful sigh.

"It was touch and go there a few times," Kit agreed, lifting Phoenix above his head as he sailed around the room. It made his forearms flex in an ungodly way, the skulk tattoos rippling.

"Stop." I pushed past him out of the room, Ember's outfit in hand. "Otherwise we're going to be really late, and I refuse to show up to see our mothers smelling like I've been freshly plowed."

Kit came up behind me, Phoenix on his hip as he leaned

forward and kissed my shoulder. "They're used to it by now. Hardly anyone comments on it anymore."

I scoffed, stepping away from him. "Akil wrinkles his nose every time we walk in the room."

"Someday, he'll understand."

Ember babbled as I put her dark hair in little pigtails, but was much less squirmy than her brother. Kit and Phoenix disappeared into our bedroom while Kit got dressed, coming out in matching flannels. My full-grown husband had an obsession with matching his infant son, and I swooned a little more each time. Maybe that was why he kept doing it.

The moment I had Ember dressed and ready, Kit scooped her up, securing her into the carseat by the front door. "Ready?" he asked, lifting both carseats.

Darn it, maybe I was ready for number 3.

Kit's eyes flashed, a smirk playing on his lips, but I shook my head. "Nope."

Wrenching open the door, I jogged to the car, buckling myself in to put some distance between us.

Inside Scallywag's, Selene and Devanna had gone all out on the party decorations. The entire bar counter was stocked with food, which was good since half the town and most of the skulk would likely stop by over the afternoon to wish the twins a happy birthday.

"Hey, little buddy!" Nadir said as he unbuckled Phoenix from his carseat. Before I could warn him, he had Phoenix's feet on the ground, and my son took off through the crowded bar. "Shit, he's fast."

"You unleashed him, you chase him," Kit said as he

lifted Ember from her seat, snuggling her to his chest as he covered her in kisses.

"You know exactly what you're doing, don't you?" I whispered to him, and Kit cast me a sideways glance, a small lift of his shoulders.

"They're so cute, how can you not want more?"

Phoenix streaked by, Nadir hot on his trail as he bent over at the waist, arms outstretched in case my son toppled over.

"Where's my birthday girl?" Aditi said as she walked towards us, taking Ember from Kit and moving into the center of the room. "You look just like your papa, you know that? I remember his first birthday like it was yesterday. Just as I got him dressed, he had the biggest blowout I've ever seen. Green poop everywhere."

"Great story, Mom. So —"

"Then," Aditi continued, cutting off Kit's interruption. "He shifted before we could clean him up, and scampered off into a pile of leaves. The day ended with the dirtiest little cub, glaring at us from his bath. We had to cancel the whole party."

Kit gave the classic grimace of a child enduring their parent's embarrassing stories, but I felt the tiniest twinge of disappointment through our mate bond. He hadn't said anything, but I knew he was waiting to see if the twins would be able to shift. With our strange magical hodge-podge, we had no idea what kind of spawn we'd created. Only time would tell.

Flannel streaked by again, Phoenix this time chased by not only Nadir but Akil.

"Hey, that's my Gobbles!" Akil called after his nephew,

triumphantly waving a Beanie Baby above his little head. "Please don't set it on fire!"

Not looking where he was going, Akil crashed into Ruby as she walked in the door with my mom.

"Careful there, dear," Mo said as she gripped Akil's wrist, then that slow smile I knew so well spread when she dropped her hand. "You know Ruby, don't you?"

The teenage witch blushed, her cheeks almost as red as her hair as she waved awkwardly. Akil did an exaggerated hair flip move that made my neck hurt just watching, then waved back before shoving his hands in his pockets. "Hey, Ruby. I think we met at the library a few weeks ago."

Ruby nodded, then quickly moved to the bar where Devanna sat, nursing a whiskey.

"The library?" Emerson gave Akil a sideways glance. "I didn't know you could read."

Akil cleared his throat, then swiped the cookie from Emerson's hand and raced off after his Beanie Baby before Emerson could retaliate. I stifled a chuckle at Emerson's resigned expression at his younger brother's antics — my brothers-in-law were a handful of their own.

Cole approached next, giving me a quick hug. "Congrats on surviving, Nimue." Cole grinned, then elbowed his mate Skylar, who blushed. "You two made it look so easy, we decided it was time to give the whole parent thing a try."

"Oh my gosh!" I exclaimed as I pulled Skylar into a hug, squeezing her. She'd been slow to open up over the last two years in the skulk, but I was elated my children would have their own generation of pack to bond with. "That's so wonderful! How are you feeling?"

"Good." She nodded. "Just trying to figure everything out for the future."

"What she isn't saying," Casey said as he butted his way to my side, wrapping his arm around my shoulder, "is she's counting the days until I move out so she can turn my room into a nursery." He squeezed my shoulder, then let go, and I found Kit's gaze across the room. He nodded, understanding my silent meaning that we needed to check on our friend — life was changing quickly in the Cove, and the last thing we wanted was for anyone to feel left behind.

"Hi baby," Mo said as she kissed my cheek, giving me a warm hug when I pried myself away from the skulk. I soaked in her warmth the way I always did — she was the best. "Happy Mother's Day to you."

I laughed, pulling away from her hold. "It's not Mother's Day."

"Sure it is. You've been a mother for a whole year, and I'm so proud of you, especially with twins. Thank you for making me a Grammy to these little hellions."

"Phoenix!" Nadir cried, and I looked around the room as Kit darted forward, already on high alert. "Kit, I swear he was right here."

A giggle I would recognize anywhere sounded from behind me as little fists curled into my jeans. My breath caught as I looked behind me, seeing Phoenix's chubby face staring up at me. Nadir stood on the other side of the room, ripping his hair out, worry written in his every feature.

"Mom," I said warily, stooping to pick up Phoenix. "Did what I think just happen, happen?"

"If you're asking if I saw your one-year-old flicker across

the room, then yes," she chuckled. "Well, this just got interesting."

"How old was I when I first flickered?" I asked hesitantly, already knowing the answer.

"Nine, dear," Mo said as she patted me on the shoulder. "You were nine."

Just as I opened my mouth to call for Kit, Aditi shouted his name. "She shifted! Kit, Ember shifted!"

Phoenix kicked his legs, trying to break free of my hold as I shoved through the room towards Aditi, spying the baby fox on the floor, a puddle of baby clothes around her. Two little bows perched on the edges of her russet fur, dark eyes staring up at me. She sneezed, and a handful of sparks shot from her snout, the gathered crowd chuckling at her display of mixed powers. Tears welled in my eyes as Kit bent down and scooped her up, holding the tiny pup up to his face.

"We got ourselves some Pokémon!" Casey hollered, money exchanging hands between him and some of the other skulk members. "Told you, boys."

Not to be outdone by his sister, Phoenix finally wriggled free, and with a pop like he'd been doing it his whole life, he too shifted into the tiniest little grey fox cub. With a shriek of pure joy, he scampered off, weaving between the crowd's feet, shooting sparks as he went.

"That can't be good," I said as I stepped up to Kit's side.

But he grinned, as big as I'd ever seen. "No, it's not good, Nim. It's perfect, just like you. Our family is perfect."

ALSO BY AIMEE VANCE

Mayhem Hockey Club

Moms of Mayhem

Call of the Norns: A Viking Time Travel Fantasy Trilogy

Fates Illuminated

Fates Promised

Fates Defied

Acknowledgments

When we started writing *Smoke Show*, the idea was to create a chaotic supernatural town where everyone could fit in. Along the way, we have truly fallen in love with this world and these characters. It has been such a fun journey to share them with each other, and now, with you.

On that note, a huge thank you to those of you who have poured love on *Smoke Show* in reviews and posts online. We are thrilled to see that you love it as much as we do! Hopefully, you enjoyed *Deja Brew* just as much, because we have so much more in store for you.

To all of you in the Bookstagram community, we appreciate your support and friendship. Thank you, thank you, thank you!

From B: To J, for supporting my writing obsession and inspiring many of the little details in this book To A.E. and C., thank you for all your support, encouragement, and for occasionally letting me rant about the process. To A.R., I'm so glad Smoke Show brought you back into my life, and thank you for joining along this writing journey.

From Aimee: To Chris and our girls, thank you for always reminding me you're proud of me. I love you beyond words!

B. Perkins has been making up stories about magic since she learned how to write words on paper. When not immersed in fictional worlds, she enjoys spending time in nature with her boyfriend and two dogs. (The cat is never invited, because it would be terrified). She has several degrees in various things, and if all they're good for is to provide background in creating fantasy worlds and systems, then maybe they were worth it.

About Aimee Vance

Fueled by peach tea and chaos, Aimee Vance writes heartwarming and laugh-out-loud romance stories. She holds a B.S. in Public Relations from Texas Christian University and has always been an avid fantasy reader.

Residing in Texas with her husband, two young daughters, and Labrador Retriever, Aimee loves to transport readers to worlds hidden between the pages where magic and love intertwine. She prefers sassy heroines, grumpy heroes, and enough humor to keep you chuckling with every page.

facebook.com/aimeevancebooks

instagram.com/aimeevancebooks

goodreads.com/aimeevancebooks

amazon.com/author/aimeevancebooks

bookbub.com/authors/aimee-vance